TIMELESSLY

Ours

Contents

To the fearless women who rise above.

Two years earlier

My required presence up in the arena's executive suite is my least favorable result of another win. Whose idea was it for the team and coaches to suit up after an adrenaline-driven game and drink cocktails with VIPs and family members of the team? Most of those whose tickets were comped today.

The Buffalo Blades scored four to two tonight against a team that managed to get in the top two in the entire league. So yeah, today's worth attending the celebration—especially as Head Coach for the Blades for the last ten years.

But I'm weary. And irritable as usual.

Despite winning tonight, the team's been struggling. Our right winger, Carter Hayes, is out for six games with a sprained wrist. Garret

Garrison, one of the defensemen has gotten too cocky on the ice and for no good reason.

And to top it off, the team Captain, Nicholas Kane, has been having trouble keeping his fists to himself these past few weeks—seeing the penalty box more than ice time.

But because I know why, I've cut him a break.

Can't imagine what's it like to be living his dream while his twin sister suffers daily with addiction. If only that were the worst of it. The Kane twins come from a toxic upbringing. One that *Nicole* Kane bore the worst of.

After swiping fatigue off my face, I crank my neck and button my suit jacket, then step out of the elevator.

I consciously join these things *after* the players have, for the mere fact that guests will be too wrapped up in conversation with each of them to bother with me.

I pause in my tracks when a man around my age clears his throat and approaches me. "Coach."

Doing my best to conceal my scowl, I turn. My brows rise respectfully, finding one of the few men I don't mind having a brief chat with.

"Bruce," I say, catching his hand. "Good to see you again." Bruce Knight is the father of Jace Knight, co-captain, defenseman, and my least favorite player on the team. Not because he isn't a solid player, he's one of our best. But because he *knows* it and acts like we're lucky to have him.

His frequent quarreling with my oldest daughter, Angel, doesn't help his case either, not that the guy cares what I think about him outside of his ability to score.

"Great game tonight."

"Thank you. And thank you for coming." I glance around at the crowd. Unfortunately, Bruce Knight is likely the better of my options this evening, but I was hoping to see Angel. My twenty-four-year-old daughter, who used to be the first one to drag me up to these events with her quirky and spirited personality. That was until her accident last year. Angel used to be a Buffalo Blades Ice Girl, until an injury on the ice—on national television, no less— deflected her desire to ever skate again.

The best thing to come out of her quitting being an Ice Girl was less time she spent around Jace.

When there's no sign of her, I turn back to Bruce. "Is Cora here as well?" It seems fitting to ask about his daughter since she's friends with mine and other than that fact, we have nothing in common.

"She should be around here." He peeks his head over the crowd, and I blow out an exasperated breath. Because *this*... is the best I could do tonight.

I should be *home*, with my younger daughter. Rory is the result of a one-night stand I had a few years ago but is by no means a mistake. Sure, the fans and media still consider it one, but she's one of the few joys I have in my life.

Best part? I don't have to raise her with anyone. Her mother left her at my door. It was years after my divorce with Angel's mother, Claire—who, to this day, I resent not changing the locks on, since she barges into my home whenever she pleases.

Absently, I turn my head from a conversation I was never quite interested in having, when my eyes lock onto one... *breathtaking*...woman.

Petite, maybe five foot, *long* dark silky hair, big green eyes—familiar eyes—and laughter that carries waves through the air like a distant song.

She's... magnetic.

"Ah, there she is. With Nicole."

My brows knit and I blink. "Nicole?"

"Nicole Kane." His brows jump. "Surely, you've heard of Nicole Kane. She's been in rehab up until last week."

My jaw clenches at his careless regard for Nicole's hardship, and I turn back. That spark of energy ignites when my eyes find her again. But I've met Nicky before. It's been a while—and it was before things went completely south for this girl—but I feel like I would have...remembered *her*.

She's *easily* the most beautiful woman I've ever seen. And my ex-wife was a supermodel.

This woman—given she's Nick's twin, makes her twenty-seven—is a whopping *seventeen* years younger than me.

I rub the back of my neck. "It was good to see you, Bruce." I don't bother waiting for his reply. My feet are already on the move, and I can't stop them.

Her laugh is like a siren, and I'm awakened.

Her hair flips and her eyes stay focused on whatever it is Cora is telling her. Her skin is glowing. Her smile—though sensing some fakeness in it—is brilliant. I can only imagine what her *real* smile is like.

I'm looking for the badass no-nonsense Nicole Kane but I don't see her. I see someone who looks nervous out of her mind. A little guilty possibly and ready to face it all.

Hell, what do I say to her? Ask her how she's doing? Will she remember me?

Snap the fuck out of it, man. She's not in the state of mind to be worried about who you are or what you say to her.

I've only met her on a few occasions... when her twin brother was babysitting his "troubled" sister. That's what Nick used to say...no one ever used the words 'drug and alcohol abusing sister' on the team. Because no one knows for sure if she did drugs. Nick didn't seem to think so. But alcohol was a definite.

Fuck, I should just leave her be. She's braving enough of the 'good to see you well' and the 'how are you...*really*?'

But when she meets my gaze, I'm caught. Whatever this is, whatever I'm feeling, it's like she can sense it.

Because she's giving me the exact. Same. Look.

She blinks away and turns back, giving her focus to a rambling Cora, who seems very apologetic about something. But Nicole watches her adoringly.

"Lovely seeing you ladies here," I say, what I feel might be a good start since I can't seem to make my mind work. I turn my focus down to the five-foot beauty. "Hi, Nicky."

For a moment, I wonder if I'm overstepping by calling her what her brother calls her. But it's also a gentle reminder to myself that she's young. In many ways.

Those striking green eyes look up at me again. Any coyness I caught just seconds ago is gone and replaced with an aura of sheer confidence. The transformation is palpable.

My God, she's beautiful. Captivating.

Her lip turns up and I fight not to let my eyes linger there. "Coach Collins. You lead a good team," Nicole says, her tone somewhat guarded. Like she's struggling to keep up with what I might expect.

I wink and give her a nudge as assurance she doesn't have to do that. Not with me. "Sorry I'm returning your brother in one piece."

There it is.

A real one. She releases a heart-melting breathy laugh and looks down coyly, brushing her hair behind her ear. "I'm sure you'll make it up to me next time." She winks back.

Holy. Shit.

I need to walk away. Right now.

I chuckle lightly and be sure to address both of them. "See you around."

And I don't go near her for the rest of the night. Because I've never felt so off-kilter.

1

Present

Ow. Fuck. My head. I wince in pain. A...familiar pain.

No. Not this again.

No no no. *Nicole*...what did you do? What did you do?

I hear myself groan and stir in bed. I'm in a bed. Is it morning? Was it...*only* alcohol? And when did I... oh dear *Lord*, please tell me I'm in my *own* bed.

I hear another breath, but it's not mine. It's deep. Throaty. And maybe...angry?

Shit. I'm not alone.

My eyes fly open, fearing the worst. But it's not the worst. Not...entirely.

It's him. He's *here*.

Coach Collins.

My vision is still a bit blurry, but from what I can tell, he's sitting in a blue leather armchair a few feet from the bed I lie on. His eyes are fixed on my face. His expression hard. Or just...empty.

It's almost like one of those many...*many* dreams I've had of him. Where he stares at me from a distance, and I wait for him to come to me. It usually ends around there. He never does come to me.

But this...is no dream. I never feel anything when I'm dreaming. Blinking past the pain in my head, I focus on him.

And nearly wince.

There isn't that... hint of a warm smile I'm typically gifted with whenever his eyes would find mine. There's nothing but a cold, hard...*glare*.

He's fully dressed in navy pants and a white dress shirt. His fingers are entwined as he leans back...probably waiting for me to come to.

"R-Royce." Not many can call him by his first name, and I wonder if I'm still allowed such a privilege. Since everyone else calls him "Coach".

I'm not sure what I expect...but he doesn't respond. He looks at the nightstand and then back at me.

Frowning, I follow and find a glass of water, which looks heavenly right now, and a small bottle of aspirin.

I sit up slowly, and from the corner of my eye, I see him flinch. Like he wants to come help me but stops himself.

My head is pounding hard. So hard that I try not to make it worse by wracking my brain as to where he might have found me.

Lying in a ditch? No, that's not like me. My twin brother, Nick, once found me unconscious, but at least I was in my own apartment.

I take the aspirin and gulp down the entire glass of water. Royce rises and approaches the bed. He swipes the small bottle from the nightstand. Smart man. Never leave a recovering addict with access to a means of overdose.

"I'll be back when that sets in a little. There's a bathroom through that door if you need."

"Where am I?" I ask. I mean to ask with more force, demanding in fact, but I'm so weak, I come off sounding like a lost fairytale princess rather than a five-foot brunette with a sharp tongue and a black belt.

"One of my guest rooms."

I nod slowly and sit up a bit more. Hesitant to pull the covers off me.

He moves to the door. "I'll give you some privacy. I'm just downstairs if you need me."

Once he's gone, I shift my gaze to the windows. A gentle glow filters through the blue curtains, so I can tell it's morning. But I don't race to them. I don't tear the heavy drapes apart like Cinderella to welcome the flood of light.

I don't want it.

I'm more of a Wednesday Adams.

So instead, I peek outside to the driveway. It's not a house I'm unfamiliar with. I've been here several times before.

My best friend Angel, Coach's older daughter, used to live here until earlier this year when she moved in with her boyfriend. Now, this enormous, five-bedroom, beautifully modern home is reserved for him and his six-year-old daughter, Rory.

I'm not surprised my car isn't in the driveway. I wouldn't have driven here. Couldn't even tell you where my car is right now...

Which means...he found me.

My stomach sinks and I swallow hard. I reek of my least favorite scent. Alcohol.

Don't panic. We can figure this out.

After a hot shower.

I sniffle along with a deep breath and hold my head high as I walk to the bathroom. It matches the guestroom with its midnight blue and ivory colors. The tiled floor is a smooth white. My bare feet move over to the plush rug in front of the sink. Gold hardware isn't what I would have imagined for a man like Royce Collins. But it does accent the room beautifully.

Not like the sad little titled room I have back in my apartment. The one that fits one person at a time with mildew growing in the corners and space for either a shampoo *or* body wash in the shower.

I move over to the toilet and wait for the urge to hurl. I feel queasy as hell but...it doesn't come.

Also, might want to rethink that, Nicky. If you deposit those painkillers, there's zero chance of him giving you another dose.

Luckily, I've always been good at holding my liquor.

Hey, some women are proud to become CEO's of million-dollar corporations. Me—I'm proud to be vomit-free since I was eighteen.

I wash my face, using the peppermint scented bar soap to wash off my makeup.

God, I was a mess last night. A real hot mess.

Way to go, Nicole. Way to prove your brother right.

I laugh at myself remembering how angry I was at him last night. At *all of them.*

My stomach churns but it's not from the alcohol consumption. It's the gut-wrenching realization I came across last night.

Tears threaten again and I turn, marching to the glass-enclosed shower that's three times as big as mine. I turn the knob and watch the room begin to steam as I strip out of my bartender uniform a tad too eagerly.

There's that queasiness again. "Slow your roll, hotshot," I remind myself.

I step in and under the hot spray. It's calm against my skin—scorching because that's how I like it—but calming. I lather the peach scented shampoo over my hair and let the water run down my body. Rinsing away the alcohol seeping out of my pores.

This time I can't fight back the tears as I replay what I remember about last night.

12 hours ago

The Buffalo Blades just kicked off their new season and won. After losing in the finals last season, they needed this win. Their *fans* needed it.

And I'm more than happy to be part of the celebration tonight.

As head bartender at their favorite sports bar, Bridges, I'm always part of the celebration.

Might as well serve the drinks since I don't drink.

I'm also celebrating something tonight.

My biggest win yet.

Sober for two years, after being released from rehab. I'm not counting the months I spent there recovering and reflecting.

I breathe in the joy and smile as I witness some of my closest friends... and my twin brother, the captain of the Buffalo Blades, rein in their victory.

I'm no idiot, I know my brother doesn't love the idea of my working behind the bar again, but it's what I'm good at. I'm quick with my hands and feet, I charm every customer in the house... even the ladies. And I'm finally making my own money. Not letting Nick pay my way, regardless of how much he makes playing pro hockey.

"Nicole," one of my best friends, Cora Knight, also my brother's live-in girlfriend, calls. "Nick and I are heading out."

I meet her across the bar for a quick peck on the cheek. "Love you. Keep him humble for me, will ya?" I tease.

"Tall order," she says back with a smirk.

"I heard that," Nick whines, wrapping an arm around Cora and winking at me.

Then he does something I've come to expect from him whenever he leaves the bar. He scans it until he sees something... or someone that comforts him, then he nods and makes eye contact before taking off.

I've never paid any attention to it but for some reason, tonight, I follow his gaze...which lands right on...

Coach?

Fuck's that about?

Shaking my head, I get back to work. I'm not here to make more drama for myself. I've suffered enough of it in my life. My mother being the root of it. The ignition starter, the spark that lit the fire that blew up my life before I was old enough to speak for myself.

Within thirty minutes, the team and other patrons slowly start pouring out of the place.

Good, I can get off my feet soon. Only one hour till closing time.

Coach takes a seat at my bar. It's casual as per usual. His eyes scan the space, and he avoids my eyes.

As usual.

"Soda and lime, please."

My brows twitch but I don't question it. It's not that I don't enjoy Coach's company when it's winding down like it is now, but something about Nick's ominous departure just rubs me in a weird way.

Or maybe...just maybe...Coach, or okay, *Royce,* actually enjoys my company as he winds down from the evening. Wouldn't that be something?

"Lime. I need more lime," I mutter before ducking under the bar. I pull the clear container of fruit from the mini fridge, looking for the freshest in the bunch. I always go a little bit extra for this man.

And these stolen nights with him sitting at my bar, chatting with me like we're friends, laughing at my jokes, it almost feels like...maybe *he's* going a little bit extra for *me.*

Or...maybe he feels like staying to...protect me...from overzealous patrons who had a few too many.

Whatever his reasons, I don't question it. I've been blushing for this man for the better part of the last two years, and I'll take whatever he'll give me.

"Hey, Coach. Are *you* doing it tonight?" Jace's voice comes from above and I stay ducked.

Coach doesn't respond. At least not in words that I can hear.

"Okaayyy..." Jace continues. "Don't know what that means but Angel and I are thinking about leaving soon and I know she's closing tonight..."

Who? Angel?

No... He means me.

What the hell?

It's gone quiet suddenly and I toss the lime up in the air and pop up catching it with my eyes pinned on Jace.

"Talkin' bout me?"

His eyes widen with shock and his lips part just a touch.

I point at him. "You're gonna catch a fly like that," I warn.

"Hey, Dad." Angel parks herself between her father and her boyfriend. "Did Jace tell you, we're thinking of heading out so—" She cuts herself off when she finds me standing here. "Oh, hey."

My eyes shift from the dumbfounded jock to my tall, beautiful bestie, who I trust with my life.

"Hey, Angel," I say seductively, shifting my gaze to her. "You wouldn't happen to know why your boyfriend is so concerned with you both leaving if I'm closing, would you?"

"Um... to see if you needed a ride." It's almost a question as she glances at Jace for help.

Coach shakes his head, pinching the bridge of his nose.

I glare at her and she squirms under pressure. Jace pushes her aside and stands in front of her protectively.

I roll my eyes dramatically. "Oh please hotshot, your girl's safer with me than anyone so take your heroicness someplace else."

Jace's jaw tightens but he bites back a comment. Especially since Angel squeezes his forearm.

But I still need answers. And I have a sick feeling I know what's going on.

"Hey bestie, maybe you can solve a little puzzle for me. Any particular reason why one of you always seem to stick around when I'm supposed to be closing alone?"

Jace and Angel exchange a lingering look. But Coach keeps a fixed gaze on me,

"Fine, then. Let's play a game." I set a rocks glass in front of me, but I don't fill it with ice. Instead, I pull a vodka bottle off the shelf and hold them side by side.

"I'm going to have a drink. I'll stop pouring when one of you starts talking—you with me?"

Angel looks nervous. Jace looks mad and Coach—well, his usual scowl is firmly in place, fixated on the contents in my hands.

"I pour on the count of three. The longer you wait, the more I pour."

"Three...two...one." I flip the bottle over. A drop barely falls to my glass before Angel breaks.

"We're babysitting you," she cries out.

Jace's head snaps to his girlfriend. "Really?"

I set the bottle down and toss the bluff juice in the sink behind me. "Tell me more."

"I'm so sorry. We've been taking turns...watching you here until you close, just...making sure you don't...that you're alright."

"Babysitting," I repeat, my vision turning hazy, a ball of fire forming in my chest.

"Please don't hate us," she whispers.

"Who's idea?" I demand.

She blinks. "Mine."

I cock my head at her, adoringly. "Angel," I start. "Have I taught you nothing?" I lean toward her. "Always look a person in the eye when you lie to them."

I untie my apron.

"Nicole," Jace starts...almost as a warning. For someone who raised the sweetest young woman I know—his kid sister, Cora—Jace has zero skill when it comes to sweet talking.

Abandoning my shift, I race out, tossing my apron at Hank, the owner. "I've got to go," I mutter.

Less than a minute later, I'm pulling out of the back lot in my car—a used sedan I managed to buy in the first few months of working at Bridges.

I don't want to go to my apartment. I don't want to be alone.

They were all in on it. All of them.

It's dark, but I know my way. I don't rationalize. I don't tell myself this is a bad idea. Okay, maybe I do. But it's immediately followed by a "fuck them all" under my breath. Bring on all the bad ideas.

While you're at it, let's make 'em the worst.

With that consent, I make the right onto a familiar street. It's been over two years since I'd been here, but I doubt anyone has forgotten me.

With my poker face firmly covering the painful betrayal, I park my car and walk toward the place I considered my second home—where no one judged me—because no one cared.

Sylvie's Bikers and Babes.

I'm not sure the reaction I'll get when that faithful bell chimes as soon as I enter the dive bar and ask for my old boss. My old friend.

"Hello, boys. Sylvie here?"

2

I T'S LATE FOR MY morning coffee and I need it. Bad.

I should have come down hours ago for it, but I couldn't leave her. If Nicole had woken up—even if she'd recognize my home within minutes—it wasn't worth leaving her alone and panicked.

I needed to ensure she knew she felt safe the moment she opened her eyes.

I wait forever for the fresh coffee to brew, wondering if she's alright up there. I'm instantly relieved when I hear the pipes work and the sound of the upstairs shower running. Pulling open the cupboard, I take out another mug—one for her—and drop in a few sugar cubes.

She's going to want to know how she ended up in my house. Where I found her. And I'm not sure I'm ready to tell her.

No. I'm not sure she's ready to hear it.

11 hours ago

By the time I pull out of the lot, I've already lost sight of which way her sedan went. There's no hiding my giant white Range Rover behind her. And I can't risk her picking up speed or shooting glances in her rearview mirror if she spots me.

I'm no amateur.

That kind of car chase is how people get hurt.

And Nicole's been hurt enough.

"Stop," I growl at myself and pull over, reaching for my cell phone. "Hey, David," I greet my old friend at the police station quickly. "I need a favor, but it's a personal favor. Off the record."

There's silence on the other line for a few seconds. "Collins. How's it going, buddy. Congrats on the win tonight."

I shake my head. "Right. Thanks. Listen—"

"Would have been good to see it..."

I sigh. "Season tickets if you do this for me. *Without* questions."

"Shoot."

"I need to know a list of places Nicole Kane used to hang out."

More silence. I'm ready to offer the guy my job for the answer since it's clear he's hesitating. "Wish I didn't agree to the no questions part."

"Dave." I resist the urge to tell him it's urgent. It would only create unwanted attention from the Buffalo P.D. And I'm seriously hoping we won't need it.

I hear typing in the back. "I don't know where she hung out, but I'm sending a list of places she's worked... and places she's been present when we made arrests. There's no arrest record for her, but she's been a witness plenty."

"Thanks, man. I'll send you those passes Monday."

"See ya at the next game," David says, like he got the better end of the deal.

People say it's always the last place you look when you've found something you lost. I sure hope that's an accurate assumption when I pull into the back alley of the last place—the most toxic of places—Nicole worked before her brother put her in rehab.

Sylvie's.

Sylvie's Bikers and Babes is known for a specific crowd. They're not dangerous or threatening. They just want to look like they are.

A guy in a black apron steps out the back door and lights a cigarette. He pauses when he spots my flashy vehicle. I jump out and close the driver door before approaching. I don't hesitate. I don't show any inclination that I'm terrified of what it would mean if Nicole is indeed in there.

It's the last place I looked for a reason.

Because I thought I knew her better than to ever set foot here again.

"I'm lookin' for a young woman about five foot. She come around here?" I give the guy the courtesy of asking before I try and power past him into a place I know I'm not welcome.

He assesses me. "You a cop?"

"No."

"Of course, he is." Another guy, taller, in his mid-thirties steps out. "He's just undercover. Look...his jacket's clean and he's sober as fuck. He's got to be a cop." They look over my shoulder. "You got back up?"

"Am I gonna need it?" I ask, letting them know I'm not here for trouble—necessarily. Not sure why I don't correct them. "I'm just looking for someone."

The first guy—in the apron, keeps his cigarette between two fingers and holds his hands up. "I don't know anything. I just work in the kitchen."

The tall one shakes his head.

I step forward. "Look, I'm not looking for trouble. I just want to know if—"

"Pete, Griff—who's that? He got a badge?" The voice comes from behind the back door.

"Says he's not a cop."

A tall, buff woman steps out—and the way her head is held high, shoulders squared, the solid silver bob of her hair—there's no doubt in my mind...that's Sylvie.

Tossing a damp bar rag over her shoulder, she squints her eyes. "Entrance is around the fron—hey, you're Royce Collins."

I don't know whether to be offended or relieved.

The woman looks like she's piecing things together in her head. "He's lookin' for Nickles," she deadpans.

The tall one lifts his head. "Nickles? You her dad?"

Sylvie rolls her eyes. Clearly, having full knowledge that not only am I not Nicole's dad, but that man is far from ever coming to "look" for his daughter.

Because I'm desperate, I assume *Nickles* is Nicole and go with it. "She's my daughter's friend and I'd like to find her. Make sure she gets home safe."

The tall one scoffs. "She's safer here than *you* are."

Sylvie pushes past the men and approaches me with a lethal tone. "You're not comin' into my bar."

"I'm not here to cause your place any trouble," I repeat, calmly. Reminding myself not to lose my patience like I would with anyone else getting in my face like this.

"You think I'm just going to let you come in and take one of my customer's off in your fancy truck?" She stares me down.

"Last I checked she was more than just your customer. She was your friend," I remind her. "I know you care about her. I just want to make sure she gets home without anyone knowing she came back here. Especially her twin brother."

Sylvie's shoulders relax and her expression softens. "She's at the end of the bar. She's had a few but I've been watering down her beverages significantly after her second. I was going to take her back to my place tonight."

Relief washes over me. It almost overpowers my anger. She should have never been here in the first place. I should have caught up with her. I should have come *here* first.

I march past the owner and burst through the doors. I scan the orange glow of the small bar but she's not in here. I weave around the small tables and chairs and push one stool against the wooden bar in frustration, then twist to the woman following me. "You said she was in here," I growl.

Sylvie looks around anxiously then turns to Griff, who'd been outside with us. She sighs.

"Hey, Sylv?" A biker in the middle of the bar calls. "Your girl caught on to your 'watered down scheme', grabbed a vodka bottle off the shelf, and took off."

"Shit." Sylvie spoke the word in my mind.

I don't ask any more questions. I don't even go back for my truck. I race out the front door and scan both directions of the street. The *empty* street.

I'm frozen as I try and figure out what Nicole's next move might be.

When I hear a car screech in the distance, I race. It's not Nicole's car. Her's was blocked in by mine in the back of the bar.

She's on foot.

And it sounds like someone had just swerved out of the way because of a reckless pedestrian.

Present

I knock on the guestroom door gently. The shower's been turned off and I imagine I waited long enough before coming back into the room with her breakfast.

"Yeah," Nicole grumbles.

I twist the handle and push. Nicole's hair is wet. She's wearing the full-length white guest bathrobe that hangs in every bathroom in the house. It's tied loosely around the front, but I'm not concerned about exposure. It's her skin that catches my attention. I set the tray down.

"Nicole, your skin is red. Are you allergic to something?"

She reaches for the coffee and scrunches her face at the bowl of oatmeal. "No."

Talking to her when she's back in her 'don't fuck with me' mood is going to be just swell. But I've raised one daughter in her twenties now, so this isn't new territory for me.

"Nicole, why is your skin red?" I ask firmly. Clearly tiptoeing isn't going to get me anywhere.

"I take hot showers."

I shake my head. "That can't be good."

Ignoring me, she looks down at the tray. "Oatmeal? I'm not your six-year-old. I'm a grown-up."

"Could have fooled me the way you ran off last night."

She scowls at me then shifts her gaze to the clothes on the bed. The ones I fetched when she was still out cold. "Angel's?"

Well, they're not mine. But instead of pointing out the obvious, I pull out the chair for her to sit and eat. "You haven't eaten anything since four o'clock yesterday."

She pins me with her eyes and I'm not sure if it's another scowl or surprise.

"You need soft foods," I argue, insisting on making a case for the oatmeal.

"I'll just have coffee. Thank you."

I draw closer. "Don't make me spoon-feed you." I mean it as a joke but there is a level of iciness in my voice. I'm growing tired of her bratty attitude.

She turns to me, not missing my tone, and steps closer. "I'd like to see you try." It's almost a snarl and I feel like I need to clutch my dick just to keep it from pointing at her. She smells like peaches and daisies, likely from bath soaps the housekeeper stocked in the guestrooms. It's not the typical Nicole smell. It's usually pomegranates and some sort of spice. Her face is clean and glowing, her eyes a sharp green. Her lips full and drawn into a slight frown.

She's so fucking gorgeous.

And the heady look she's giving me right now...egging me on, like she knows there's something I've been holding back on since the moment I laid eyes on her...isn't helping.

I flex my jaw. "I'm not your enemy, Nicole."

"Where'd you find me?" She doesn't look at me when she asks. But appears to be deathly afraid of the answer.

I sigh. "You move fast, I'll tell you that much."

"Where?"

"About midway through the side street of Main and Twelfth." She wasn't exactly passed out. But she'd settled herself in a spot by a parking meter, leaning against the pole.

The bottle beside her empty.

I'm not sure how much of it she drank, but I know it wasn't all of it. A lot was spilled around her, and I wonder if it was intentionally dumped.

"So, about three blocks away."

My brows twitch. "You remember being at Sylvie's last night?"

She nods. "Up to a certain point." She glances at me and covers her face, groaning. "I must have been a hot mess."

I was so relieved to find her...somewhat conscious and in one piece...that I didn't care what she looked like. Just that I'd found her. She was safe. I'd carried her back to my truck, put her in the backseat and drove home.

To keep things completely confidential, I relieved the sitter for Rory before bringing Nicole inside.

"You're safe, Nicole. That's all that matters." I don't mean for it to sound as biting and heartless as it probably does, but I don't know how she can be so concerned with how she must have looked instead of being relieved I didn't find her half-dead from alcohol poisoning.

"Is Rory home?" she asks after a moment.

Since her release from rehab, Nicole's been working on certain improvements in her life, including who she chooses to spend time with. That being her brother and the team and my oldest daughter, Angel. So naturally, she's around my little girl, Rory, quite often.

"She's in school."

"Would have been nice to see a friendly face. She's the only one in town who doesn't judge me."

She's right about one thing. I'm no friendly face. I used to be—with *her*. Especially after learning the full story about her past from her brother, who spent many nights after aggressive games in my office telling me the source of his rage on the ice.

Not the Nicole Kane story heard through the grapevine over the years. Not the one that's been lost in translation. The real story—from his point of view. I'd have given anything to hear her version of it, though.

Nick's version is that Nicole didn't just develop all her problems by hanging around the wrong group of people. That lifestyle was forced on her. When, at the age of sixteen, her mother, Terry—who was involved with some drug dealers, left Nicole as collateral when she was being threatened for money she owed. Terry was gone for one hour. One hour. It was all it took for Nicole's life to be ruined. They didn't rape her.

But they did touch her.

Since she was scared shitless, they shot her up just to calm her down. No one knows if she was violated in other ways after that. The whole thing still makes my blood boil.

Luckily, when they were seventeen, Jace's dad, Bruce, helped enroll both Nick and his sister in Taekwondo, when he realized self-defense was necessary. Nick and Jace spent more time at the local ice rink than karate, but Nicole broke the town's record, earning her blackbelt in six months.

Unfortunately, her defensive, badass attitude attracted the wrong group of friends, and it was all downhill from there. It was almost like she thought she didn't deserve better.

Her beauty was her curse. Long dark hair, bright green eyes, high rosy cheekbones, and a smile—if you're ever so lucky to see it—fucking breathtaking.

Tearing my eyes off her, I step to the door. "She'll be home at three. I'll take you to Nick's after."

She frowns. "Nick's?" The stubbornness in her eyes is suddenly replaced with panic. "Royce, you can't—" She swallows. "You can't tell him how you found me. You can't tell him I...relapsed." Liquid fills her eyes and the pleading in her voice slices through me. "*Please.*"

If that wasn't enough, she pulls on the arms of my long-sleeved shirt, lifting her chin to me like I'm her only lifeline.

"Nicky," I rasp, her hands on me making it hard to breathe.

"Please, you can't. Just take me to my apartment. I'll be fine. You can search my place. I don't care. Just please don't tell my brother. I've been trying—I've been so good for two years." Her voice breaks. "I didn't even want it last night. I was just—so angry with all of you..."

I know the first thing Nick would do—that is if he doesn't haul her back to rehab—is put her on a leash. Which is what drove her to what she did last night.

I need a new plan.

It's the very last thing on earth I should be doing and the one thing I've been longing to do. I pull her into my arms and hold her. Her body tenses at the sudden invasion of space—but within seconds, she clings to me, burying her face, hiding her tears.

Tears I didn't believe she had.

Tears no one believed she had.

My whole body is on fire and I can't think straight. I swallow hard, release her, and hold her at arm's length. "I'll give you a few minutes to get dressed. Meet me downstairs."

She sighs defeatedly. "I have no control over my life."

"Fifteen minutes, Nicole."

3

12 hours ago.

Everyone turns. Everyone always turns. The country music plays on but the chatter and laughs stop instantly.

"Look who it is."

I ignore Bud Singer and the unwavering trail of his eyes on the side of my face as I walk past him and up to the bar.

"Hey Griff," I greet the bartender and my old...let's call him colleague.

He doesn't look surprised to see me. Or at least he's acting like he's not surprised. In a better—less cloudy mindset, I'd be able to tell, but not tonight. I only want one thing.

"Is Sylvie here?" I ask flatly.

The kitchen door bursts open behind the bar and out walks Sylvie Greene, the owner. Her hair is a silver bob that always grows out a little too long before she manages to cut it back to her signature length. She's a tough biker-babe type in her mid-fifties. Save for the last two years, Sylvie and I were friends. If you could call it that. She was more of a mother-figure. She looked out for me as long as I kept trouble out of this place.

I bartended here for a bit. Brought in the crowd with what Sylvie insisted were my good looks since it certainly wasn't my charming personality.

I came in here for a drink after getting thrown out at my last job for cursing out a handsy customer. A bar was the only place I could go where people didn't look at me with pity.

Oh, there's Nicole Kane, who's drug-addict mother pimped her out when she was sixteen.

Not true. My mother left me with a man by the name of Frank Lidowsky, her dealer, at his warehouse with his friends, as assurance that she would get him his money within the hour. But I won't get into that right now.

I heard she does so much drugs...

Also not true. I don't do drugs.

She was probably fired for drinking all the inventory.

Fake news. I don't drink on the job. There's plenty of time—and booze all over town—for it after I get out of work.

No one knows the real story. And no one dares to ask. In this town, I'm either feared or pitied.

I prefer feared, so I play into that image of me.

Go ahead—believe what you want. The worse, the better.

And that's where Sylvie comes in. I came in and asked for a job five years ago. When she laughed in my face and told me to "take a hike kid", I was about to tell the old hag off when someone behind me commented on my having "better luck as a barista, sweets."

I twisted his arm and kicked him against the back wall, causing three picture frames to come tumbling down and told him to never call me *sweet*.

Sylvie hired me on the spot.

But I practically signed my own death sentence working in this place. Unlike me, Sylvie *drank* on the job. And she *loved* company.

"Nickles! Well, well." Sylvie throws her rag over her shoulder. Her eyes stay locked on mine when she reaches for the vodka on the shelf and sets in on the bar. "Am I asking Griff for one glass or two?"

Knowing the rules, I toss the bartender my car keys. "Two."

Present

Exactly twenty-two minutes later, I make my way downstairs. I'm dressed in Angel's clothes. The one's she'd left behind before moving in with Jace. My hair is still damp and my coffee is cold.

The oatmeal I'm bringing back down went untouched for the most part.

After a once-over, Royce takes the dishes from me.

"Is there more coffee?"

He glances at the oatmeal before dumping it. "There is. If you have a banana first."

I'd laugh if I had the energy. "But *dad,* I don't want a banana," I say dryly.

He sucks in a deep breath and pours the hot coffee into my mug like someone is making him drink cough syrup. "Don't do that," he mumbles. His fingers brush mine when he sets the mug in my hand.

"Sorry," I offer, meaning it. "I know. You're not my enemy. But my fate is pretty much in your hands right now."

"That's a little extreme. I'm not going to tell your brother about last night. But we can't pretend it didn't happen. Is there...someone you should talk to? Is there a protocol?"

"I don't want to think about it right now," I mutter absently.

"Nicole," he growls in frustration.

My eyes lift to his, my stomach flipping at the gravelly way he says my name.

"I'm sorry," he offers softly.

I glare at him. "Did you see me flinch?"

"Just because I don't scare you doesn't mean I have the right to bark at you."

Christ, this man. He's *profoundly* gorgeous. Now that my head is numb with painkillers, I can appreciate every delicious inch of him. Chiseled jaw, pacific blue eyes, rock-hard body, and a panty-melting scowl that is right up my alley.

I cross my arms in front of me, willing my racing heart to calm the fuck down. I *don't* show fear—but I'm terrified. There's no ignoring what happened. I'd have to start over.

Back to square one.

But before I dwell on that, I can't shake the image of the way he found me. Jesus why did it have to be *him*?

And yet...I want to go back to the moment where I was wrapped in his arms just a few minutes ago. Where he held me and let me cry against his chest.

No. No Nicole. That is not who you are. You don't show vulnerability. You don't show fear. And you most certainly don't show loneliness. So snap the fuck out of it and have your coffee while it's hot.

With that little pep talk, I take a sip.

"What are you thinking about?"

Even hungover, I'm quick on my feet. "It was two years yesterday," I say just above a whisper.

He turns and grips the edge of his kitchen counter. "I'm sorry. For my part in this. For all of our parts in this."

I frown. I want to be angry. I should be blaming all of them for what happened last night. But I'm no amateur. I slipped. One little trigger and I was out that door and heading right back down that hole.

"Turns out you were right."

He looks like he wants to say something but holds back.

"If anything, I suppose I owe you," I say.

"For what?"

I shrug. "For those nights you watched over me." I try to hide the bitterness in my voice. "Solely so that I would...close up safely and go home."

He looks at me like he doesn't believe me, then dumps the rest of his coffee. "I'm going to run to the office for a meeting this afternoon but I'll be back by the time Rory gets home. After that, we can talk about what we'll do."

"We?"

He turns to me, his eyes as sharp as his statement. "You're not alone, Nicole. We're all responsible. We'll figure this out."

I glance around and resist the urge to rub my arms. "Do I just hang out here?"

"I'd like it if you did. I don't think you should go until we talk later and come up with a plan."

I nod, knowing a good place to start is probably quitting my job at the bar. "I'll call Hank."

He nods agreeably and leaves like he can't get out of here fast enough.

Sleep. Sleep is exactly what the doctor ordered. I was so exhausted. At some point in the day, I take another shower and change the sheets I was sleeping in. Then head downstairs to wash every piece of linen I've touched.

The laundry room in my apartment complex is shared and the machines needed to be replaced about ten years ago, so this is somewhat of a luxurious task for me.

I found a phone charger earlier and plugged in my dead phone. As I wait for the dryer, I turn it back on and brace myself for a slew of messages.

Or worse—none at all.

Angel: *Hey. I can't reach you and I'm really worried. Can I come over?*

Angel: *Okay, this isn't funny. I know you hear me knocking, let me in.*

I hit play on a voicemail she left me early this morning.

"Nicole. You can't ignore me forever. Look, I'm sorry about lying to you these past few months. But it was a group decision and it made sense to us at the time. Also, I swear half those stories I was telling you about Jace and me those nights...were true. You know when I used our fights as an excuse to not go home? Hold on...what?" She trails off as if talking to someone else. "And Jace says that *all* the times he complained about me during his nights to watch you...were true... Wait, what did you say about me?" she hisses at her boyfriend.

I should be fuming, but I laugh and then press the delete button. "Just because I'll get over it, doesn't mean I need to call you back just yet," I say quietly before setting my phone aside.

I'm seated at the kitchen island halfway through my herbal tea and sports magazine when I hear a car pull up in the driveway.

The sound of an argument outside the door has me on alert. Having a full view of the front door from where I'm sitting, I stare and wait for it to swing open, my defenses gearing up.

A petite brunette with dyed red hair streaks pushes the door in. "Will you just calm down and get inside?" she howls. My face twists when I see who's behind her.

Rory stomps into the house. "Daaaddddyyyy!"

I hop off the kitchen counter. "Whoa, whoa, Rory, what's going on?" But my eyes don't leave the stranger who walked her in.

Rory's eyes beam when she sees me. Her backpack falls to the floor and she rushes over. "Nicole." I move in front of the counter, holding my arms out, mostly for fear of her knocking her head against the corner edge. I'm not much of a hugger, but it does the trick since she lunges herself at me.

"Is Angel here?" Her big brown eyes search for her older sister, since I'm only ever here to see Angel.

"No."

"Oh, is she coming?"

Darn it. I hadn't thought about that. But Angel does technically still have a room here. What if she stops by before I get a chance to come up with something? "I'm not sure. Maybe."

I hear the babysitter with the red streaks chuckle. "Rory, I don't think she's here for your sister. I think she's here for your da—"

I straighten and pin her with an icy gaze. "What'd you say your name was?"

She folds her arms defiantly and cocks her head. "Don't worry, he's too old for me," she assures me.

"Her name is *Kathy*," Rory responds with added disgust to the name.

I smile brightly. "Kathy, maybe you should spend more time touching up those roots than making inappropriate comments."

She shrugs. "I never said anything. Rory, take your shoes off."

"No."

This is a common word from the defiant little daredevil before me.

"Rory, I said take them off now. You're tracking dirt everywhere and it's not like you have a mother to clean up after you."

Rory's face falls and my jaw hardens. I'm still not entirely well but I don't remember blurred vision being a hangover symptom.

Cool it, Nicky, she can't be more than seventeen.

I bend to my little friend. "Rory, why don't you go take out all your favorite toys and I'll come play with you in a minute."

"All of them?"

"Just go on and lay them all out on the carpet. I'll grab a juice box for you. Oh, but take your shoes off…wouldn't want those toys getting dirty."

The little girl scurries off to the other room and I pin my *I don't give a shit who you are* gaze at the only real brat in the house.

"*What* did you say?" I demand, steady and hushed.

Kathy has the gall to roll her eyes at me. "Look, she can be a little bratty, she needs to be reminded that her dad isn't going to clean up her mess."

I push a chair under the counter to eliminate any barricade between us and step forward. "Look around. Does it look like he's struggling to keep the place in order?"

"It looks like—" She looks over my shoulder and her expression softens as she steps back, defensively. "Alright, I'm sorry, I was just leaving. You don't need to threaten me."

I jerk. "What? No one was—"

"Nicole!"

I freeze and twist my head back to glance at Coach. His eyes full of question and warning, but I ignore it. Turning back, I smirk at *player number two*. "Nice. I suppose you're going to stumble out of here acting like I've scared the living lights out of you?" I make a motion with my hands as if shooing away a stray cat. "Well go on then."

Kathy holds her hands up and starts backing up. "Fine. I've had about enough anyway. I could take the girl but if *you're* going to be hanging around here, I quit."

"Kathy, wait." Royce goes after her and I clench my teeth that he's buying into her bullshit. But instead of trying to get her to reconsider, he hands her two large bills.

"But... I didn't finish off the week."

"Until you find something else," he mutters and thanks her.

I ignore the glare he gives me across the hall and turn on my heel. As promised, I go back into the kitchen and grab the juice box for Rory from the pantry.

"Nicole," Royce starts sternly.

I twist defensively. "I know how that looked but you didn't hear what—"

He pinches the bridge of his nose. Something I found strangely sexy in the past—until now—when the headache is *me*. "I didn't need to hear what happened before. While I'm sure you weren't *threatening* her, if she felt uncomfortable in the slightest in *my* house, I could have a big problem."

Shit. I never thought of that.

My eyes drop—but not my head—I don't drop my head for anyone. He moves past me to the kitchen, not bothering to wait for my response or apology. I swallow and remember I have a little girl waiting for me.

Rory didn't waste any time unloading all her toys onto the rug. Barefoot, I step over a few hard objects and nestle myself about a foot from her. "What are we playing with?"

"Here." She pushes a set of colorful magnets in my direction, and I connect them with no particular thought as to what I'm supposedly building.

"Daddyyyy." Rory skillfully jumps over the toys scattered all over the floor before running into her father's arms.

"Hey, kid. How was school?"

"I had a good day," they both say simultaneously, and it drags a smile out of me. Royce's version comes with a nod and is a little flatter as he openly calls out her predictable response.

He sets her down and his eyes land on mine. I look away and open the juice box for Rory, luring her back to me for it.

"Thank you." She sprints over and grabs it, then gulps down the entire box in less than sixty seconds.

"And how was your day?" Royce asks me.

I ignore the question and level his gaze, my jaw tight. "I didn't realize that could have...caused problems for you—I apologize."

I *haaaate* apologizing. I don't know how to do it. And it's just not in my blood. But I would never want to get him in any trouble.

He lifts a brow as if I've taken him by surprise, then looks at his daughter. "I'm sure you had your reasons."

It's subtle, but I'm relieved he recognizes that I was being protective of Rory.

I stand. "On that note, I'd better get going," I say casually, pretending to have forgotten our earlier conversation that I might need my brother's supervision again.

"Nicole." There's almost a warning in his tone. Almost.

"I'd love to stay and play some more, but I need to pick up my car."

One of the last things I remember before setting my ass onto a barstool is tossing my keys to Griff. Because unless they had your keys, you're on a tight limit for the night.

"No need. It's in the driveway."

Frowning, I move to the window, and wouldn't you know it—my sedan is parked next to his Range, practically invisible by comparison.

I turn back to him. "How did you get the keys?"

"I looked for you at Sylvie's. A smart gentleman who knew better than to argue with me gave them to me."

Feeling more mortified by the minute, I shake my head. "Alright well, are they in the car?"

"No." He sets his hands in his pockets casually.

Closing my eyes, I release a steady breath before opening them again. "What exactly are we waiting for?" I poise my question carefully.

I will not be irrational. I will not be forceful. I will not lose control.

"Dinner is at six." He glances at Rory. "We can talk shortly after."

I follow his glance, knowing why we can't have this conversation now. "And exactly what time does she go to bed?"

"Eight."

I nod once then squint at him. "Remind me why I'm being held hostage?"

He rolls his eyes. That's a new one for him when addressing me. "You're more than welcome to leave. But I'd need to call your brother first."

I cross my arms. "What's for dinner?"

4

NICOLE DID ME A favor. Kathy was a pain in my ass. But at least she'd tolerated Rory for more than a month.

Her only job was to take Rory to school in the mornings, pick her up, and care for her until I got home from work. They'd spend maybe a total of three to four hours together per day and could barely stand each other. The girl had no filter and my six-year-old didn't care for her very much.

Okay. Rory hated everyone but she particularly didn't like Kathy. Over the last few years, Rory complained about a lot of things concerning her babysitters; *her hair's too long, she's always on her phone, she's always looking at you funny, Daddy.* But I never heard her complain that someone yelled at her.

I was just hoping to find a temporary replacement until I *gently* let her go.

A word that is clearly not in Nicole's vocabulary.

Something I always liked about her.

I set a bowl of water down for Rover, my Rottweiler, since he'd already wolfed down his dinner before I even set the table.

Rory is sitting at the dining table with a coloring book, her hair still wet from the bath I'd given her an hour ago.

Nicole strolls into the kitchen, sets some things on the table, and pulls herself up behind my daughter, gathering her damp hair.

"Where'd you find that?" Rory asks.

I glance over between plating dishes. In addition to a conditioning spray that doesn't do anything for Rory's wild curls, and a pink comb, Nicole holds a little bag of colorful ring bands.

"In your room," Nicole answers flatly.

"I use those to make bracelets."

"Well, now I'm using them for your hair. Sit still."

Quietly, Rory turns back to her coloring book. She's not one to let people touch her hair. But I can tell my little girl is curious if nothing else.

By the time I'm done setting the table, Rory has two even braids on either side of her head with colorful pink and purple ties at the ends.

Rory strokes them once but doesn't look up from her coloring book. I smirk when Nicole leans in. "Well, you're very welcome."

Rory side glances at her. "I didn't say thank you."

"I *noticed*."

Rory shrugs. "I haven't seen it yet."

Nicole laughs. "Ah, you make a great point. Well, go on then. And clear the table, I might think that orange crayon is a carrot and bite into it. And take it from me, it takes weeks to get crayon bits out of your teeth."

Finally, my little girl giggles as she collects her things and runs to the nearest mirror.

Nicole glances up at me. That's what it's been the past few hours. An occasional spared glance, but barely another word has been spoken between us.

I remember when those glances would linger just a little. When one of us used to have to break our gazes from each other at the arena or after parties.

Now she looks like she can't get away from me fast enough.

It shouldn't gut me—feeling like I'd betrayed her trust. If her actions last night proved anything, it's that we'd all been right all along.

Fuck. Just saying the words in my head leaves a bitter taste in my mouth.

"Hope you're hungry," I say, setting the main dish in the center.

"It smells alright." Nicole swallows and takes a swig of her ginger ale.

"Are you feeling ill?"

Her eyes dart to mine. "I feel great." Her words are sharp and as if needing to prove something, she lifts the serving spoon and scoops up a piece of eggplant parmesan onto her plate. She cuts half of it and puts it on Rory's plate.

Rory strolls into the room and pointedly looks at Nicole. "Thank you."

Nicole laughs.

"Aren't you going to say you're welcome?"

Nicole's shrug matches the one Rory gave her earlier. "I already did."

Throughout dinner, Nicole took maybe two bites of the half eggplant parm she had on her plate.

Okay. It was *exactly* two bites.

But it's not like I was being creepy about noticing. My vision is trained to detect everything happening in a two-hundred-foot-long hockey rink. Keeping an internal scoreboard of how many times Nicole managed to swallow her food sitting right across from me was an occupational hazard.

She did, however, eat most of the celery sticks on the table. Including the ones Rory passed her.

I'm upstairs with my daughter, reading her favorite Halloween book. As soon as hockey season kicks off and Daddy's back to work full time, my little girl knows one thing; Halloween is coming.

Tucked under my arm, Rory follows along the pages and I'm battling with myself internally about what I refused to ask Nicole this afternoon.

"Hey, sweetie." I set the book on the nightstand and begin to tuck her in. "Did...Kathy say something to upset you today?"

She shrugs but keeps her eyes on the book. "I dunno. Whatever it was, Nicole didn't like it."

"Do you remember?"

"Something about me not having a mother to clean my shoes or something." She squints at the memory. "Then Nicole asked me to set up my toys so we can play."

Rage and gratitude fill me, but I set it aside. "Has she...or anyone else said something like that to you before?"

She settles onto her pillow. "I dunno. Goodnight, Daddy."

I shake my head. With the revolving door of nannies and sitters I've had over the years, who the fuck knows what someone might say in front of her, or worse...*to* my little girl about her mother.

The gossip about Rory's mother abandoning her as a baby isn't something I expect to keep her sheltered from forever. I was just hoping it would be when she was older. Like when young adults start digging into their family tree or some shit like that.

I'd been mentally preparing—even rehearsing—for years. But no matter how I phrase it, she'll only hear one thing. Her mother didn't want her.

Years ago—almost seven actually, I met a young woman at an NHL event. She was a big fan and seemed genuine and sweet. It was rare that I took someone to bed so soon after meeting them but...she was willing, we'd been drinking, and...nine months later, our lives changed.

Actually, my life changed.

Vicky was in her late twenties at the time and had zero interest in starting a family. She signed away all rights to the child and handed her over.

It wasn't easy, but I managed to keep it out of the media for a while. But eventually had to come out and announce the new addition to the Collins name.

Kissing my girl goodnight, I sneak out of her room and head downstairs, preparing myself for battle with the last person I'd ever want to fight with.

There's a breeze coming from the back of the house, near the kitchen and I notice the sliding back door is pulled open. Nicole's car keys are safely hidden in my truck, but I wouldn't put it past her to go searching at the first chance she got.

I move fast toward the open door just as the jarring sound of glass shattering and profanity echoes from the kitchen. Switching direction, I race to the root of the noise.

Nicole's hands are in the kitchen sink—along with the array of dinner dishes. But it's all hazy in the background. The blood running down her palm is all I see.

I'm at her side in an instant and shut off the water, then tear a few sheets off the paper towel roll, immediately securing the wound with a tight grip.

"I would have taken care of that," I tell her calmly.

"I wanted to help," she says absently. Her hands are shaking, and I grip the other one.

"Wait here, hold this tight against your palm, and *don't* pull it off."

I return with a first aid kit and pull out the items I'll need. Gently, I open her palm and look her in the eye. "This might sting."

Her tone is as sharp as the glass that sliced her flesh. "I think I'll be alright."

She wasn't wrong. Nicole doesn't flinch when I remove the bloody towel from her hand and rub alcohol over the wound. With a generous amount of antiseptic applied, I roll the bandage over her hand a few times and make a small knot on the side.

"I'm a mess," she whispers, then looks up at me. "What now?"

And in her eyes, I see it. The one thing Nicole never shows. The one thing I personally know she'd die before admitting.

Fear.

"Come here." Taking her other hand, I lead her to the den and settle her on the loveseat, kneeling in front of her.

"You have to understand, I feel like I have an obligation. Not for my sake, but for yours. There's probably some kind of...protocol that I'm not experienced in. Your brother, he's—"

With eyes full of unshed tears, she looks down at me. "Don't call him. Please. He's...he's finally got his life together. Controlling his temper. He's in an *actual* relationship. I don't want to move him backwards. My brother will never blame me. He'll blame himself...and he'll go off again." She shakes her head. "I will handle this. I can't bring him down with me. What good is it if we're both fucked up?"

I swallow. "Is *that* what you're worried about?"

She shrugs. "I don't really believe that Nick will send me back to rehab. But I'll be under his constant supervision. You remember what it was like. He wouldn't go anywhere without bringing me along. And where do you all go after games?"

I nod. *To drink.*

"I know I can barely stand straight now, but I can take care of myself. Last night was a mistake. It won't happen again."

I can't fight it when my hand reaches up and strokes her cheek, then my fingers do what they've been itching to for the last two years. I push her hair behind her ear and hold the side of her face. "Are you angry with me?" I ask, my voice hoarse.

She smiles weakly and leans into my hand. "I don't have the right to be."

I inhale deeply. I know the right thing to do and I just can't find it in me to do it. I can't call him. I need more time to think.

Fuck, I need more time with *her.*

"Why don't you get some sleep," I suggest softly.

She sighs. "I feel like I've been sleeping all day."

"You need rest. Your body is still recovering and if I'm not mistaken, you've been stressing out all day about what I'm going to do with you. That's not resting."

She lifts a brow as if to say we still don't have that answer.

"Come on." I stand her up and help her up the stairs.

"Sorry for the broken glass." She offers when we reach the guestroom door.

"Remind me never to ask you to walk my dog. You might sprain your ankle." I nudge her chin.

She laughs and a tear falls on my thumb. A single tear that carries the weight of so much emotion.

I swallow hard as I come to a decision, I have no right to make.

I'm going to take care of this.

5

T HE MAN WASN'T WRONG.

I needed a night of uninterrupted, peaceful, sleep.

I groan as I remember last night. God. Had I really begged him to keep my dirty little secret?

Seriously, Nicole, get a fucking grip. You're supposed to be the big bad bitch in town—next to Sylvie, of course.

Two years with Cora and Angel as friends, and I turn soft.

The biggest thing that still guts me is that *I had this*. I was so good. I don't even want to drink. I don't want that life of being dependent on something.

I just want normal.

Cora and Angel—as much as I love them—are the exact kind of boring I need in my life. Sure, they each had their fair share of drama—especially recently. But let's not forget who helped them pick themselves up and dust the fuck off.

Yours truly.

Sadness and misery are for the weak.

And I'm anything but.

I close my eyes, repeating these lies in my head.

It's early and I need coffee. The bedroom Coach put me in is glorious. High ceilings and windows with velvety curtains. A luxurious queen bed with five-star hotel quality sheets. What more could a girl ask for?

But what I love most, it's *quiet*. There were no sirens and loud late-night comradery outside like on my neighborhood block. There were just...well, crickets literally. But even those were soothing last night.

Hell, I wouldn't fight Coach too hard on one more night.

I thought I looked halfway decent yesterday after my second shower, but today, you can really see the difference. The color has returned to my cheeks, my eyes are wide and on alert, my bones don't hurt, and I don't feel like I'm going to be sick every five minutes.

Coffee.

And maybe I'll take him up on that oatmeal again.

With my bare feet and a thick bathrobe tight around my body, I slip down the hall to Angel's room and help myself to another outfit out of her closet. Since Angel is nearly a foot taller than me, I can't pull off her pants, so I opt for a mini skirt and a long sweater before making my way downstairs.

The tension in my chest over the consequences of my actions hasn't subsided—much. But at least I'm not in pain anymore. The headache was nearly unbearable yesterday when it returned. And I was afraid to ask for more aspirin.

The less dependent on painkillers I appear, the better I can prove that I'm perfectly fine.

Coming down the hallway that descends from the stairs to the kitchen, I find Rory perched on a barstool, swiveling as she eats her pancakes.

"Hurry up and eat the yogurt too, Squigs."

My lip perks and I find myself wondering what his nickname would be for me. *Wrecking ball* comes to mind.

Shaking the awkward thought, I step into the room. He's in sweat-pants, which I've never seen him in before and a white t-shirt that hugs his biceps. A stubble lines his jaw and my mouth *waters*.

Get a grip, Nicole.

Royce glances back at me. And then...he does an actual double-take. "Hi."

I smile. "Morning."

He sweeps his gaze once more. "You look...good."

"I'm rested."

"I'm glad."

Tearing my eyes off his for what I know won't be long, I slip next to Rory onto a bar stool.

Now, I'm not speaking for myself when I say Coach Collins looks great in just about anything, and top-notch in a suit. But damn the muscles straining out of that t-shirt and the slight peek of the bulge I caught when I scanned him is enough to melt me into a puddle.

It's why I'm not standing beside him right now, pouring myself a cup of coffee because, of course, he's standing right by it. He probably *smells* clean too.

I distract my wandering eyes by fixing Rory's hair, which is separated into two ponytails, and not even close to being symmetrical.

I get a whiff of his familiar clean cedar scent when he approaches the counter and *moan*. "Mmm."

Royce grins. "Hope it tastes as good as it smells," he says as he sets something down in front of me.

I blink at the cup of black coffee in front of me. "Oh...I'm sure it does. Thank you." I sneak another glance up at him and pray he doesn't see right through me because that would be so embarrassing.

He clears his throat and steps back to the stove. "Rory finished the last of the milk. I'll need to run out to get more later." His tone suddenly distant, professional.

Maybe he's just getting into work mode? Or maybe he's ticked off he needs to babysit me. He reaches for his own and twists back, leaning on the counter, his eyes on us.

"Black is fine." I take a sip and notice him tense. "What?"

"It's scorching," he points out like I'm about to walk into the sun.

I laugh and wink to see if I can loosen him up. "Throw an ice cube in yours, then. I'll take this as is."

Shaking his head, he turns back to the stove and slides pancakes onto a plate. "I happen to like my coffee hot. But I prefer to keep the feeling in my tongue."

My cheeks burn.

Maybe this coffee *is* a little hot.

Or maybe you're blushing because he called attention to his tongue.

His cell phone rings, and he answers with a sigh. "What?"

I turn my focus back to Rory and peek at her untouched yogurt.

"Perry, I can't make it, you need to move the meeting to later." There's a beat before he shakes his head. "This meeting wasn't even my idea. Reschedule or cancel. And while you're at it, tell him I'm leaning toward canceling." He hangs up with frustration.

"Couldn't find the right tie to go with those sweats?" I tease, seeing as how he doesn't look at all ready for a work meeting.

"I need to take Rory to school first. I don't like to wear a suit when I'm dropping her off."

"Because you're afraid the fabric will get caught on the fence?"

He looks at me like I've annoyed him for the third time this morning. "I just don't."

I nod once and try not to laugh. Angel has shared her father's pain of excessive female attention, especially when dropping Rory off at her private school.

For the next few minutes, I sip my hot coffee and listen to him re-arrange his schedule for the day. All to fit in his meetings between ten and two.

"You know...I can take Rory to school today."

He looks up at me. Yep, me again. The annoyance in the room.

I blink innocently. "And pick her up."

He assesses me, leaning an elbow over the kitchen counter. "How's your driving record?"

"Been driving for ten years. Never had a speeding ticket or violation or a court order."

He glances at Rory. "So if I were to call up a friend of mine at the station to pull up your driving record..."

I sigh. "*Six* years. One DUI and the court order was for an unpaid parking ticket."

He raises a brow and I roll my eyes. "Okay fine, it was for failure to appear in—you know what, forget it. Sorry I offered." I've had just about enough of his holier-than-thou attitude.

Not that I blame him for questioning me. This is his daughter's safety we're talking about. And Nicole Kane is a known pathological liar.

I abandon my coffee and step out onto the back porch. It's large and elevated. There's a white swing bench to the left and a fairly sized hot tub on the right. A set of steps leads out to a grassy field with one giant tree in the middle.

I suck in the crisp October air. Cursing myself for acting like an idiot. It's got to be the residual alcohol that's impairing my brain function. He'd be a fool to trust me with his kid. Especially since the image of me passed out on a street corner is forever drilled into his brain.

I hear the door swing open behind me. "Nicole."

When I don't turn around, he steps up behind me. "Will you look at me?"

"Just go. The sooner you take Rory to school, the sooner you can get back and call whoever you need to so I can get out of here. Be it your buddy at the station or my brother."

He curses under his breath. "I'm sorry. You were just trying to help."

I twist, surprised to see the conflict in his warm eyes. This hot and cold game isn't working for me.

"Better yet, I'll do it." I lift my phone out of my back pocket. "I think a screaming match with my brother over the bullshit he's been feeding me is exactly what I fucking need."

I press ignore over the seven missed calls from my friends and find Nick's name just as my phone is swiped from my fingers.

He turns and takes three steps before turning back to me. He tosses something in the air and on instinct I reach up and capture the dangling metal.

Looking down, I find a set of car keys in my hands. *My* car keys.

"Hammock Academy. She starts at nine. Pick up is at three."

Maybe it's the scowl that persists on his face. Or maybe it's the iciness in his voice. But I toss my car keys right back at him. "Sorry, I've got other plans today." I turn and walk down the porch steps to the grassy field where a tire hangs from a tree branch. I stop and give the rope a tug.

"Hey, Nicole?" he calls.

I turn just as he tosses the keys at me again. I lift my right hand and catch them like a baseball.

He grins. "Your reflexes seem to be in order."

"My reflexes are better than anyone in this town," I mutter, giving the other side of the tire a tug as if I'm inspecting it for safety.

"It's been there since Angel was eleven. I guarantee you, it's safe."

There it is.

That reminder. This isn't just some man I had the tiniest of crushes on for the past two years. This is my best friend's *dad*. Seventeen years older, a supermodel for an ex-wife, and most definitely out of my league. Royce Collins could do way better than someone with a growing list of red flags.

He steps closer and hands me back my phone. Then in a soft, almost puppy dog tone, he says, "I would very much appreciate it if you took Rory to school for me today."

When I narrow my eyes at him, he rolls his playfully. "I mean, it's the least you could do. You cost me a babysitter yesterday for no reason."

I bite my lip and he looks as if he's waiting for me to tell him why I'd gone off on Kathy.

"I had a reason. Just can't remember what it was." I rub my chin.

"Right."

I shrug, stubbornly. "I suppose I could help you out today."

Rory steps out onto the porch. "I ate all my pancakes!"

Royce keeps his eyes on me and grins. "That means the dog had a mighty big breakfast." He holds out his hand to me.

With a soft laugh, I take it and follow him inside.

6

ROBERT HASTINGS WALKS INTO my office at eleven o'clock on the dot. I didn't bother moving our meeting back to nine a.m. as initially planned. I had a point to make.

Robbie is in his early fifties. A retired pro-hockey player on the New York Blue Wings. There was a time I'd looked up to him. In my college years, when I was coming in and he was on his way out. He was the best in the league. Speed, agility, leadership, he had it all. Until a cracked wrist ended his career prematurely.

Along with my dream to play against him one day. Or better...beside him.

My rookie year in the NHL was his first year in early retirement. I still remember being somewhat star-struck when I met him at my first big event with the league that year.

I'll never forget the bored expression he had when I introduced myself as the new center on the Buffalo Blades. His eyes averting mine as if he'd been looking for someone more interesting to talk to.

The man was my inspiration, my "hashtag goals" as Angel would say when she watched Olympic skaters do an axel jump.

I'd walked up to him feeling small and honored after following his career for so long—and within seconds, he'd crushed my existence down to nothing.

He was the last person I ever let myself truly admire.

Because years later, I found out exactly how he broke that wrist. It wasn't an injury during a playoff game as we heard in the media. It was a fist fight with one of his teammates, who was trying to pull him away from a young woman Hastings was coming onto at a club—after she'd clearly and repeatedly expressed her disinterest.

After a few years coaching, he was replaced abruptly and went on to be a commentator for the league, but there's been talk of him leaving the business. Which was fine with me.

Until I heard the man is gunning for my job as Head Coach of the Buffalo Blades.

"Thanks for meeting with me." Robbie makes himself comfortable on the black leather sofa.

"Had to move some things around so I sincerely hope this isn't a waste of my time," I say, not bothering with pleasantries.

He gives me a tight grin as I lean against the edge of my desk with my arms crossed. "This won't take long. As you may have heard, I'm retiring from the broadcasting business."

I raise a brow. "I haven't actually." There's no way I'm admitting to the rumors I'd heard. "Finally decide to move to Florida and take up golf?"

He chuckles insincerely. "No, no. I'm moving here."

"Here?" I repeat with as much boredom as I can muster.

He stands with a sigh. "Yeah, why the hell not? Buffalo weather's pretty much the same and I got a kid goin' to a university nearby. Maybe even see if I can patch things up with my ex-wife. Well, one of em." He chuckles.

"Congratulations." I nod.

He fixes a piercing gaze at me. "Royce."

"Coach Collins," I deliberately correct.

He half grins. "I'm interested in coming on board. I think you and I will work well together."

"I didn't realize there was an open position with the commentators."

He glares at me. "As head coach."

"Last I checked, I'm not retiring."

"I'm not asking you to retire. I want you by my side. I don't have to tell you; you know I brought the Blue Wings to finals year after year. We brought home the Stanley Cup for three of them in my ten years as Coach. When was the last time the Blades won?"

We've won twice. But it's been a while. And the last two years, we haven't got very close at all. Earlier this year, it was because we lost Jace for the season after I found out he'd been hiding an injury. Without him, we didn't stand much of a chance.

"If this is why you're here, I'm probably the wrong person to be having this conversation with." I round my desk and take a seat, finished with this conversation.

Hastings doesn't move. "I was hoping we could come to some sort of a mutual agreement on how we can work together before I talk to the execs, but..."

I point to the door. "But you were wrong. I have no desire or intention of working with you. Please see yourself out. And don't go calling my assistant, demanding a meeting with me. You can put in a request for one and someone will get back to you...like everyone else."

Ouch. That may have been a little out of line, but what do you expect, the guy marched into my office and basically told me to hand over my job.

It's after six o'clock by the time I leave the arena. Nicole didn't give me a chance to worry much between all her text messages throughout the day.

I've been checking as often as I could without much of a chance of responding, but it's the two voicemails she left I choose to replay on the drive home.

"She's dropped off...By the way, the woman with the blonde hair who took Rory from me at the gate—gave me the side eye. Not cool."

I hit play on the next voicemail, like it's my new favorite song. The kind of song you know you're too grown up to like but you just can't help yourself.

"Picked her up. This time, blondie brought a friend. But don't worry, I kept my mouth shut. Ugh. Fine, no I didn't. I might have said something along the lines of.... 'If you keep looking at me like I'm the floozy who slept

with your husband, I'll make it happen.' Ha – you should have seen their faces. Don't worry, Rory didn't hear me. I mean, give me some credit, I have class!"

I chuckle for the third time and check the recent texts I missed.

Nicole: *Where do you keep the mac and cheese?*

The next one came through thirty minutes later.

Nicole: *Never mind. I gave her a blue lollipop earlier so she's all set.*

Nicole: *Didn't you have a dog?*

Jesus Christ.

I race into the house at a speed I haven't known in years. I march to the back of the house where I hear Rover's paws against the hardwood coming toward me.

"Hey, boy." I ruffle his head and nose and he follows me into the kitchen.

Nicole is clearing dishes from the table and putting them in the sink.

"Daddy." Rory jumps off the chair and wraps her arms around my leg.

Nicole tosses a dishrag down and turns to me. She's just as stunning as she was this morning...with maybe a little bit of a day.

"See you found the dog," I say, treading in warily.

Rory frowns. "Rover was here the whole time."

I cup my daughter's head and lift it. "Stick out your tongue."

"Ahhhh."

I hear Nicole chuckle.

"No evidence of a blue lollipop," I mutter, shifting Rory's head in every direction to fully inspect before releasing it.

"Blue lollipop? She made me have buttered pasta and chicken fingers." Rory turns a treacherous glare on her temporary caretaker. "You have candy?"

Ignoring my daughter, Nicole laughs and points a wet wooden spoon at me. "So you *were* getting my messages." She doesn't seem the least bit insulted, but thoroughly amused as she hurls over in laughter. "Man, you're easy."

"Hey." I start in a low voice to my little girl. "You take Rover out back yet?"

She shakes her head and sighs. "Come on, boy." My dog leaps, beating Rory to the back door, wagging his tail.

"I'm sorry *dear,* busy day at the office," I mutter mockingly to Nicole, nudging her away from the sink so I can take over the dishes.

"Hey, I'm not offended, but I question your parenting had there been a real emergency."

If I were being honest, her messages throughout the day—no matter how absurd—were comforting. In her own rebellious way, she was checking in with me, letting me know everything was fine.

Minus the looks *I'll* now be getting from Blondie—I mean Mrs. Matthews.

She looks at the clock on the wall and stiffens, then removes the apron I hadn't noticed she was wearing. I almost wish she'd put it back on—and I don't know why.

Swallowing, she steps up to me. "Listen, um...I really appreciate the time you've given me here, privately, to recover and...well, hide out for a bit." She glances out the window as if expecting something—or someone.

Squaring her shoulders, she looks up and squeezes my arm.

It sends a shiver down my spine. Because Nicole *doesn't* touch people loosely.

"I know you worry about me." She starts tenderly, and it feels as if she's finally voicing the one thing we both feel but never act on. "I can see it in your eyes. And I know you were disappointed—just as everyone else will be soon. But I promise, I'm going to take all the right steps. I—"

The sound of a car door slamming from my driveway cuts her off. I realize my jaw's been tight the entire time she was talking. As if I'm bracing myself. Why does it sound like she's saying goodbye?

Nicole sighs expectantly. "I called Nick for you."

"What do you mean *for* me?"

"It's alright, Coach." She shrugs with a defeat that tightens my gut. "Let's just get this over with." She hangs up the apron just as Rory and Rover come back into the house. My dog looks relieved and less jumpy.

Coach.

I'm back to being Coach. Not the man who's been a little more on her side than anyone else.

"Rory, go play in the den," I growl, following Nicole, who's halfway to the front of the house.

She pulls the door open before her twin brother has a chance to ring the bell.

He sighs dramatically. "Nicky, thank God. What the hell do you think you're doing ignoring my calls?"

She steps back to let him in.

My team captain looks up at me and I nod him in. "I told Jace and Angel where you are by the way. They've been worried sick since you ran off—*seriously, Nicky?* Where did you even go? I wiped all of your contacts."

I jerk back and glance at Nicole, who's glaring at her brother like she's waiting for her moment to speak.

"I'm fine—now."

"What does that mean? Where did you go?"

She crosses her arms. "I'll explain everything but first—"

He holds up his hands. "I know. I know I messed up arranging this whole *spying* thing but sis, you've got to understand, it's not easy for me seeing you behind the bar."

She swallows and the onset of tears touch her big green eyes.

And I can't do a damn thing about it.

Fuck.

She looks like she doesn't have a leg to stand on. She didn't get her chance. We'd all taken it away from her. Because of what we did—the trust we broke—she ended up in the last place she ever wanted to be again.

"It's okay," she says softly. "I understand. You were...right to not trust me."

My insides twist. Because there isn't an ounce in me that believes it.

"What do you mean? What happened?" He looks up at me but addresses his sister. "And why are you here?"

"Coach—found me. He...helped me."

Shaking his head, he levels my gaze. "Where did you find her?"

"Don't look at him like that," she finally snaps. "He—and all my friends sacrificed many nights because *you* wanted eyes on me. Don't you dare take that tone you so leisurely take with me, on people who were loyal to you. And don't act like I'm not in the room, either. You want to know where he found me? Just ask."

Nick swallows hard. His expression softens and a hint of guilt crosses his face before he's hard as stone again. "I swear to God, Nicky, if you say Sylvie's—"

"Sylvie's?" I cut in, moving toward them until I'm right beside her. "Nicole barely made it up the block from Bridges before she turned back to finish her shift."

Both sets of green eyes turn to me.

I ignore Nicole's. Between her wincing at the name of her old boss and the threat behind her brother's tone, I'd heard enough.

"But she was clearly—and rightfully—upset so we stayed outside until she cooled off. And since I was equally concerned about her being alone, I offered her my guestroom to spend the night."

Nick blinks but doesn't look away. "I appreciate it. Get your things, Nicole, I'm taking you home."

I step forward until I'm between them. "That's not necessary. I'm already arranging for Nicole's things to be picked up this weekend."

"Excuse me?" my team member snaps.

Nicole steps around and looks up at me. Her green eyes narrowing, but only slightly, as if waiting to see what I've got up my sleeve. Trusting me just enough to not contradict me.

"She's moving in. As Rory's new full-time nanny."

7

"CAN I SPEAK TO you outside for a moment?"

It takes me a moment to blink into awareness. My eyes have been glued to Royce's. The sizzling look that's daring me to trust him.

The nanny?

When I finally look at my twin brother, I realize he's talking to me.

"Nicole," Nick calls again. "Outside?"

"Yeah," I mutter before stepping out the front door and onto the patio. Nick stays behind muttering something to his coach before following me out.

It's chilly outside, but I welcome the cool breeze to put out the fire burning my skin.

Not because of what I'm going to say to my brother when he confronts us of lying about this whole nanny thing, but where I go from here.

What's in store for me after two years of sobriety?

Two solid years.

Wasted.

There was a time when I thought I could eventually go back to "normal social drinking" but if the other night proved anything, it's that I'm incapable of anything normal.

"Hey." My brother's voice comes from behind me just before the door shuts.

With a deep breath, I turn and wait for bullshit to be called.

But instead, he grips the porch fence beside me and releases a breath into the crisp fall air.

"How much do you hate me?" His voice is raspy and low. His eyes are zoned in on the quiet neighborhood street rather than on me.

"What?"

He swallows and turns to me. "How much do you hate me? For the last several months." He motions absently toward the house. "For getting everyone on board with...watching over you each night you closed."

Sharp, familiar pain reaches my chest. "I don't hate you, Nick."

I'm afraid of disappointing you. Of being a disappointment.

"I was angry. I felt betrayed by everyone around me. Everyone in my life who was supposed to count. You, Cora, Angel—you're all I have. Do you know how humiliating that was?"

He nods. "I wasn't thinking about how it might make you feel," he admits sadly. "I was more focused on what I didn't want happening again. What I never want to see you go through again. I hated the idea of you working at a bar."

"I would have been fine, Nick," I say, trying to believe it myself.

He nods. "I know. I'm so sorry, Nicky. I'm sorry I dragged in everyone you trust—"

"I'm surprised you asked Coach."

He scratches his head. "I didn't. He found out and offered to give each of us a break once in a while."

I glance weakly back at the house.

Nick steps over to me and lifts my chin. "You forgive me?"

"No," I snap stubbornly. Then let him embrace me. "Don't touch me," I mutter as he chuckles against the top of my head.

"I love you too. I won't doubt you again. You had your chance to say 'fuck it' the other night and you turned around."

Fresh tears prick my eyes, but I swallow it down. Hiding guilt is something I was always best at.

After a long moment, he releases me and I avoid his eyes like the plague. He'll see right through me. It's a twin curse.

He leans back against the railing and looks at the house. "So is this for real?"

I follow his gaze and manage to avoid another lie. "I guess we'll find out."

The house is quiet other than the faint sound of a little girl playing by herself in the den.

Rory is sprawled on the floor playing doctor to some of her stuffed animals.

Wordlessly, I join her on the carpet.

"Wanna be the doctor?" she asks without looking at me.

"I've never been the doctor," I admit cheerfully. "Usually on the other side of that," I add, muttering the inside joke.

"You wanna try?" She hands me a pink stethoscope, which I slide around my neck. I hold the end up to her heart.

"Hmm...a little fast," I muse, not entirely sure it's a lie. Rory hasn't looked me in the eye since I walked in from the porch. "Is something bothering you?"

I've always considered Rory a girl after my own heart. Someone who keeps things bottled up because she's not sure anyone needs to hear what's on her mind. That, and the fact that she's stubborn, likes giving grownups a hard time, and well... beautiful.

I'm not conceited. But Nick and I come from some good physical genes. We both contain some sort of super strength. He uses his on the ice. I use mine...well, by any means necessary.

"I heard Daddy say that you're moving in and you're going to be my new nanny."

I swallow. The man really needs to be careful about what he says in front of this girl.

"Oh," I laugh nervously. "Honey, he didn't really mean—"

"There you are." His deep voice cuts into the room and I look up.

Royce's eyes sweep past mine and focus on his daughter. "Rory, sweetie, go upstairs and change out of your school uniform."

She sighs but pushes her toys into one central area before getting up. "Can I just change into my jammies? I don't want to have to change again later."

He huffs. "Nice try. I need to give you a bath before bedtime."

She grunts and marches up the stairs.

I have a strange urge to clean up her toys but resist because I'm not trying to prove I'm nanny material here. Especially because he and I both know it.

My chest flutters annoyingly when he draws closer. I'm still kneeling over the toys when he reaches me and extends a hand. I choose to stand without his help.

He's considerably taller than me so I move until our gaze is level—but it still feels like he's a giant comparatively.

A giant who wants to play hero.

"I appreciate you buying me more time, but I think continuing to lie is only going to make things worse when I finally tell Nick the truth."

His eyes sweep over the distance I just put between us. "I realize it's probably something I should have discussed with you first, but—he was here and"—his jaw tightens— "he was threatening you."

"Nick doesn't threaten me. That's just his way of—"

"I didn't like it."

I blink up. He's been moving toward me slowly and everything in me tightens.

Ever since I was seventeen, when a man comes near me—if I wasn't backing away from his threatening approach, I was drawing close to whack him in the jaw.

Everyone except for my brother, of course, who I only punched once but I wasn't myself that night and thought he was a threat. And the few—and I mean very few—men I've been with intimately.

Royce seems to pick up on it because he stops his advance. "I've seen you with my daughter. You're protective of her—"

"You can't be serious," I whisper, cutting him off.

"You've helped me with her on a few occasions in the past two years and...she seems to like you."

"In small amounts..." I remind him loudly. "Rory might like my dropping by with a cake pop once in a while, but she will not like my taking over her life. And I'm pretty sure the feeling would be mutual," I add haughtily, crossing my arms.

He takes a breath. "Sit down, Nicole. You're going to give one of us a migraine with all this forced hostility."

My brow perks and I move to the sofa. He follows me but sits on the coffee table facing me. "Nicole, I'm not a threat. I'd never do anything to hurt you. I promise you're safe in my home."

I put up my hand. "I think you're a little confused. I'm not afraid of you."

"I intimidate you." It's a statement and it's fucking ballsy.

I mean he's not wrong. But I'll be damned if I let him have the upper hand in this conversation.

"Not in the way you might think."

Silently, I dare him to challenge me. To ask me in what way he intimidates me. Hell, he might already know.

I'm not even sure how discreet I've been over my crush on Coach Collins for the last two years, because every time we're in a room together, my whole body reacts. I go rigid when he's near, tingly when he speaks, and every inch of my body *melts* when he smiles at me.

Smiles from Coach are rarer than the total solar eclipse for anyone that's not his daughter—but even Angel has been getting less of those lately, now that she's living with Jace—his least favorite player.

Instead of pressing me for details, he stands and places distance between us. "I'll pay you well. You can stay in the same room. There's also a guest room down here if you prefer—"

"You...trust me?"

"I trust you—with Rory. It's the highest level of trust I can give anyone."

I nod. "Royce, I don't know anything about—"

"I'll teach you." Again, as if he can't help it, he draws closer. "Everything you need to know—I'll teach you."

I shake my head, still doubting this is a good idea. It would have been. Maybe a week ago, before I fell off the wagon. Before I ended up in the last place I ever thought I'd step in again. I would have thought this might be worth a shot.

"Why?" The word comes out in a breath.

He considers it for a moment before his features turn hard and his eyes drift. "You don't have a lot of options right now, Nicole, and I—"

"Stop," I shout. My eyes narrow on his. "Stop being so stone cold," I hiss. "I have a lot of options. I'm no one's charity case and I will not be pitied."

"I don't pity you in the least, Nicole. I care about you," he shouts back, before catching himself. "You're Angel's best friend, you're my team captain's sister. The season just started and I need someone with Rory almost every night. She knows you. She trusts you. *I* trust you." He catches my elbow and once again invades my space. "And fucking sue me, but yes, I want to help you."

I blink and look down at his hand under my arm. "Do you...*know* how to help me?"

He shakes his head slowly. "Not a damn clue."

I nod and sniffle. "Then I suppose we're even."

"Do you trust *me*?" he asks.

I don't need to think about this the way he did. "Probably more than I should."

He nods and releases my arm. "I won't let you down."

I glance up to Rory's bedroom. "Wish I could say the same."

8

I RINSE THE SOAPY suds off my little girl's silky auburn hair until every trace of it is washed off. When her hair is sleek and shiny down her back in deceiving straight locks, I set the rinse cup down.

"So, what do you think, Squigs?"

"What if I get tired of her? Or what if *you* get tired of her?"

I nod. "Hmm...what if she gets tired of *us?*"

Rory bobs her head at me. "She will."

Part of me wants to chuckle as I imagine a more mature response from my feisty little one, saying *I could pretty much guarantee you she will.*

Hell, it's what I'm afraid of. But hopefully, by the time Rory has driven the last nerve out of her, Nicole would be...better. Whatever that word means for her.

As usual, I humor my daughter by rinsing bubbles off the two mermaid dolls she has in the tub with her.

"Let's not worry about that right now. I want to make sure you understand that Nicole isn't just going to be here once in a while as Angel's friend. This is going to be her job. It's what I've asked her to do on a regular basis."

"On a what?"

"Day and night," I say as I drain the water in the tub and give her one final rinse. "So...she'll take you to school, pick you up, help with homework, give you baths and put you to bed."

"What about dinner time? Last year, we had dinner when it was still light outside and sometimes when it was really *really* dark."

I release a breath, remembering off-schedule dinners with Rory and Angel based on practice and game schedules—sometimes skipping dinner altogether.

I wrap the large pink towel around her. "Well, that's one of the good things about having a live-in nanny. She'll be here to make sure you have dinner at the same time every night. And you don't have to come to work with me all the time."

A little more routine in her life would be good.

A flash of fear crosses her face. "How will she know what to do? What if she does everything wrong?"

"I'm going to show her the basics, but Nicole might have her own ideas. She's a girl, so you might like them better."

"Like what?"

After quickly towel drying her hair, I lift the wet locks over her head and tie them into a little bun. The way Angel taught me when Rory's spirals started growing in.

"Like how to do your hair. I could never do what she did last night with the braids."

Rory doesn't argue. But the girl doesn't exactly dish out compliments either. It took weeks before she admitted to liking my Mickey Mouse pancakes.

"Do I have to brush my teeth tonight?"

"You have to brush your teeth every night. *And* morning. I know you skip sometimes. Oh, and a word of advice; Nicole happens to be an expert at calling B.S. so don't go lying to her that you did if you didn't."

My daughter rolls her eyes. "We'll see who's the expert around here."

"Rory," I warn.

My six-year-old is just about the only one who isn't afraid of my raised voice or my tone.

Nicole isn't either. And yet I do...intimidate her somehow. When she told me that it's not the way I think, it took everything in me not to ask her exactly how. I don't even think she realized she licked her lips when she said it. I had to turn away to avoid staring at them like they were a tall glass of lemonade on a hot day.

Any stray fantasies I'd had about Nicole's full luscious lips have to stop tonight. No—*last night.*

Hell, she's been off limits to me since the day I laid eyes on her.

Nicole's beauty is no secret. But there was always so much more that struck me about her. The woman had been through utter hell—and yet lit up the room with her positive energy and strong personality. She didn't shy away from attention or hide when people pointed and whispered to their friends. Nicole is fearless and strong. She looks everyone in the eye and connects with them individually.

But no one knows what she's thinking. And that Mona Lisa glimmer of a grin tells me she knows more than anyone in the room. Any hope I had of one day uncovering those secrets needs to disappear.

And replaced with more realistic dreams.

Like making sure Rory never feels like she's missing out by not having a mother. That she doesn't get teased in school, the way Claire predicted she would.

That one day...in the far, far future, she'd know how to be one despite my stubborn desire to never remarry.

I watch Rory climb into bed, her gray terrycloth bathrobe still on. The first yawn of the night surfacing.

Nicole has been eyeing my daughter's bookshelf. "What are we readin', Ror?"

Rory looks up at me tentatively and I give her a reassuring nod. Moving to her bookshelf, she pulls out a short book. Her favorite Halloween book is slightly long, and I wonder how intentional this is. If Rory isn't quite ready for someone else to read her favorite...or if she isn't ready for Nicole to read to her at all and therefore picked a quick one.

Either way, I secretly grin with pride. Collins' blood is naturally untrusting. Our trust is earned.

Somehow Nicole stole mine the first time she whisked Rory off my hands at Bridges one night when I couldn't get a sitter. She sat at the bar with her, chatted up a storm, and taught her about a drink that was named after an iconic child actress, whose hair was as twisty and shiny as hers.

Like me, Rory gravitated to her each time she saw her after that.

Nicole settles comfortably on the bed and scans the book. "Wow. You're easy. Is this like the prequel to another book?"

Rory shakes her head. Clearly not interested enough to ask what a prequel is. I bite my lip, wishing I had asked Nicole to ease Rory into the bedtime thing.

"Okay." Nicole picks up the tiny book. "Lost Litte Cricket." She flips the book to the back. "The end."

Rory blinks. "You didn't read it."

"Sure, I did."

"You skipped all the pages."

Nicole feigns shock, inspecting the book. "There are pages? Where?"

Rory opens the book for her.

"Huh. Almost didn't notice. Say, what do you like about this book? You like crickets?"

"No. They're loud and scary."

"Ugh, I know. When I lived with my brother, sometimes I felt like they were in my *room*."

Rory's eyes widen. "Me *too*. We have so many in the summer."

Nicole gasps. "How do you sleep?" Then gently pokes at Rory's ribs with the edge of the book, making her giggle.

"Okay. Well, you do get *one* book so...let's make the best of it." Nicole flips open to the first page and I'm not sure Rory will be sleepy enough or satisfied in the sixty seconds it will take to read that three-year-old level book.

"Actually, can I pick another book?"

Nicole's mouth turns up on one side. "I'll wait."

I retire to my bedroom for a long hot shower, trying not to argue with myself. Try to rationalize that I'm not betraying a team member's trust and putting someone's recovery in danger by keeping my mouth shut.

I'm not one hundred percent sure if anyone—least of all her brother—will believe this was a one-off mistake. An out-of-her-mind, driven by hurt and betrayal, mistake.

But I can't fight this urge to want to take care of her.

What could Nick do for her under his roof that I can't? We practically have the same schedule.

I'm done lying to myself that this has nothing to do with the pull I've had toward her. It might have something to do with it.

But for Christ's sake, she's only a few years older than Angel.

Not that age is relevant right now. Neither one of us is in any shape to get involved.

This should solidify my restraint. She needs to get better. And I need to focus on keeping my fucking job.

Taking my mind off my situation for a few minutes, I open up my laptop and go over the schedule for the next few weeks. I make a few minor changes, send my assistant an email, and print a copy to hang on the bulletin downstairs.

It's a relief knowing Nicole will be here.

A constant for Rory.

The agency has been good about getting people who would be discreet over the part-time job of babysitting for a former player and now the head coach for the Buffalo Blades. But despite the convenience, I've turned down live-in requests on many occasions, and for many reasons. Like the fact that I don't need anyone getting the wrong idea of what living with me could lead to.

I don't have to worry about that with Nicole. We're both well aware of how off-limits this is.

It's almost midnight when I slip downstairs to hang up the schedule in the kitchen. Something I know I'll forget to do if I wait until morning.

The light is on and Nicole is sitting at the kitchen island, swiveling back and forth on the bar stool. She has a steaming cup in front of her with a used t-bag set aside on a napkin. She's in that guest bathrobe and her hair is damp over her shoulders. The worry lines over her brows relax when she sees me.

"Hi," she says, scanning me in my gym shorts and black t-shirt.

"Hi." I clear my throat. "Sorry, I wasn't expecting anyone down here."

She shrugs. "It's your house. You shouldn't apologize. Did you need to be alone?" She starts to stand.

"No." It comes out quicker than I intend. "Please stay. I just wanted to hang up the game and practice schedule for you." I hold it up briefly before pinning it to the center of the board on the back wall.

"Oh, sweet. Now I know when I can throw parties and how long you'll be gone." She winks.

I grin. "I'll send a warning text when I'm thirty minutes out."

Her smile fades when she looks at her phone again. The one she immediately placed down when I walked in.

"Something wrong?"

"Nick told Jace I was here and…"

I nod once. "He told Angel." I haven't given much thought to how my older daughter would feel about the arrangement. Nick showing up and barking at her like he owned her fucking did me in and my instincts took over.

"And?"

She sighs heavily and reads. *"What's this about you being Rory's new nanny? I mean if I didn't think you'd laugh in my face I'd have recommended it a year ago, but still… I have questions."*

I release a breath. "Okay, well that's good…"

Nicole holds up a finger and continues to read.

"Hello? Okay fine, forget the questions. I just want to see you. I know you're mad, but you can't hide from us forever. Besides, I know where you live…and I have a key." Nicole rolls her eyes and smirks.

I pour myself hot water and sit across from her on the island, reaching for the used tea bag beside her and dipping it into my mug. "You're still angry."

She shakes her head. "I have no right to be."

"Stop saying that. You have every right to be. Just because something… happened doesn't mean we had the right to assume it would."

"She used to sit there and make up stories about her and Jace fighting as an excuse to not go home just yet. She made up stories while I sat there and gave her *real* advice. Do you know at one point, I was so sad for them? I thought they had something so amazing after everything they'd been through together. And then there were nights I thought; wow, if they can't make it, there's zero hope for me."

I wince. "You're right. That wasn't fair to you."

She shrugs like it's no big deal. "I mean, I didn't buy a lot of it. A bullshitter can pick up bullshit, but I just thought I was getting the edited version of the story—not that it was entirely made up."

I nod with understanding and she sighs. "I'm sorry, she's your daughter. I forget that sometimes."

My stomach vaults. I love how open she is with me about her anger. I want to be that outlet for her. "You want me to tell her you need space?"

She looks up at me. "You'd do that for me?"

"I don't think it will keep her away, but I can try."

She smiles gratefully. "I appreciate it. But I should probably deal with my friends sooner than later." She picks up her phone and sends off a quick text, then sets it down and releases a breath. "Dinner was really good," she comments with some cheer, changing the mood.

"Notice you didn't touch the plate full of celery sticks I prepared for you. Guy at the grocery store asked me if I bought Rory a pet rabbit."

She laughs, swinging her head back and exposing her neck. It's slightly red again and I guess she'd taken another scorching hot shower.

It's too easy to picture my fingers around it, soothing the irritated skin.

Her phone dings and she swipes to read the message. A smile curls her lips before she reads out loud. "*Awesome see you tomorrow morning. Oh, and I'm bringing Cora. I love you but I'm still a little afraid of you.*" Nicole chuckles and rolls her eyes.

I shrug. "So, what, Cora isn't?"

She shakes her head. "That girl isn't afraid of anything."

I'd have to agree with that. Jace's little sister fell in love with one of my most aggressive team members with a raging temper. One he supposedly has under control now that he's committed to being a better man for Cora.

I stand and set my mug in the sink. "Well, good luck. I'll be around if you need backup, then heading to the arena for practice."

"And it's okay if we tell her..."

"The same thing we told your brother. No one needs to know anything else."

I start to leave the kitchen and hear her behind me. "Royce, wait."

I stop and turn abruptly as she crashes into me. "Sorry," she breathes, bouncing off my chest. "I just..." she swallows and takes a breath like she's winded. "Wanted to say thank you."

I sizzle all over from the contact. "Don't thank me just yet. Have you *met* Rory?"

She laughs and that's when I notice her bathrobe has loosened around her waist. I blink away before my eyes travel any lower than her chest.

"Sorry." She adjusts and tightens the front.

"No harm done. I should apologize, I should have taken you home at some point today to get some of your things. At least something to sleep in."

She waves a hand. "Oh, I don't sleep with any—" Her eyes widen. "I mean, yes, that would be great. Maybe tomorrow?"

I nod curtly. "Tomorrow." I climb the stairs too quickly—before my cock starts showing evidence of my understanding of her sleeping naked.

Right. Next. Door.

This won't do. This won't do at all.

I step into my bedroom and pull out a shirt from the dresser. She's still downstairs when I slip into her room and leave it on her bed.

I just have to believe *this* is what she'll be wearing tonight—before my mind dares to picture anything else.

9

I OPEN THE FRONT door to a smiling Cora—her dark hair cut to her shoulders. The magenta streak in her hair freshly dyed. It's barely nine in the morning and I just returned from dropping Rory off at school.

Royce is in his office upstairs taking a call—or at least that's what he told me he was doing when he saw Angel's car pull up in the driveway a moment ago.

I'd spent the night wearing a t-shirt he'd so generously left out for me after I let it slip that I don't sleep with any clothes on.

I'm pretty sure I fell asleep grinning. Between the heat in his eyes and the smoke behind him as he raced out of the kitchen, I didn't know whether to be flattered or mortified.

It smelled *heavenly*. Fresh cotton with hints of lavender and rain from being laundered. But woven into the fabric was a masculine undertone of cedarwood and an earthy musk that pierced my senses.

All night.

I wonder if he wants it back...

Still facing me with a big Cora-sized smile, my friend reaches beside her, pulling on someone's arm.

I frown as she yanks Angel from behind the wall to the front door.

"We're here," Cora chirps, letting herself in.

Angel on the other hand winces and gives me a tentative smile.

"Hello, friend," I offer as sweetly as I can.

"Can I come in?"

I roll my eyes. "Angel, it's your house. Come on in." Following Cora, I yank my other best friend inside. "Jesus, woman. You keep this up, I might just have to hurt you."

Angel's hands shake nervously when I lead them both into the den. "Don't make jokes. You know how sensitive I am—after everything that went down between Jace and me last year, the last thing I want to do is betray someone I care about...again."

That earns my friend another eye roll—two actually. Cora spent most of last winter convincing Angel that she hadn't betrayed Jace's trust by accidentally slipping his secret to her. One that nearly cost him his playing career after Cora went to Coach with her concerns that her brother was playing with a bad shoulder.

"I know, honey." I pat her gently. "Here, come sit."

"Sit? I can't sit. We're going to talk about this nanny business in a minute. But first, please tell me you don't hate me—I mean us," she adds with a squeal, pointing to Cora. "She was a part of it too."

Cora sets her arms on her hips. "Really? *Now* you throw me under the bus?"

Angel turns and points her thumb back at me, hissing to Cora. "She could snap my neck."

I sit back with my arms crossed, mildly enjoying this. Then turn to the other brunette in the room. "Hey, babe."

Cora shakes her head at Angel, who is still pacing the room and moves to sit beside me. "I'm so sorry," she whispers. "We all knew it was a risk doing this behind your back but...we were all so worried. It's not that we didn't trust you." She puts her hand on her heart. "I trust and believe in you with my whole heart. But I also never want to see you in a situation where...you feel alone. I don't know much about recovery, but I work with children whose parents have...similar battles and...it could take years."

Or a lifetime. "I know."

She swipes at a tear that falls from her eyes. "I love you. And I totally get it if you need to stay angry...or hidden for a bit longer. Believe me—I know all about needing space after someone hurts you."

"Dammit, you're good," Angel grumbles.

I hug my friend. "Thank you, Cor. That means the world to me. And I know you all had my best interest at heart. And that you do trust me—" I swallow hard. "I just hate having to let you all down."

Cora shakes me as if to wake me up. "But you didn't."

"Right." I nod and flick her pink streak back. My bright yellow one has grown out and I make a mental note to head to the mall with her sometime soon to have it redone. Angel still has her blue one but doesn't upkeep as diligently as Cora does.

Dyeing vibrant streaks in our hair is our version of friendship bracelets. Cora started the trend with her hot pink one and I just had to follow with highlighter yellow. The boys still make fun of us for it.

Cora glances at her phone. "I'm already thirty minutes late to work. I'm going to go make a coffee to go—do me a favor and throw this one a bone before she has a breakdown?" She points at Angel.

I look up at my tall blonde friend and raise a brow.

Cora leaves and I stare at Angel. I don't know why lying to her breaks me more than it does anyone else.

Angel breaks into tears. "I was so scared. So scared that you—when you left, you would—and then we couldn't find you—" She sucks in a breath and I go to her, wrapping my arms around her.

"I'm sorry. I should have called."

She nods vigorously and hiccups. "It would have been nice." She scans me. "But you're okay..."

"I am."

"I guess we all made it worse by assuming the worst, huh?" she asks, wiping away a tear.

"No, honey. I would have thought the same thing if it was the other way around. I'm so sorry I made you worry." I grip her hand meaning the next words more than I've ever meant anything else. "Thank you so much for being my friend. For worrying. For shedding these tears for me. I can honestly say, no one's ever done that for me."

She chuckles as she swipes them away. "Well, you're welcome." Her head bobs again and she looks at me. "I love that you're here. I think this is perfect for you."

I laugh. "Are you kidding? I think your dad just feels sorry for me."

"No. You're great with Rory. I think you're exactly what she needs."

"Angel, you got any to-go cups here?" Cora calls from the kitchen.

"Far left cabinet." The voice that makes my stomach flip comes from the bottom of the stairs.

"Dad!"

"Hey, sweety." He frowns. "Everything alright here?"

I hold up my hands. "I swear she came in tears. I didn't do this." I point to her red face.

Angel chuckles. "I'm better now." She crosses to him and lifts her toes to kiss his cheek. "Thanks, Dad. I think this is perfect for her."

"Still in the room," I say, grabbing my iced coffee and standing to leave them alone.

"No, stay." Angel reaches for my arm and pulls me to stand with the two of them. "Tell me, how did this happen? Nick was all grumpy about it on the phone, he didn't give us a chance to ask any questions."

I look to Royce for help and he doesn't miss a beat. But it's what he says that was unexpected.

"Don't thank me. Nicole is the real hero here. Rory needs someone constant in her life. She needs routine. And next to you...Nicole was the next best thing. I'm just relieved she accepted." His eyes are on me and I get the hint that he wants me to truly believe it.

"I can't reach it." Cora's strained voice calls from the kitchen.

My tall friend sighs. "Be right there." She nudges my shoulder. "Thank you for not hating me." After another quick squeeze, she leaves us. At least I think she does, because I can't see anything but Royce.

His gaze is soft. "You doing okay?"

"That was...very generous of you."

"To offer you a job?"

"To call me a hero. I know it's just a cover—but a little bit of a stretch, no?"

He tears his eyes from mine. "Think what you will, but I do believe I'm getting the better end of the deal here."

And that's all he says before he walks away.

That crack in his wall now seamlessly repaired.

I'm in the kitchen busying myself over chores after the girls leave. Royce hasn't given me any actual chores around the house but I can't just sit around and do nothing. I'll end up thinking. That's never good for anyone.

Still, while my hands are in the sink, my mind goes back to my friends and what seemed to be an endless array of apologies, gnawing at my guilt.

I hate lying—I'm good at it. Or at least I used to be, but I hate it. I'm going straight to hell for lying to my brother and making Angel cry when she was one hundred percent right for not trusting me.

And Cora—I swear that girl knew something was up and leveled it up a notch just to fuck with me. She was always smarter than she led on.

I sigh. And yet...she was my very first real friend after I got out of rehab. The one who welcomed me into her life, no questions asked, and told me she *needed* me. Needed someone to look up to, like an older sister.

The bitch was also the first one to make my eyes water.

My skin tingles. And I don't have to turn around to know why.

"You don't have to do that, you know?" he says, stepping up behind me.

I twist my neck. He's in jeans and a white long-sleeve shirt that seems soft to the touch. His biceps stretch the fabric, making my fingers itch.

"Afraid I'm going to break more dishes?" I avoid looking directly at him again since I can't seem to do anything but make him turn away from me the first chance he gets.

He steps behind me, brushing my arm with his built chest as he shuts off the water. It's...innocent, but scorching. "House chores are not part of our arrangement."

"Fine." I throw off my rubber gloves, feeling my cheeks heat. My frustration is likely misplaced, but I'm fueled with way too much ammunition. "Once you figure out what I'm actually good for, why don't you let me know." I pick up the rag I'd been drying with and toss it at him on my way out. He catches my arm and twists me back. I gasp, my face nearly colliding with that broad chest again.

"Don't take that tone with me." It's a sexy growl that makes my heart slam against my ribs.

My lips part and I'm ready to push until more of his goddamn wall is broken. "Is this going to be a regular occurrence, because I have a hard time keeping a filter on it."

His grip tightens around my wrist and I wince. Not from pain. But what in the actual fuck I was doing to him.

This is your boss, you idiot.

He drops my hand and backs away. "Of course not. I apologize. I um...I came down to see if you'd like to go over to your place now for some things."

Flustered, I nod. "I'll go grab my keys."

We're both quiet on the ride downtown to my place. Royce offered to stop by the hardware store for boxes and I told him there was no need. Everything I plan to bring, I can fit into one large duffle bag.

"You know," I finally snap, breaking the silence in the car. "I shouldn't be apologizing because I did *nothing* wrong, but...I'm sorry for earlier."

He inhales, his chest rising as he watches the road.

"But what do you expect?" I continue. "You hired a bartender. *This* is how we are. We're loud and forward and..." I trail off, wondering why I snapped the way I did in the kitchen. What had set me off? Guilt over upsetting my friends? Or did it have something to do with the man sitting next to me being so hot and cold?

"And what?" he asks, too calmly.

I hesitate and lower my voice slightly. "Defensive."

"You're right." He glances at me. "You shouldn't be apologizing."

I nod slowly.

"But you do know what this means?" he asks.

"What?"

He turns to me with a raised brow. "I'm making you a chore list."

I smirk. "It's the least you can do."

We return to the house an hour later with the one bag I'd prepacked in my head before we even got there.

He puts the car in park in his driveway and takes a breath instead of stepping out.

"Are you sure that's all you need, Nicole? You seemed to leave a lot of stuff at your place? There's plenty of storage here if—"

"This is all I need," I assure him.

He glances at his trunk. "It can't be more than a few weeks' worth—"

"I know."

"Nicole, this isn't a temporary gig. This isn't a 'until you get back on your feet', it's—"

"Royce. I snapped at you twice before noon today. You're going to lose your patience with me. Rory is going to realize I'm not as cool as I appear to be from a distance. I—I could get drunk and come on to you."

He shakes his head. "That's ridiculous, Nicole." He sweeps his eyes over me. "You and I both know you don't need to be drunk to come on to me."

I raise a brow and he smirks with a wink. "Come on. I'll help you with all your *bag*."

I chuckle and hop out of his truck.

I heat up meatballs for Rory and me for dinner. Royce had premade them earlier for us and I mashed some potatoes to go with it. Apparently, Rory likes hers cheesy with extra bacon bits, so I pile it on at dinner time.

It's the first evening I'm alone with her and I do my best to hide my nerves. Jesus, a group of bikers in leather and tats could walk into a bar and I wouldn't flinch. This tiny little beast walks into a room and I'm practically shaking with anxiety.

"Wow. You really polished those off."

"The potatoes were extra cheesy," she says appreciatively.

"You're welcome." I stand. "Okay. Come help me clean up and then we'll check your school folder."

Ignoring me, Rory jumps off the chair and heads to the den, pulling toys out of the bin.

"Rory," I call with a little warning in my tone. "Come help me clean up."

"Aren't you supposed to do that?"

I laugh. "I'm supposed to be taking care of you and teaching you responsibility is part of that. So, put those away and help me. Just...bring the dishes to the counter for me. That's all."

She taps her chin. "No."

I sigh. "Okay. Carry on."

After cleaning the kitchen, I meet Rory in the den with her backpack. She didn't want to look at her homework when we got back this afternoon and I figured she'd already spent the entire day at school, so the kid deserved playtime.`

Then I lost track of time and didn't start dinner until nearly seven.

I lean against the arched wall of the open room. "Well good news is you don't have any homework, but your teacher left a note saying you didn't finish this in class because you were playing."

She glances at the paper I wiggle in front of her, then looks back at her toys and I'm pretty sure that was an eye roll.

Okaaayyy...

"Why don't we take a stab at it together? I mean it's been a while since I've been in kindergarten, but I think it might come back to me." I chuckle.

"Then you start, and I'll look at it later."

Taking a breath, I come sit next to her and begin cleaning up her toys.

"I'm still playing," she shouts.

"It's almost bedtime and you still need a bath. We'll have to do your homework instead of reading later."

She crosses her arms. "You still have to read to me."

I cross mine. "You still have to do your homework."

She snatches the paper and pencil from me and starts to circle objects next to the letters. Then on the opposite page, writes the letters next to the images indicating what they start with before shoving it back at me.

"There, that wasn't so hard, was it?" I'm about to put it away and then notice one thing she missed. "Oh, you forgot to write your name on it."

She looks up at me and grins. "That one is easy. You can do that one yourself." Then she calmly keeps playing with her toys like I'm not even in the room.

Breathe...

The rest of the evening isn't any better. Rory refused a bath, I had to bribe her to brush her teeth and prayed she was too tired for a story because I needed to lie down.

I'm exhausted beyond words by the time Rory is asleep. One hour past her bedtime.

I make my tea and go up to my bedroom, knowing that Royce will be home any minute from practice and I don't want to face him. I don't want to tell him how horrible the evening was. He'll never want to leave for work again. I have no issue admitting that I'm no nanny. But I hate admitting defeat. That a tiny six-year-old had driven me to a point where I wanted to scream.

What did I do?

Rory always *liked* me.

Then I realize something. It was from a distance. I was fun, I brought her cake pops, taught her how to order sugary drinks with little umbrellas at the bar. I defended her to her babysitters and made fun of them with her.

Now I'm on the wrong side.

I want to be all that for Rory, but I also want to take care of her...the way she needs.

I don't bother showering or brushing my teeth—or changing for that matter. I set my alarm for the morning and lie over the covers until I'm fast asleep.

10

I WAS HOME BEFORE ten last night and Nicole was already asleep. At least I assumed she was. After checking on Rory, I walked by the guestroom. The door was closed, and lights were out.

I was hoping to ask how her first night alone with her Rory went but judging by the clean kitchen, completed homework and nothing out of the ordinary, it couldn't have been bad at all.

Maybe Nicole was the answer all along.

The thought makes my stomach clench. Nicole being the perfect caretaker for my daughter is the last thing I need to think about right now.

They're both already in the kitchen by the time I come downstairs. I'm dressed in jeans and a blue dress shirt for a press conference about the fake news of my retirement Robbie and his people started spreading.

Looking forward to setting that record straight.

Nicole is leaning against the double wall oven sipping her coffee. Rory is swinging her legs under the kitchen island with a plate of scrambled eggs in front of her.

"Morning." My voice cuts into the eerily silent room.

Nicole barely looks up from her coffee. "Morning."

"Eggs?" I ask my daughter, impressed with the amount she'd eaten.

Rory shrugs. "Hi, Daddy."

"How was your night?" It's more directed at Nicole, but since she's turned away, I keep my eyes on my daughter.

"Really good. I ate all my dinner and did my homework. Nicole was great." She beams up at me.

Dumping the rest of her coffee in the sink, Nicole turns with a smile that doesn't exactly light up her face. "Yeah. We had a great night. Rory was an angel."

"Like my sister."

Nicole nods once and turns to me. Her tired eyes scanning me. "You look sharp."

"Media stuff today," I say flatly.

"Coffee will help. I made plenty."

"I see." I step over to her and reach for my tumbler in the cabinet above the coffee machine.

"Breakfast? I made scrambled eggs."

"Thanks. No. Just coffee today. I need to prep for the conference later."

"Sounds exciting. What's it about?"

"My guess, Robbie Hastings expressing interest in becoming Head Coach for the Blades."

Her brows knit. "But *you're* Head Coach."

"And I have no intention of stepping down."

She nods understandingly, her features softening. "Good luck. I'd offer to make that coffee Irish for you, but your liquor cabinet is shockingly empty."

I hold up my full coffee mug and refuse to take the bait. "This is perfect as is, thank you."

"Rory, if you're done with breakfast, go brush your teeth," Nicole instructs dryly.

She sighs sluggishly and hops off the stool. "Come on, Rover."

I wait until my girl is out of the room before turning to Nicole. "Okay, really. How was last night?"

She gives me a warm smile. "She was perfect."

"Really?"

"Yep. Everything we needed to do, we did. Dinner, homework, bed-time reading..."

"Bath time?"

She blinks twice. "Mmhmm." She nods and turns to dump the fresh coffee she'd just poured. "Better make sure she's brushing well. Good luck today."

With a narrow gaze, I watch her rush the room.

Shit.

I don't bother calling bullshit. I need to get my head on straight for the press conference and deal with whatever really happened last night later.

It's no wonder Rory ate her eggs quietly this morning. She was making nice—at least while I'm still home.

It's no secret Nicole isn't the most honest person in town, but lying to my face when it concerns my daughter is becoming a habit I need to put an end to.

I make a mental note to be home earlier this evening and head out.

"You ready, Coach?" My assistant, Perry peeks into my office, letting me know they're ready for me.

No.

"Yes." I stand and button my suit jacket. "Where are they set up?"

"Same as last week, Coach."

I arrive on location just down the steps from the front entrance of the arena and greet management, stepping around them to take my stand at the mic.

The moderator addresses the crowd. "Thank you for joining us, I'm now going to welcome Coach Royce Collins, who has some news he'd like to share. Coach Collins, the floor is yours."

"Thank you, everyone. It's not so much that I have news to share, it's more to set the record straight. I have *not* announced a plan to retire or step down. Robbie Hastings' move to town is certainly exciting and I'll be the first one to welcome him. But his return...and the fact that he's...here today...does not mean a change to the coach team. From my understanding"—I glance at Robbie—"he's reuniting with the family he left behind here in Hollyville."

"Coach Collins, what about *your* family? Have you given any thought about spending more time with your daughter?"

I know they're referring to Rory—and the rumors from six years ago about my sleeping around landing me a child at my doorstep.

"I have two daughters and just like other single parents with full-time jobs, I make plenty of time for them."

"Who's your younger daughter with now?"

"She's with her nanny. Were there any other questions regarding my position as head coach?"

I give it two seconds before signaling to the moderator that I'm finished and step away from the stand.

A knock on my office door minutes later ticks me off, because I half expected Robbie to follow me up here. Saying things like, "nice try, but the seed is planted".

"What is it?" I bark.

The door creaks open and Jace's head peers through. "Bad time?"

I release a breath. "Always. What do you want?"

Glancing behind him, he steps in and closes the door. Then settles into one of the chairs at my desk and watches me. "What really happened?"

"Jace, I don't have time for this. I have another meeting with the owners later this afternoon and I'd like to not think about the joke back in town."

"I'm not talking about Hastings. That creep has moved around so many times in the last fifteen years, whatever he's selling, no one is going to buy."

I nod. "You just bought yourself five minutes. What's up?"

He sits up. "I'm talking about Nicole. You told Nick she never left the lot."

"That's right." I flip through papers on my desk, not sure I like where this is going.

"I went out there after you. Both your cars were gone. And then she ends up at your place? Please tell me you didn't—"

I point a finger at him. "First of all, it's none of your goddamn business what I do. Second, time's up, get out."

He leans back. "I'm getting warm, aren't I?"

I throw my arms up like I'm the only sane person in the room. "You haven't said anything."

"And I won't, Coach." He pins me with a glare that tells me he's serious. "Where did you find her?"

I release a slow breath, pull off my glasses, and pinch the bridge of my nose.

"How bad was it?"

"She blacked out. Brought her to my place to sleep it off."

He curses and rubs his forehead. "Nick would have had a fit."

"I know."

"On and off the ice."

"Yep."

"Is she really your nanny?"

I nod. "She's great with her," I respond, doubting it for the first time after she lied to me this morning.

Jace rubs his chin. "Who are you protecting? One of your players, or the woman you can't seem to tear your eyes off when she's around."

I glower at him. "Get out."

He leans back, satisfied with himself. "Ahh, the latter."

"I'm not interested in Nicole. I'm helping her."

He releases a breath, giving up the interrogation. "Look, I get it. Telling Nick doesn't sound appealing to anyone, but you can't keep this to yourself."

"I'm not. Now *you* know," I point out with a shrug.

He stares at me. "Angel still feels like hell. It's not fair."

"And you won't say a word. Some things are more important than easing guilt."

He drags a hand across his face and stands. "You're right. Are you sure you know what you're doing?"

"Not a clue."

He nods and opens my door. "If you need anything..."

"Thanks," I mutter, pushing off my chair and locking the door behind him.

My emotional capacity is reaching its max today and it's barely noon.

Parking my car in its usual side of my driveway, I hop out and head toward the front door—until I hear screaming coming from the other side of the house and run.

11

A few minutes earlier

The pep talk I gave myself earlier—the one where I reminded myself that I'm the grownup and *she's* the child. The one where I assured myself, I can handle this...it's failing me *miserably*.

Rory was quite smug with herself this morning when I didn't say anything to her father.

I'm no fool. I know I'll need to admit defeat eventually, but he's been so hot and cold with me—and likely regretting hiring me—that I didn't want to let him down again. I don't want to add to his list of reasons to doubt me.

I just need to figure out why the hell this girl's giving me such a hard time.

So far today, I practically did her homework for her, let her get away with zero vegetables during dinner, gave her two pouches of juice instead of one as directed, and now...she's refusing a bath.

Again.

"Rory," I beg. "You didn't bathe yesterday either, and we told your father that you did. I think he'll notice the mulch in your hair and patches of dirt on your legs when he gets home."

"I'll just wash my face." She stuffs the folder with her homework in her backpack and heads for the stairs. "It's okay. You don't have to read to me today. I'm going to bed early."

"But it's still light outside..." I let my voice trail off since she's already gone, and stare absently at the dog. The only living thing in this house that seems to like me.

After a long moment, my anger turns vengeful.

Careful Nicole, she's six.

"Oh, this won't hurt a bit," I mutter with a smirk. "Hey, Rory," I call up the stairs.

"What?" she snaps.

"I think the dog needs to go."

She stomps down the stairs. "No, he doesn't. He just went."

"Well, he's doing that thing where he—oh forget it, I think I know what to do. Come on Rover, let's go outside."

"Wait," Rory calls after me.

I step out back with the dog and scratch his ears. "Just play along, okay boy?" I whisper.

Rory snatches the leash from me and takes him down the steps over to his tree. I glance over at her in between my sneaky task as she waits impatiently for Rover—who isn't sure what he's supposed to do.

"Come here, boy," I call and the rottweiler races back toward me. "You want some water?"

Rory shakes her head. "See? He didn't have to—"

Aiming the spout directly at her bare feet, I turn up the pressure and squeeze the nozzle.

"Heeeyyyy," she shrieks as cool water bursts over her. Tiny hands reach up, shielding her face from the heavy cascade.

Relentlessly, I trail the spray up her body, following her as she jumps around between screams and laughter. I aim it over her head, watching pieces of mulch flow out of her messy hair and onto the ground.

Rover jumps around with his tongue extended, catching as much of the action as he can.

"Stop, stop," Rory shrieks through her giggles.

The word strikes deep in my chest and I *freeze*. I can't move. I can't breathe. I can't even stop the flow of water. All I feel are the chills that run down my arms and spine.

"Nicole, that's enough!" The roar comes from below the elevated porch, and I blink, snapping out of my daze, then finding Coach heading our way. I release the nozzle and turn my head slowly to the drenched child and one excited dog. Coach races over and shuts off the water.

Quickly, he snatches the throw blanket off the swing and wraps it around Rory. "Get inside, now." It's a low order directed only at her and his little girl is inside in seconds.

Rover follows but not until he stops to shake himself dry in front of me. I hold up my hands and turn my face from the sudden strong mist.

"What the hell was that?" he shouts.

"She needed a bath. So I gave her one," I answer steadily.

"Is this some kind of joke? Nicole, this isn't a game. She's a child. She...she could get an ear infection, she could catch a cold. It's *October*, not July."

Come to think of it, it is a little chilly now that I'm all wet myself.

Royce scans me slowly and swallows, then opens the back door. "Let's get inside."

I step in and stop in the hallway, Rory's screams echoing in my ear.

He removes the leash from Rover and hangs it up. "Rory," he calls. She appears with the throw blanket around her little body. "Go upstairs and run warm water in the tub. I'll be up in a minute."

"I can do it," I offer.

He holds up his hand. "You've done enough."

"Fine. Maybe you'll have better luck," I mutter before he storms off.

I grab a kitchen towel nearby and dry off Rover instead of myself, then fill his bowls. Resigned, I settle next to him on the floor, rest my head against the wall and pet his thick fur.

"You're not surprised, are you boy?"

He licks the palm of my hand before moving back to his feast.

"Yeah, me neither. At least I can make one customer happy. I have zero regrets, isn't that awful? She had it comin'."

After about thirty minutes, I hear him descending the stairs. It doesn't take him long to find me still in the corridor by the back door. He's changed into a pair of black sweatpants and a white t-shirt. He holds a fresh towel in one hand and reaches the other down to me.

Sliding my hand off the friendly dog, I take his hand and let him pull me up.

He leaves me with a towel in my hands and crosses to the other side of the kitchen.

"I think we need some rules," he says.

I frown. "What? No. I can't do this."

"Number one, you need to be honest with me," he continues, ignoring me. "I need to know if my daughter is acting up, you can't—"

"You're not listening. I'm not doing this. I don't need your rules or how-to's, I am done. You want to know how last night went? I'll tell you. I wanted to *scream*. I'm no expert, but I don't think nannies should scream." I start pacing the room as he watches me. "She was impossible. If I was behind a bar, I would have thrown that little patron out."

"Nicole, you can't hose her down in the backyard if she's refusing to take a bath," he adds with a softer tone.

"She's clean, isn't she?" I shout defensively.

"That's not the answer."

"I agree. It's how to get things done. When vendors were late with deliveries, we were late with payments. Guess what, they were never late again." I dust my hands for dramatic effect. "Problem solved."

"You can't do that every time. It doesn't teach her anything. And my yard is a mess."

I glance absently in that direction and lower my head. But it's not because he's yelling at me.

Stop, stop.

I close my eyes. It was nothing. It's not the same thing. I wasn't hurting her.

"Why didn't you tell me last night was hard?"

I open my eyes warily. Now is not the time to have a mental breakdown.

"Why didn't you tell me you knew I was lying?"

He raises a brow. "Because I was disappointed. Not only did I take you for a better liar, I thought you'd be just a tad more mature."

It's a punch to the gut. Both those statements. The second a little deeper.

"Are you firing me?"

"No. But I am putting you on probation. If you keep lying or...going off script...we'll need to revisit this. One month." His voice is strained, like he's sorry to have to throw me out in that timeframe.

He must be forgetting who he's dealing with. Challenges and ultimatums are my love language. I walk up to him and shove the unused towel into his chest, which hitches under my palm.

"One week," I grit.

Tearing his eyes off my lips, he looks into my eyes. "Fine."

Royce

I'm on the balcony in my bedroom, shirtless and frustrated. If I still smoked, I'd light one up right now. Followed by another one.

And then.... I would jerk off picturing myself shutting that sassy mouth with mine. Gripping her damp arms as she struggles free because she's not done mouthing off at me and then succumbs to my demanding mouth. Her slim but strong body would melt into me with a moan. Our tongues would dance while I lifted her and pressed her against the wall. She'd respond by rocking her hips against my erection.

Fuck. I run my hand through my hair when the woman of my dreams drops to her knees in my mind, sucking the anger out of me.

I shake off the image and step back inside, needing a cold shower.

Fifteen minutes later, my hand is on my cock and it doesn't get any better. Because I still see her coming toward me, pressing herself to me with nothing but a towel between us; not only accepting my terms but raising the stakes the only way she knows how.

How could I expect any less from her?

Nicole Kane always fights fire with fire.

Nicole doesn't speak to me the next morning. Her hair is tied in a ponytail loosely over one shoulder, her expression is flat and her eyes are tired. I can tell she hadn't slept much. It's the first time all week I'd walked into the kitchen in the morning and she was actually sitting at the counter across from Rory.

Usually, she's washing dishes or double-checking Rory's bag and the morning checklist on the bulletin board.

This morning, she's made mini pancakes. A little on the clumpy side, but my daughter doesn't seem to mind. For herself, Nicole made a bowl of blueberries and coffee.

"I don't want sliced banana," Rory whines.

Nicole takes a slow casual sip. "Then I'll give you a whole one."

"I don't want any banana. I just want pancakes."

Setting her coffee down, she glares at my little girl. "You either eat the banana or last night's broccoli that I let you toss in the trash. I'll go dig it out right now, it's your choice," she growls.

Rory stabs a slice of banana with her little fork and shoves it in her mouth.

Rover abandons his breakfast bowl and is at Nicole's feet. She absently scratches the top of his head between slow sips.

So far, the dog has been the first to acknowledge me when I walked in—but still doesn't leave her side. Other than him, no one spares me a glance as I move about the kitchen. Rory out of guilt because I called her out for her behavior last night during bath time. And Nicole because...because I yelled at her and she's giving me the cold shoulder.

Okay. I didn't just yell. I was unsympathetic and cold. The probation warning probably didn't help matters either.

But it's for the best. If this isn't working, then everyone suffers. Especially Rory. It's why I've avoided live-in nannies in the past. I don't need someone moving in here only to be scared off by my daughter.

I walk over to the counter where they both sit and kiss the top of Rory's head. "I'll see you later, sweetheart. I'll be home in time for dinner, okay?"

"Okay, Daddy."

I glance at Nicole, who's expression is stoney as she picks off blueberries she doesn't like, still pretending I'm not in the room. "You should wait until she's done with her coffee before you argue about anything."

It's my first attempt at damage control but it does nothing.

Rory follows my glance and nods. "Like with you on Saturday mornings?"

I chuckle. "Yes. Like with me on weekends." With a final kiss to my girl, I grab my jacket and head to the arena hours before I need to be there.

I don't miss having a wife. That's for damn sure.

After Claire, that's the last thing I need. My ex-wife is unfortunately far from gone from my life. Since Angel moved out, her visits have been less frequent, but I've had to repeatedly make it very clear that I'm not interested in a friendship much less giving us a second chance.

But there is a very distinct difference here. When Claire and I fought, I never felt the urge to make things better just so I could see her smile again.

12

"**G**OOD MORNING," THE RECEPTIONIST greets me with a warm smile as usual.

"Morning, Rosie." I smile back and hand her a pumpkin spice latte. "It was buy one get one free today at Starbucks."

"No, it wasn't." Rosie blushes gratefully.

I wink. "Give this compulsive liar a break, and take the coffee, will ya?"

"Thank you."

I smile again and take a seat in the waiting room of Dr. Pamela Heart's office. She's been my therapist since I was twenty years old. I hated the guts out of her back then.

I hated the guts out of everyone except my brother—as annoying as he was. But Dr. Heart has been with me and helped me overcome so much over the years. Sure, there were a few times I went off the rails and kept getting mixed up with the wrong crowd again...and again. But she's always seen me for the person I am deep—and I mean *deep*—inside.

Not the lost soul that will never find her way back.

"Nicole, she's ready for you."

"Thanks." I stand with my usual raised chin and plastered smile while my insides turn with a mixture of nerves, emotion, and the need to run for the nearest exit.

"Hi, Pamela." The first name basis was insisted on about a year ago and it's made a world of difference for me.

She stands from her desk and moves to the couch where we sit on opposite ends.

"You're not due to see me until later in the month. Everything alright?"

I grip my knees. "No. It's not. I... had a setback. A small one. Okay, maybe not so small. It was Sunday night."

Her smile fades and she looks down at her notebook. But her pen doesn't move.

"What happened that night?"

"I ended up at the bar where I used to—"

"No. Start at the beginning. What happened *earlier* that night?" she asks calmly. Just her voice, her rich, understanding, soothing voice makes me release a breath and start over.

Pamela nods slowly as I walk her through it all, only making minor notes every so often but staying focused.

I pause and wait for her to say something.

When she doesn't, I continue. "I realize I should have been here the very next day."

She shakes her head. "Your timing is just fine."

"I know I should have gone to my brother instead of accepting the offer from his coach, but...I'm just not ready to have my life taken over again—or screw with my brother's, you know? He'll keep me from working, he'll have me tag along everywhere. I can't live like that. And neither should he."

She nods. "I agree."

"You think he's crazy—for hiring me?"

"We're back to Coach Collins now?" She blinks and glances down, choosing her words. "I think he's giving you a very generous shot to prove yourself. He obviously sees your potential."

I scoff. "He's just desperate."

"How are you doing? With Rory?"

"She's... just a dream," I say.

Pamela waits patiently for the truth. "More of a nightmare, actually." I look up at her guiltily. "I'm screwing up. And last night...I thought I was hurting her. Realistically, I didn't, but when she screamed—" I choke on my words and my hand shoots to my left arm.

Pamela is silent, which is odd for her. She picks up the phone and asks the receptionist to extend my visit today, at no additional charge.

"Nicole," she starts when I explain what I did in the backyard. "You are not your mother. You are not those men from the warehouse. You had *fun* with her. You got creative. She was *laughing*. Her father may not see it now, but I bet you earned her respect."

I nod absently.

"And how is your communication? With her father?"

I scoff. "He's caught me lying on three...maybe four occasions now."

She cocks her head. "And how easy are you making yourself be...caught?"

"I don't enjoy lying. It's not a game for me anymore. It's not who I am anymore. But—I feel like the real me is..." I shake my head. "No one would want the real me around their child. And this job, this chance...it seems like something I really want, but don't deserve."

She nods then looks at me like I know what she's going to say.

"You think I'm sabotaging myself."

"Why is that the first thing to come to your mind?"

Ugh, therapists.

"I don't think I'm making Rory hate me. I think I really want this to work. You're the first person I've told this to."

She frowns. "You haven't expressed your interest of making this work to your new boss?"

"No. Our relationship is complicated."

She sets her notebook down and reaches for her iPad. "How so?"

"I...well, he's my best friend's father. My brother's coach. I've known him for years and...well..."

Her eyes drop to my twined fingers, squeezing my knuckles. "This is the coach for the Buffalo Blades we're talking about?"

I nod.

She types into her iPad and waits for the results, then lifts a brow. "Do you...find him attractive?"

Yep, she Googled him.

How do I answer that? I'm more than attracted to him. My whole body responds in unspeakable ways when he's near.

"He put me on probation," I blurt, sidetracking from her question.

She nods once. "What were his terms?"

I scrunch my nose. "That I stop lying and going off script—whatever that means."

"Are you not following directions? You've never cared for a child before," she reminds me.

"I'm doing what feels right with that little—" I force a smile "ray of sunshine."

Pamela smirks and reaches for her notebook again. "Given your trigger last night with regard to Rory, I'd like to put you back on your anxiety medication. Only to be taken as needed. Anxiety strikes unexpectedly, and with your new responsibilities as a full-time nanny, I want you prepared."

I nod.

She looks at me sympathetically. "Do you have someone who can dole them out to you?"

I take a breath. Nick would dole out my meds. But I can't ask him. Not yet, at least. "I'll find someone."

She nods and reaches for her prescription pad. "The person you give it to should—"

"Be aware of the count. I know."

"I'm glad you stopped by today. Would you be comfortable switching back to weekly?"

I nod out of obligation. *I don't have a choice.*

I've used up all my fake smiles at my therapist's office and have zero left for the rest of the day. It's Friday, thankfully, and I get a two-day break from the ugly glares from Rory's teachers and the moms at the playground.

They act like I can't read their minds—or their lips when they whisper to each other.

Rory has been quiet too, but strangely obedient.

We're finishing her homework when we hear the back door open and Rover appearing out of nowhere, barking and racing past the kitchen to the back door.

"Hey, boy. Yeah, I missed you too."

I curse my thumping heart at the sound. For that part of me that melts a little when I hear that mature, gravelly voice.

I quietly wonder which tone of his I'll get tonight. And which one I *want*. Whether it's the gentle one I'm used to... or the hard one he introduced me to last night.

I stand as Rory runs to the door with her arms spread.

I can't do this again tonight. I can't argue with him. He's still my boss. As hurt as I am that he's giving up on me, that he's expecting me to fail so gave himself an out from this arrangement, I have to respect that he's just looking out for his daughter.

I don't blame him. I'd do anything to keep this little girl safe too. But the fact that he wants to keep her safe from *me* hurts to the core.

Needing some distance, I hold my hand out to Rory. "Come help me fold laundry upstairs while your dad cooks."

She hops off the stool obediently and follows me.

An hour later, I'm both famished and nauseous with nerves as we head down to dinner. I take Rory to wash hands with me and we sit at the table.

"Everything looks delicious," I say flatly, my eyes scanning the table dryly. I'm still not smiling. I'm no longer bothering with pleasantries with this man.

"If you hate it, I do have plenty of celery sticks," he says, with a smirk. Rory chuckles.

I turn to her, the first hint of a smile touching my lips. "Don't laugh at me, I'll make you eat them."

I do well to avoid Royce's eyes on me throughout dinner, which is quiet for the most part.

"What about you, Nicole? Do anything interesting today?" Royce finally asks when I've avoided every other topic of conversation.

I know he's making a show of including me for Rory's sake, but I'm not interested in chatting. Hell, the way he spoke to me yesterday, I feel like I shouldn't even be eating at this table.

Atta girl, Nicole. Be offended, not turned on.

"Not much," I answer.

"Didn't you say you were going to the doctor this morning?" Rory asks.

Royce shifts uncomfortably. "Rory, it might be personal."

"Did she give you a shot?" she asks, practically horrified.

"No," I answer softly. "This doctor just...talks to you, mostly."

Rory's brows knit and she almost looks sad. Her voice drops. "Because you have no one else to talk to?"

I turn to her and still don't bother with fake smiles. "No, she's just very smart and tells me things I can do to feel better."

Royce's eyes are on me again. "How'd it go?"

I glance up but don't respond.

"Is that why you're so quiet today? Because you talked enough?" Rory asks, and it releases a soft chuckle from my lips.

"Yeah, probably."

She blows out a relieved breath. "I thought it was because of me."

Instead of reassuring her, I fork away the rest of my salmon and finish my sparkling water. "Rory, if you're finished, go upstairs to get ready for your bath."

In front of me, Royce stiffens as if preparing for battle with his daughter. He leans his head toward me and whispers, "I can handle it today—"

"Okay," Rory chirps. "I'll go get my bath toys."

I stand and pick up both mine and Rory's plates and set them neatly in the sink.

He stands as I move past him toward the stairs. "Nicole."

"I've *got* it, Coach."

His eyes meet mine and I'm not sure if it's the edge in my voice that stops him in his tracks or the fact that I'm no longer using his name.

He puts his hands in his pockets and nods. "Yeah. It looks like you do."

Rory is playful during bath time, but not very talkative. It's the first time I'm giving her a real bath and I'm enjoying myself. I'd apparently put in way too many bubbles, but she's totally here for it from what I can tell.

I lather soap off her silky hair.

"I like the way you do that. Daddy always does it too fast."

"Maybe he just doesn't want you to get cold."

She shrugs and it makes me smile. How easy she can be when she's not deliberately trying to make me dislike her. I'll likely never admit it out loud—especially not to her—but I liked the fire in her. The stubbornness, the bossiness, that need to challenge me. It makes me a little proud.

I never want anyone taking advantage of her.

"Did you think I was sad because you haven't been very nice to me?"

She nods, keeping her eyes on the bubbly water.

"And my being sad, made you sad?"

Another nod.

I lower myself a bit. "You know you can tell me anything. We used to be friends."

She looks up at me and gives me a look as if that was a thing of the past.

"Just because I'm your nanny doesn't mean I'm not your friend."

"It just means you're going to quit."

I frown. "What?"

"Angel and Daddy always talk about how my babysitters always quit."

"But I'm not—" I blink.

Don't make promises you can't keep.

With the reminder of my probation period—for which I have six days left, I flick her chin. "Regardless of who I am—the nanny, Angel's friend, or your local grocery store checkout girl, I'm always going to be your friend. I'm always going to defend you and laugh at others with you. That's our thing. You're my favorite little girl," I add with a whisper.

I may not be Mary Poppins, and I'm likely to screw up again, but no one can deny me my friendship with this girl.

And the fact that she was just ripping off the band-aid because she thought my leaving was inevitable...breaks my heart.

"Let's rinse you off."

13

THE OTHER NIGHT, I took a tone with her only my players, occasionally my assistant and certain reporters get to hear from me.

That raw, unfiltered fury that unleashes when I'm provoked. When I'm challenged by someone who thinks they know better.

And dammit if I don't love the way she fights back. The way she doesn't cower. Sure, I'd gotten the cold shoulder all day but if she taught me anything last night, it's that she's not one to be threatened.

Nicole went straight to her room after putting Rory to bed—at eight-thirty, no doubt avoiding me. I waited for her to come downstairs. To be grown up and talk to me. Hell, if nothing else, to gloat that whatever she's been doing with Rory—and yes, including the whole backyard mess—is working.

But she never came down.

On Saturday morning, I'm lifting weights in my gym by seven. Rory will be up soon, and I want to spend as much time with her this weekend since we're traveling to play in Seattle next weekend.

Moving to the elliptical, I try not to spend too much time wondering what Nicole discussed with her therapist during her visit yesterday. I try not to be offended that I didn't know about it. Not that I had a right to after I was a dick to her and set a clock on her time here.

My gut twists every time I think about it.

An apology is definitely in order, but I'm not sure how much I'm ready to bend my rules. I despise lies so that needs to stop.

But I suppose I could make it easier for her to be truthful.

When I've worked up enough of a sweat, I grab a towel and toss it around my neck. I'm in my gym shorts and black tank. There's a shower down here, but I don't bother with it, since I may just go for a run with Rover in a bit.

I make my way to the kitchen to start breakfast when I hear the coffee machine already brewing. Nicole has her back to me, making pancake batter—or trying to.

"You're up early," I say.

Jumping, she turns.

"I'm sorry," I offer quickly and pull out my earphones. "I've had these in for the past hour so I'm a little loud."

Nicole blinks but doesn't respond. Big green eyes scan me sultrily. Her lips part and she quickly spins back to the bowl on the counter. "It's fine," she breathes.

I *shouldn't* be satisfied with that reaction. But I am.

And I need more of it.

"Really, I didn't mean to scare you," I say softly, unable to keep myself from moving toward her. "But Rory won't be up for a bit, I thought you might want to sleep in for a change."

Against my better judgement, I gently twist her to face me. Because I'm sick of being ignored.

By *her*.

I hate that she can't look at me. That I pushed her to that point.

Her breath hitches and she stares at my chest before lifting her chin. And just when I'm expecting her to push me off her and tell me how inappropriate I'm being, she *breathes* me in.

Can she see the way my heart beats for her?

Does she know what she's doing to me?

Blinking, she breaks free and moves to a paper bag on the kitchen island. She pauses for a moment before pulling something out. It rattles like a bottle of pills.

With firm, steady hands, she stretches them out for me. "These are prescription. It's for anxiety."

Slowly, I take them from her, my eyes flicking back to hers.

"There's exactly twenty in there," she says, mechanically. "Count 'em."

"I don't need to. But I can if that's...what *you* need...I will." I want to help her, but I need her to tell me how.

"No. If I need them, which I haven't in a while, I'll need you to give me one—just one."

Understanding settles and I nod. "Of course." I grip the bottle and look back at her. "Am I the reason you need..."

Her eyes flash. "No. It's not you." She closes her eyes. "The other night, I thought I—hurt her—out there." She opens them and lifts her chin. "But I didn't. I know that now." She looks down at the bottle in my hands. "These are supposed to help in case..."

I pull her into my arms vigorously. "Honey, you didn't—you couldn't."

She nods against my chest, letting herself go for a moment that's way too brief before pushing me away and grabbing an empty mug.

"How many sugars?" she asks, her voice steady, like the last three minutes didn't happen.

I don't push. She doesn't need that. "One, please."

She moves back to her batter and I know she's no longer paying attention to the mix. I step behind her, unintentionally towering over her small frame as she struggles to smooth the lumps with the whisk. "Do you mind?" I ask softly, taking the whisk from under her fingers.

I don't miss the goosebumps along her arms before she steps aside. "Be my guest. I've made it four times... can't seem to get it right."

"It's not you. It's the whisk."

"Is it breaking up with me?" she asks, looking up at me for what seems like the first time in forever.

"'Fraid so, but you're better off." I reach for the sterling silver serving spoon. "A rubber whisk won't help the clumps. I use this to smear along the bowl. And if that doesn't work, a tinge more water or milk."

I smooth out the batter and reach for the scoop spoon, handing it back over to her, which she accepts with hidden appreciation.

"Ding dong."

I release a breathy groan at the shrill voice coming from the front door and wait until my ex-wife finds us in the kitchen.

"For the last time, Claire, it doesn't count if you *say* it, you need to ring the fucking bell."

"Oh hush and drink your coffee." She waves me off but her eyes land tauntingly on Nicole and I instantly want to move in front of her.

"Oh, hello, Mrs. Collins."

I grit my teeth and decide to correct Nicole later. Even though Claire never bothered to change her last name back to her maiden name, because it's "better for her professional image" to still be associated with me, doesn't mean Nicole should have to use it.

"Oh good, Angel is here?"

"No," I say dryly. "Why are you here?"

Frowning at Nicole, who smartly pretends not to notice, my ex-wife shamelessly asks, "Then why is *she* here?"

"Maybe I'll tell you if you try that entrance again and this time ring the bell like everyone else."

As usual, Claire rolls her eyes at me with regard to her manners.

Nicole dries her hands on her apron, which Claire scans suspiciously. "It's alright. I'm Rory's new nanny, temporarily," she adds that last part and it singes my gut.

Claire raises a brow, then turns to me. "This is a joke, right?"

"Claire, why are you here?" I demand, keeping my cool in front of my house guest.

She holds her head higher as if establishing some authority between the two women. "I saw the press conference."

Now it's my turn to roll my eyes. "If you have questions, call my assistant."

"This has nothing to do with your supposed retirement, I know damn well you're not. But what *else* you mentioned during it." She nods at Nicole, who excuses herself to go check on Rory.

Once she's out of the room, Clarie hisses at me. "Are you crazy? You hired Nicole *Kane* to watch your daughter?" The way she says her last name, like she's the shame of the city, infuriates me.

"It's bad enough that she's friends with *our* daughter, who unfortunately tunes me out when I try to talk sense into her, but you're willing to let this woman take care of Rory?"

I'm not about to defend Nicole to my ex-wife. It would be the equivalent of defending her to the whole town since Claire is where town gossip starts.

"Have you completely gone off the rails? Do you enjoy making these career sabotaging mistakes?"

She'd said the same thing when I found out about Rory. Claire and I had long since been divorced but she staked claim to staying in my life. Which I allowed, because of Angel.

"And if you stopped caring about your career, then think about your daughter. She's not safe with her."

I pinch the bridge of my nose. "Claire, please stop, or this conversation is going to go somewhere you don't want it to. And now that Angel isn't here, I have no issue being vocal about it."

She jerks like I'd just slapped her.

"Royce," she starts in a lower, calmer voice. "I don't know what kind of midlife crisis you're going through but fuck her if you so please and get *rid* of her. Don't use your child as an excuse."

I close the distance between us so that I can say this without the possibility of Rory hearing. "Get. The fuck. Out of my house."

She doesn't flinch. It's not the first time I've thrown her out in such a harsh manner.

She shakes her head. "You really are so crabby on Saturday mornings." She puts a hand on my chest and speaks tenderly just as Nicole and Rory come down the stairs. "Call me. We'll discuss it over dinner."

Nothing's changed with this woman. Moving to the door, I yank it open and glare at my ex-wife. "Don't hold your breath."

Nicole keeps her hand on Rory's back as she guides her to the kitchen, away from the front door.

"I'm sorry," she starts when I re-enter the kitchen after a moment alone in the foyer to compose myself.

I frown in confusion because that was supposed to be my line.

"I couldn't keep her from coming down the stairs. She was practically on her way down already."

I scratch my head. "Yeah, um..."

"It's fine. Angel's mom never liked me—and it takes a lot to offend me."

I raise a brow.

"From certain people," she adds, then turns to the pancake batter.

Unfortunately, I'm *not* immune to Claire's remarks and I'm pissed off for Nicole.

I need to run. I need to burn off this frustration. Between Nicole still being angry at me, and Claire working on my last nerve, I'm about to blow and I don't want to do it here.

"You okay if I go for a run?"

She eyes me with concern. "Of course. Thanks for—the batter."

A tinge of relief washes over me when she offers me a small smile. *Maybe I didn't screw up all that bad.* "I'll be back in a few."

I return thirty minutes later. Rory is watching cartoons in the den and Nicole sits on the bar stool with a bowl of berries. "Pancakes came out great. I left some for you."

I glance at a plate she prepared for me. A pair of pancakes, a side of eggs that look like they might be scrambled, a banana, and some peanut butter. I give her a crooked smile. "That's a big plate."

She shrugs. "It's what Nick eats after a workout. Minus the pancakes."

Glancing at my distracted daughter in the other room, I inch toward Nicole, who stiffens. It's subtle, but I don't miss it.

I can't help but hope that one day, she'll respond to me differently when I come near her.

Very differently.

"I'm lifting the probation."

Her brows crease. "You can't lift something I put in place."

"I just did. And you didn't set it in place, you adjusted it."

She considers it for a minute, then looks up at me. "Why?"

"Because there should have never been one. I hired you because I've been watching you with my daughter for the last two years and you've got a way with her no one's ever had."

I've been watching you *without* my daughter too, but I'll leave that part out for now. "I also promised I'd teach you and I didn't follow through. Instead, I yelled at you. It's something..."

Her green eyes lift to mine when my voice turns gravelly.

"Something I never thought I'd do."

It's another admission to the connection we have.

Understanding and something like resolve settles her features and the pang of guilt hits harder.

She slides off the chair, but I barely give her breathing room. I don't move away. She looks up at me. "She's not safe with me," she whispers.

Shit. "You heard that?"

She shrugs. "I've known it all along."

I need to change the fucking locks on my doors. "Nicole," I start, but she holds up a hand.

"Nothing is lifted. The probation stands. Tuesday, right?" She nods, answering her own question. "We'll see then." She moves away from me and starts clearing the counter.

I feel like I broke her.

It was just five days ago when I walked into my kitchen and she was glowing, laughing, teasing me that she'd lost my dog and fed my girl candy. Thanking me for what I'd done for her.

I don't recognize the person I unleashed.

But I can't blame her. I *shouted* at her and then backpedaled my offer of a safe place to live and a steady job. I'd given her a chance only to put a timer on it two days later. And now, she can barely look at me for more than three seconds.

Relenting for the time being, I ask. "What will you do today?"

"What do you mean?"

"You're off this weekend. You need time off so I'll try to arrange for at least one to two days a week, depending on travel game schedule. But I'm home until Monday so, you have the weekend off."

"Oh."

"And I paid you this morning."

"You did?" She picks up her phone and must see the notification of transferred funds. Her brows rise appreciatively. We never discussed the amount, but I meant what I'd told her; I'll pay her well. More than she was making at the bar in tips and salary combined.

With her poker face on, she sets her phone down. "Thank you."

"Like I said, I'm getting the better end of the deal."

14

I SPEND THE DAY at the mall with Cora, feeling guilty for leaving Rory. Like I should have brought her along or something. She would have loved the caramel pretzel dip.

And then maybe I'd take her for frozen yogurt...*instead* of lunch. That's one way to prove to Daddy Coach just how wrong I am for this job.

Maybe that's the answer. Maybe I could beat him to the punch. Why wait for Tuesday for him to change his mind—or worse—decide to keep me? We both know it won't last. And I don't want Rory to grow attached. She's already expecting me to leave.

And with the sweet deposit into my account this morning, I could probably buy her something that screams bad influence.

I'm not sure what I had in mind but I pause when I see something in a window similar to what...well, to what I would wear.

What'll Daddy think of that? Would it give him a coronary?

"Hold this." I hand the sticky snack to Cora. "I'm going to stop in here for a minute."

"But this is a kid's store."

"I'll be quick. I know what I want."

Five minutes later, I saunter out with a smug look on my face. This should *unseal* the deal.

Cora catches the smirk on my face.

"You going to tell me what that's about?" She points to my mouth. "Or feed me some bullshit?"

"Cora Knight." I press a hand to my chest. "I am hurt. You know I never feed my girls bullshit. Just the boys." I snake my arm in hers. "Let's go look at some leather jackets."

Thirty minutes later, I'm checking out of the kid's superstore with a vegan leather jacket and a cool studded baseball cap for Rory to match mine. A token of appreciation for the past day and a half of finally being on my side.

And maybe a little guilt gift if I have to leave her in a few days. I want her to know we're still buddies, with matching jackets, glammed-out hats, and colorful skull tank tops.

Cora nudges me. "You know, usually when people get paid, they pay some bills, buy themselves something pretty. You only bought yourself a pretzel and stuff for Rory."

I scrunch my nose. "The pretzel is for her too. Plus I finally got my bright yellow streak back." It doesn't start at the root, the way Cora's does. Since my hair is long, I started it midway and down to the ends, so it's classy and can still be hidden if needed. I gasp and grip Cora's elbow. "I forgot. I need one more thing. Then I promise, I'll shop for me."

We find a vendor that sells girls' hair accessories and I pick out two yellow clip-on hair pieces, holding it up to mine. "Which one matches best?"

Cora examines and points. "That one."

I squeal and purchase the artificial hair.

Cora shakes her head and strolls along with me. "So... how's it going?"

I release a groan. "It's hard. But I think I'm getting better at this, at least I hope I am."

"And how's it going with Rory?" she asks innocently.

"I was talking about Rory."

Cora smirks. "Oh were you? I thought we were talking about how you're handling living under the same roof as the man you want to bang."

"What?" I stop dead in my tracks and glance around us, as if we'll see someone from our circle of friends. Or Royce himself. Which is ridiculous. He took Rory to the movies and probably lunch at some fancy place. "I don't want to *bang* Coach Collins."

"Mmhmm...Nicky, I had a crush on your brother for eight years. I know googly eyes when I see it. I recognize the blush when he catches your eye from across the room and you turn away."

"Now that's B.S., I *never* turn away." I roll my lips together. *The little witch.*

A sly grin stretches her lips. "You're right, you don't. Usually, he's the one to do it," she says matter-of-factly and keeps walking like we're just talking about the weather.

I return to the house with a semi-warm new pretzel for Rory since Cora and I demolished the other one.

Rory and her father are in the den. He's flipping through streaming cartoons.

"That one, that one," she demands.

"No. I hate that one," he retorts.

"That's because you hate slime."

My eyes drop to my bags. *Slime*? That would have been a lot cheaper than a leather jacket. Even a faux one.

Well, at least I know what I'll be picking up when I go out tomorrow.

After unpacking my shopping bags, mostly facial creams, makeup and—okay, a new pair of boots I totally didn't need, I call Rory up to my bedroom to play dress up.

I glam her up in her killer new outfit, hair clip, and shimmery lip gloss, and send her downstairs to show Daddy.

She tugs my hand. "Will you come with me?"

I hesitate. "Umm...well, I really need to clean up here. But come back and let me know what he says."

"Pleeeaaseee."

Pouting, I follow her out.

Fine, I wouldn't want to miss his reaction to the mini me I've created, anyway.

When we get downstairs, Rory sprints into the kitchen, where her dad is cleaning up a tea party set from the counter.

His jaw drops as he stares at his sweet little girl. Realization crosses his features when he finds me behind her.

Pressing my lips together to fight my grin—to his reaction and the fact that he was playing tea party with her on his day off—I move to the refrigerator for a bottle of water.

"Can I wear it to school on Monday? Can I?"

"Umm...it's not exactly uniform...and I don't think Mrs. Matthews will appreciate it...as much as...I do." His voice trails off and he sneaks a glance back at me.

"Awww." She pouts.

"I'm sure you can still wear it plenty, but for now, why don't you go change back to house-appropriate clothes?"

He watches her skip out of the room gleefully then brushes my shoulder and leans down to whisper. "Nice try. I happen to think she looks adorable." He pulls back and catches the new yellow strands of my hair, curling it around his finger. "Oh and...I missed this."

He doesn't give me a chance to respond, he releases my hair and leaves me there with my skin *sizzling*.

Since it's turning out to be the longest day ever, I decide to burn off some energy in the basement gym. Can't exactly stay locked in my bedroom all weekend because I'm trying to avoid my mouth running off again.

After about an hour, I head back up and sigh when I realize I still have hours of avoidance ahead of me. And of course, Royce is in the kitchen when I emerge from the stairs.

With a glance over his shoulder, he asks if I can get Rory and Rover from the backyard because dinner is almost ready.

Instead of the cold shoulder, I fire off a snippy comment. Because, as we've established, I can't keep a lid on it. "Sure you trust me not to make a mess out there?"

He rolls his eyes along with a head shake.

Feeling slightly guilty for the grudge I'm apparently still holding, I go outside in my workout clothes; a loose, white t-shirt and leggings.

The sun is starting to set, but it's not too cold. I catch Rory tossing a frisbee in the air and Rover racing for it over by the tree. It's a good thing her little hands can't throw too far down the open, extended backyard, so they both stay close.

"Rory, just one more time, okay? Your dad's making dinner."

"Four more times."

"Two," I compromise, with a swirl toward the door, just as Royce steps out. With a mischievous grin, I twist back. "You know what Rory, make that ten. Go nuts."

With another headshake, he smirks at my defiance.

Yep...just another child here.

Joining her, I toss the frisbee a little higher, which Rover seems to appreciate.

There's a whistle behind me and Rover abandons us, obediently racing toward his owner. "Come on Rory, looks like the fun's over. Let's go inside," I say, resigned.

She pouts and I take her hand.

But when we turn, we face the spout end of a long hose aimed directly at us. Royce standing devilishly behind it. I barely have time to shriek before the water bursts out with a strong mist.

Rory and I scream and try to race around the attack. I shove her in the other direction, so we split up and the devil—the fucking devil—follows me with the hose. I can't see his face, but I hear the unmistakable rumble of Coach laughing along with us.

I try to tackle him, but he's too quick. Not surprising. He's made a career of dodging people coming at him on the ice.

So instead—I grab the next best thing.

I hold Rory up in front me and shout through all the laughter. "I will use her as a shield, don't test me."

Rory giggles and wiggles in my hold. "Do it, do it, Daddy. Do it."

He smirks, toying with the hose beside him, contemplating his next move. Rover is at his side kneeling and gobbling up as much as his long tongue can gobble.

He moves to my left and I mirror him, holding onto Rory to keep her in our game. Mostly because I'm afraid of what this is without her.

"Put the girl down, Kane. My quarrel is with you."

I twist her to face me. "You wouldn't leave me to fight my own battles, would you?"

She shakes her head and we both turn smugly at him.

He shrugs. "Suit yourselves." Pointing up, he squeezes the nozzle and water shoots high into the air, crashing down on us like hail.

Screaming and laughing, Rory and I duck around the armed enemy, trying to trick him. I give Rory a shove up the stairs and tell her to shut down the water.

Reaching behind me, I find a flailing extension of the hose and pull to gain control. But my opponent uses the opportunity to his advantage and jerks me toward him. When I'm dangerously close, I release and turn but he grabs my waist and pulls me hard against his chest.

I inhale sharply as a bolt of electricity surges through me.

"Stop fighting this," he rasps against my ear.

Blinking, I twist my neck to look up at him. "What?"

His strong arm is wrapped firmly around me like I'm a flight risk. "Stop trying to prove that you're not good for her." He releases me slowly, his arm slipping reluctantly.

He jogs up the porch steps and praises his daughter before tightening the knob. He tosses me one of two towels he conveniently placed on the bench, and I drop to quickly dry off a shivering Rory. I tear the soaked shirt over her head and wrap the second towel around her before she races into the house to get warm. Rover shakes himself off in front of us again and I swear we get a look that tells us to stop making this a regular occurrence before the dog follows Rory inside.

A thick blanket is wrapped around me from behind, and his arms—his big strong arms, securing me, warming me. It almost feels like he's giving in. Like he's ripping through all the unspoken boundaries we'd set.

Or maybe...this is the *hot* of the hot and cold game we play. And tomorrow—he'll be putting up that wall again.

"I should go get her in a warm bath," I say, resisting the urge to turn into him.

"It's still your night off."

I twist my neck to look at him. "Then you'll owe me one."

"Deal."

After a quick bath, I style Rory's hair with some leave-in conditioner to bring out her natural curls and send her back downstairs for dinner. By the looks of it, she won't make it much longer tonight. She looks ready to pass out—and it's barely seven.

I don't follow her downstairs. I attempt at my own hot shower, but the water is too cool and the pressure too low.

Not surprising, given my daily piping hot showers and the obscene amount of water we just wasted so Coach could prove a point.

Deciding to wait rather than suffer through a cool shower, I shut off the water and towel dry my damp hair, then style it into a bun over my head.

Outside my door, I hear Royce taking Rory to her room for bed. She whines about why *Nicole* isn't doing it and he tries to explain "time off" to a six-year-old. I almost follow them to her room, but I don't want to climb onto her bed until I've washed up.

An hour later, I still can't take a warm enough shower, so I head downstairs, needing to distract myself with a task—any task to get my mind off him.

I weave through the halls and find the kitchen spotless. Fine. I grab Coach's hoodie which hangs by the back door and zip it over my flimsy clothes before stepping outside. Figuring I could tidy up the mess we all made in the backyard earlier.

But the vibrating sound to my right catches my attention and all my plans to keep it together around this man go out the window when I find him soaking in his hot tub.

15

OVER THE LAST TWO years, I've lost count of how many times I've wanted to wrap my jacket around Nicole Kane. I've been keenly aware of every shiver in the cold arena, every visible puff of air from her lips in the winters, every shudder at the mere mention of her past.

But now, seeing her wrapped in my favorite hoodie, which I'd left hanging behind the door before I came out here, it's better than anything I let myself imagine.

Her legs are bare, but the trim of her shorts peeks from under the hem. Her hair is loosely tied above her head.

She shoves her hands in her pockets uncomfortably. "I thought you might have fallen asleep with Rory. I just came out here to tidy up. Know how much you hate a dirty yard."

I roll my eyes. "Appreciate the effort, but no need." My eyes roam over her. "How was your shower?" By the tone of her skin and the lack of redness on her chest, it doesn't appear she'd taken one.

She draws closer. "Umm, I'll take one later. The pressure is a little low now and I seem to have used up a lot of your hot water this week." She winces.

"I'm sorry. I should see what I can do about that tomorrow." I chuckle, but inside, I feel awful that she couldn't get warm after I'd hosed her down with cold water on a cool fall day. "Hop in," I offer without a second thought. "It's pretty hot in here."

She blinks. "It's like forty degrees out."

"Fifty, but trust me, you won't freeze." I point up. "There's a heat lamp and I practically live in here all winter without getting pneumonia."

Biting her lip, she inches closer, debating. Then unzips my hoodie and hangs it gently on a chair. I take her in but try not to gawk at how fucking sexy she is. She's wearing a white crop top where the bottom looks like it was torn purposely. The outline of a dark sports bra is visible through the thin fabric.

She must catch me staring because she apologetically says, "I don't have a swimsuit."

I move my eyes to hers—where they need to stay. "The only rule is you need to be dressed—and even I break that one sometimes."

What. The fuck?

I catch her eyes flash at my comment but thankfully she doesn't call attention to it.

I watch her climb into the tub, her jaw dropping with an orgasmic-like O that makes me adjust my trunks. "Holy shit, this is amazing," she breathes. My traitorous eyes sweep her once more in the clothes that now cling to her body.

I clear my throat. "Feel free to use it anytime."

When her eyes open, they flash to my tumbler. "You making your own cocktails now? I'm hurt."

"Tea. Chamomile. You're welcome to give it the taste test."

"You're out here soaking in your glorious hot tub and sipping tea rather than a good smoked whiskey? Shameful."

She moves to sit across from me which helps matters for distance but also doesn't because now it's hard not to notice all the places her shirt molds to her body.

"Nicole, I meant what I said earlier. You're good for her. Stop trying to prove you're not."

She watches me as though waiting for something more convincing.

"I'm lifting the probation period. It's not one month, it's certainly not one week. I knew you were no Mary Poppins when I hired you—but I think you're doing just fine."

"Alright," she says defiantly. "But on one condition."

I raise a brow. "You have a condition?"

She stands, making a small splash and moves toward me. "I won't be treated with kid gloves. I'm not your daughter's friend. I'm your employee. I'm not the sister of one of your players who you've been looking out for as a favor to him."

I have the urge to correct her. To tell her it was no fucking favor. But I don't.

"I work for you. So if I'm screwing up—handle me like you would anyone else."

Fuck. Me. Between her sassy mouth right now and the glistening glow of her dripping upper body, I'm in danger of a very showy hard-on; one that I can't take care of at the moment.

I stand and push her back under the warm water that bubbles around her until it covers her chest.

"I'm not cold."

"I did that for my sake, not yours. If you're done—I have a few conditions too."

She rolls her eyes. "I'm not going to lie again—"

"Doesn't matter. I can already tell when you're full of shit."

She blinks up at me and it's impossible not to want her. So much so that I can't help what I'm about to tell her. "I won't handle you like I handle anyone else. You're not just anyone and I think you know that."

She pushes back up. Finding herself facing my chest, she doesn't bother looking up.

Nope.

Instead, she lifts herself onto the top step of the tub so we're at eye level. If I wasn't so intrigued, I'd laugh.

"Could have fooled me," she remarks, sweat and water dripping down her neck and chest, making me swallow hard.

Before I have a chance to respond, she swooshes out of the water and storms off.

I blink. What the hell? Was there more to that? Do I even dare ask?

Before I know it, I'm behind her as she enters the house, twisting her and pushing her against the wall. Rover's head popping up from the den watching us.

She doesn't gasp when I twist her this time. It's like she expected me to cave. And I am. I'm fucking caving.

"Care to elaborate?" I demand.

"You should be careful. You might burst a pipe running hot and cold as much as you do."

"I thought you didn't want special treatment."

"That doesn't give you the right to be a total dick," she bites back.

My jaw tics. "I'd been more than fair to you considering—"

"Considering I'm such a tragedy?" Her lips twist tauntingly at me and I can't look away.

"I'm getting quite tired of that mouth of yours." It's a low growl but it's out before I can stop it.

Her eyes dip to my lips mockingly. Then she lifts to her toes, holding my biceps for support as she murmurs. "That's because you haven't seen everything it can do."

16

THE NEXT FEW DAYS, I pretty much stay out of Coach's way—because that's the mood he's been in since the weekend—Big Bad Coach mood. Where everyone and everything annoys him, save for his dog.

I knew something was up when Angel came by one evening and he snapped at her out of the blue. She wasn't fazed by it, but I worried that his mood had something to do with me.

Until I sat down Thursday night to tune into a live game.

The Buffalo Blades have been *losing*.

After starting off the season strong, they've lost five games in two weeks.

I winced when I caught a glimpse of Coach on TV. When he brushed his hair back and looked like he wanted to punch through the plexiglass.

I've seen his rage during a game. It always seemed appropriate somehow. Competitive and aggressive, but all in a fair game way. But this week, he seemed stressed on an entirely new level.

On Friday night, I catch replays on the post-game show when Rory's asleep and am surprised to see most of the attention on Coach Collins rather than the team. I watch him give a thirty-second interview to a pushy reporter before storming off. Nick right behind him and filling in to avoid them going after Coach.

I'm about to shut it off when I hear the question thrown at my brother.

"Nick, everyone wants to know. Are the rumors true about Coach Collins stepping down after this season for Robbie Hastings to step in?"

Nick's jaw tics in that familiar way but then he smiles politely and gives a soft chuckle. "I believe he's already addressed this and I haven't heard anything otherwise."

Pulling up my phone, I google what this Hastings business is about and find the press conference Royce was talking about last week. I pause the television and tune into the video on my phone.

Agree with my twin—asked and answered.

Shit. I remember him mentioning this guy was gunning for his position but he didn't seem all that concerned—just annoyed that he had to deal with it.

I didn't even ask him about it. I was too busy challenging him and causing all kinds of drama while he's been struggling to keep his job.

Mature, Nicole. *Real mature.*

It's after nine and the house grows a little colder as the wind picks up outside. I know that despite the loss, the team has gone to Bridges for their usual gathering.

As much as I want to not miss it—my old job—I do. Not the waiting on people, but the comradery, the laughs, the teasing and...spending time with Coach on a not-so-tension-filled level. When I wasn't his employee. When I wasn't constantly feeling the need to lie.

When he looked at me like someone he could talk to all night rather than someone he couldn't get away from fast enough.

I'm about to turn up the heat in the house when the doorbell rings.

"Nicky, it's us, open up." My brother's familiar voice comes from the other side of the front door.

What the hell?

I pull it open and two large hockey players and my best friends step into the house.

"Surprise," Angel sings.

"Umm...yeah, you can say that. What are you guys doing here?"

Nick and Jace b-line for the kitchen and I hear the fridge pulled open.

Oh dear.

"If you're looking for beer, you won't find any here," I call back.

Cora shrugs. "They were insistent on coming to check on Coach instead of going out—he looked like he was ready to strangle someone when he left."

Great. So not only is my boss coming home angry, but I now have uninvited guests in his house.

"You guys, I don't think—"

Angel tugs my arm. "Come on, I know where he hides the good chocolate."

"Now you're talkin'." Cora follows eagerly.

We find Nick and Jace leaning against the island counter across each other muttering something about the media.

Cora immediately goes to an overzealous Rover, petting and cooing.

Jace shakes his head. "Cor—Rover's a big dog. You don't *coo* a grown dog."

"What...he likes it." She continues to rub under his ears.

"He's laughing at you," her big brother says wryly.

Meanwhile, Angel is pulling at random bagged items from the pantry. "Where is it? Dammit."

"Okay, why are you all here? You guys are going to get me in trouble. And can you keep it down? Rory's asleep."

Angel waves a dismissive hand. "Oh please. Nothing will wake that child."

I start taking a few items out of the fridge for them, since they're clearly not leaving until I feed them. I pull out leftovers of fried dumplings and cucumber salad I made for dinner earlier.

"So... how's it going, sis?" Nick asks, stabbing a dumpling. "You made it two weeks without getting fired—congrats."

I cross my arms. "Coach happens to like my way with Rory."

"I meant fired by the kid herself."

"Rory and I are getting along great." *Now.*

Jace eyes me suspiciously and I'm on alert. I *know* that look. Either that, or I'm paranoid. "You doin' alright here, otherwise?"

"Why wouldn't I be?" I deadpan.

He hesitates and glances at Nick, buying time with a bite of a dumpling. "You know, uh...that little problem you have...that makes you unfit to be Coach's nanny."

Nick turns a hard glare at his friend.

But not as hard as mine. I cross my arms. "What problem?"

He leans in across the counter. "The one where you have a secret crush on daddy..."

Nick shakes his head and turns away, pretending he didn't hear that. While I—instead of denying it like a fourteen-year-old—own up to it.

"At least I didn't pretend to *hate* my crush for five years the way *you* did."

Guiltily, he glances at his girlfriend, who shoots us a pointed glare through her search for chocolate treasure.

Just when I thought the heat in my cheeks couldn't get worse, the back door squeaks open and Royce enters the foyer leading to the kitchen.

"Coach," Nick calls cheerfully.

My stomach drops.

He looks *tired*. No. Dreadfully tired and maybe a little bit resigned. He's in the suit he wore to the game. It's a little more wrinkled and disheveled now and I subtly breathe in to see if I can pick up the scent of alcohol.

Nope.

"What's...going on?" His eyes sweep past each of our uninvited guests and land on me.

My mouth opens but I don't know what to tell him. Thankfully, Nick steps up and pats his shoulder. "We were worried about you, Coach."

He brushes it off and takes off his jacket. "A phone call would have sufficed," he mutters grimly. He gives a quick, warm smile to Cora, then sighs and walks over to the cabinet Angel tries to rearrange.

Reaching for the top shelf, he pulls out a plastic bag and hands it to her. "Here. Can you all go now?"

"Coach, come on, talk to us," Jace urges, his serious voice taking the stage.

"Not in the mood."

"You heard the man, get out," I hiss at my friends, who I know only meant well by stopping by.

Jace leans down to me and winks. "Why, you two want to be alone?"

I shake my head and slap his arm with a forced chuckle. "Stop."

Royce's eyes pierce in our direction. "Something funny?"

"No," I say quickly, then instantly feel bad. Because it almost feels like I'm making him an outsider in his own home. But can I admit to what Jace was teasing me about? If I try to cover it up, does it only make me look guilty of it?

Would it... be so terrible if I actually said it?

"They were just teasing me of how ironic it is that I ended up working for you...when there were a few months a while back where I kind of had a little crush on you—but I mean, who hasn't, right?" I laugh nervously.

Coach's scowl doesn't alter as he ponders on what I'd just said...out loud...for some dumb reason. He reaches for a bottle of water. "Doesn't seem like an appropriate conversation between my employee and members of my team."

Ouch.

Jace seems annoyed at his response and shoots me an apologetic look.

"Told you guys you'd get me in trouble. Now finish up and leave."

"That's alright. I've lost my appetite," Nick says, then nods to the rest of them toward the front door.

On the way out, Angel leans down and whispers, "Smooth." before following the others out—full bag of chocolates in hand.

I can't say I'm surprised by my best friend's nonchalant attitude toward my so-called crush on her dad. I know she's caught me staring on more than one occasion.

But she never called me out on it. Probably because she didn't want to tell me he's out of my league. Or something crueler, like "Yeah, if my supermodel mother couldn't hold on to him, you don't stand a chance."

But like the good friend she is, she'd turned a blind eye and kept her mouth shut.

I lock the door after the last one steps out and silently sigh, wishing I could follow them. But I have one angry Coach to face and probably a lecture on appropriate topics of conversation.

Returning to the kitchen, I avoid his eyes on me and start clearing the counter.

"Nicole, you're not in trouble."

"You're obviously in a bad mood. I saw it in tonight's replay. I felt it when you walked through the door. Your kitchen is a mess, you came home to uninvited guests and you're short one supposedly amazing bag of chocolates."

He grins and moves to a cabinet above the fridge—one that even Angel would need a step stool to reach. "That's alright," he says as he pulls at something stuffed to the side. "She only took my Angel stash. These"—he strides over and hands me a small blue box with rich gold lettering—"are my personal stash."

I look up at him from the box in my hands. "These don't look like the ones she took."

He shakes his head. "They're not. These are handcrafted in Japan. Made with high-quality ingredients. There is one store in New York City that has these delivered regularly and every time there's a new shipment, I'm on the next plane down."

"For *chocolate*?"

He scrunches his nose and nods like this is some guilty pleasure no one knows about.

"Impressive," I say. "And also a little bit snobbish."

"Well." He snatches them from me playfully. "I haven't told you what makes them special."

"What?" I blink innocently. "Unless it's too inappropriate to share with your employee."

He gives me a playful side eye and smirks. "Sometimes when I'm having a rough day or I feel like I haven't been honest with myself, I play a game of Truth or Chocolate."

My brows crease and he breathes a soft laugh.

"When I feel like I've been in denial about something or just aggravated, but can't pinpoint the cause, I go see my therapist." He holds it up again.

"A...box of fancy chocolates?"

He shrugs.

"How do you play?"

"This one is called Bittersweet. It's a mix of sweet and bitter chocolates. I don't like the bitter ones."

"Can you tell them apart?"

"Yes."

"So then just eat the sweet ones."

He watches me and grins. "That's not playing by the rules."

"I'm confused."

"When I'm stressed, I sit with a box of Bittersweet and ask myself some questions. Questions I would normally avoid because the answer might be difficult to admit." He holds up the box. "My therapist."

I nod slowly, taking in this piece of him he's unexpectedly sharing with me. "Sounds easy."

"Not always. If I don't play by the rules. If I lie to myself, I have to eat the bitter chocolate. If I feel like I've gotten to the root of what's stressing me out, then I pop a sweet one."

"I see," I say, smiling. "Do you and your therapist need to be alone?"

He laughs. "Care to play with me?"

I toss down the rag and cross my arms. "I would," I say squinting.

He rolls his eyes. "But?"

"But I'd like to add a rule—at least for this round."

"Okay..."

I bite my lip, my courage suddenly leaving me. "Well, I think it's cheating if you're the one who decides if you're lying or not. What if...for tonight, the other person decides if you're telling the truth...and then picks the appropriate chocolate."

I realize his scowl is now long gone and he's staring at me with intrigue. "You're on."

I smile brightly and jolt in excitement before turning back to the mess. "Just give me a few minutes to finish—"

He grabs my wrist and pulls me back, rasping against my ear. "Loser cleans the kitchen."

I turn my face up. "I warn you. I've been in therapy for eight years. I'm going to *crush* you."

"I'm counting on it," he says, then leads me into the dark living room. He settles me onto a quilt on the carpet in front of the fireplace before walking over to the small metal door that covers a bed of cold, burnt wood. He opens it and arranges fresh logs inside.

I watch as a flame catches and soft crackling starts to fill the room, warming me instantly. I scooch backward until I'm leaning against the solid wood coffee table behind me.

Royce settles beside me and watches as the flames grow. "Better?" he asks without turning to me.

"Hmm?"

"You were cold," he says matter of factly.

I blink. "Oh, yeah. I was going to turn up the heat earlier but this is..."

"Better," he repeats.

"Although I'm afraid our fancy goods might melt."

He turns to me with a naughty grin. "Then let's get started." He reaches for a throw blanket on the couch, placing it between us as if he needs that barrier.

"Do you want to start?" he asks.

I shake my head.

"Alright." He hands me the box and takes a deep breath. "I've never actually done this with anyone before so it might take me longer to…admit to what's on my mind."

"I'm least likely to judge," I assure him.

He lifts his chin, considering something, then nods. "Yes. I am stressed." He pauses and I wonder if I'm supposed to encourage him.

"Does it have something to do with this Robbie guy coming back to town?"

He watches the fire. "Maybe. Probably. I'm not threatened by him for my job, but his presence ignites…all my insecurities about my coaching, my team, and the media. I feel like every wrong move is under a microscope now that he's here and…" He shakes his head. "I need to snap out of it, I guess."

He turns to me, and I give him a small smile. Opening the box, I pull out a small, rounded piece in the sweet side and place it in his hand.

Tasting it, he grins. "Thanks." He takes the box from me. "Ready?"

Blinking, I shift away and face the fire, loving the crackling sounds it makes. The peacefulness of it. The warmth it spreads.

"I'm sorry," I start. "You didn't need all that drama from me last week. I've been so wrapped up in…" I spare him a glance, "fighting this…that I only made things more difficult for you."

He shoots me a cocky grin.

"Look, apologies aren't my strong suit, will you just say you forgive me so I can be done with it?"

He chuckles. "I forgive you." He picks up a piece of chocolate but doesn't give it to me. "But you go again. While I appreciate it, it doesn't count." He pops it into his mouth instead.

I laugh. "Okay, umm...Oh, I've got one. So, tonight, before my friends came by, I was missing being at the bar, hanging out with all of you guys, celebrating—or cheering you up after a loss. I was worried when my friends showed up at your house uninvited, but I was really happy to see them. Even if they were here to check on *you*." I roll my eyes.

His grin is never-ending as he plucks a sugar-dusted ball from the box and looks at my mouth. Without hesitation, he brings the piece of chocolate to my lips, and I part for him.

His fingers barely graze my bottom lip before dropping the ball on my tongue. My eyes are glued to his as I suck on what might be the best thing I ever tasted.

"Good." He turns to the fire and hums as if he's thinking about what to 'admit' to next.

"Can I help you out with a topic?"

He turns a suspicious glare at me and I bite back a smile. "Claire."

He inhales through his nose. "Angel's mother doesn't stress me out. She's a pain in my ass, but she doesn't bother me."

I nod and pluck a piece from the box and turn to him. He watches me coyly and I bring my fingers to his lips.

And holy shit.

They're fire under my skin. My fingers tingle and I almost drop the delicacy. Thankfully, he opens and I release it into his mouth and pull away.

He groans when he tastes the bitterness. "I was afraid of that." But he doesn't seem at all disappointed. He's watching me like I'd just stripped naked for him. Like he can't look away. His eyes dip to my fingers. "Can I go again?"

I nod.

"Clare is not a topic I want to discuss with anyone because she doesn't deserve it. I don't hate her. I tolerate her for Angel's sake. The stories you hear about us staying good friends or that we're secretly still in love are lies beyond measure. Ones that she fabricated."

I bite my lip. "I'm sorry."

"It's alright. It just means I get to give *you* a topic."

I brace myself for the worst. How I started drinking. If some of the rumors about me are true. I can't help the anxiety. I'm used to men making me uncomfortable.

"Rory," he says flatly.

I frown. That's not at all what I was expecting.

"Rory? That's it? If you want to know one truth from me, you're going to make it about your daughter?"

He smiles brilliantly. "She's my favorite topic."

I breathe a sigh of relief and then smile when I picture her. "I adore her. She's forward and unafraid. She chooses when to be wild and when to be tamed. She's freaking beautiful and..." I look up at him. "She's yours."

Without tearing his eyes off me, he lifts his fingers to my mouth again, this time, letting his fingers linger as he drops it in, then swipes along my bottom lip as I taste the sweet treat.

His eyes settle longingly on my mouth but there's almost a hint of regret in them and I'm almost afraid to ask. "What is it?"

17

CHRIST.

I've never been so envious of a piece of chocolate before. Watching her suck it so deliciously, I just had to fucking feel it. Am I crossing the line when it comes to her?

Knowing her past, how much is too much with this woman?

"I um...I like that you share my taste in sweets."

She watches me and I know she sees right through me. The way only Nicole always seems to. "I haven't tasted the bitter one yet," she whispers.

I smirk playfully and lift one. "You know the rules. You need to feed me some bullshit first."

Her eyes wander as she thinks, then lift to mine again. "I lied earlier. When I said I had a crush on you. *Total* lie."

I nod slowly. "Is that so?"

She shrugs.

I hold the piece between us. "I call bullshit." Then I place the bitter chocolate in her mouth, slipping my thumb in with it.

And she doesn't miss a beat.

She sucks on my thumb, swirling her tongue around it, licking it clean of the sugar dust. I'm entranced by the way her lips move around me. I need to taste them.

I swipe my thumb along her lip. "Nicole." It's almost a question as I stare at her mouth.

She nods urgently. "Yes."

I cover her mouth with mine in a fierce, hard kiss and she moans like she'd been dying for it all night. I rope my arm around her waist, pulling her on top of me. I take her kisses like she's the only raindrop in the desert. My thumb strokes her jawline, reveling in the skin I finally get to touch, trace, taste. A groan escapes my throat and it's unfamiliar, feral, like we're both in some sort of danger.

I taste it all. The sweet, the bitter, the hunger, the longing. And I can't—no, I will never get enough of her.

I press my thumb back on her lips as I break our kiss but hold her jaw between my palms.

She's breathing heavily, her eyes slowly lifting from my chest to my eyes.

"How did you like that one?"

She blinks in confusion. "The bitter one?"

I nod.

"Hmm," she hums appreciatively, still straddling me. "It makes me want to be bad more often."

I laugh and she breaks into a soft laugh with me, burying her head on my chest. "I'm sorry. I'm totally devirginizing your therapy game."

"De-virginizing?"

"Or...deflowering?" She scrunches her nose, then swings her leg over me, awkwardly shifting back to her spot on the floor.

I'm left facing the fire again. "Are you warm now?"

She nods. "I think it's safe to say I am very warm right now."

A few minutes later, I take her upstairs and it feels a lot like I'm walking her home after a date. Seeing her to her door. She turns and looks up at me. "Better hide those chocolates now that I know where you keep your stash."

I smile. "Good night, Nicole."

She bites her lip. "Royce." She pushes her hair behind her ear. "I wasn't planning to...act on my...crush. I respect you and I care about Rory. I don't want you to think I—"

"Nicole. I kissed *you*."

"You never told me why."

I grin. "Guess you'll have to wait until we play again."

The next morning I'm packing for an away game for the weekend when my phone buzzes.

Robbie: *Good luck in Seattle.*

Hastings isn't getting to me today. I don't have the time or patience for his taunting. I have more important things on my mind.

And one of those things just walked into my bedroom.

"Daddy." She leaps into my arms and I lift her. "Are you going on an airplane again?"

"Yes, I am. But I'll be back after two sleeps." I hold up two fingers for her which she tugs as if sealing my promise.

She nods as if that's what she expected, only she's not as miserable for my short absence as she usually is. And I wonder if the reason is the other beauty that just walked into my bedroom.

"Rory." I set my little girl down. "Why don't you get changed out of your pajamas. There's no school today. You can wear whatever you want."

"Yay." She races out the double doors and down the hall to her room.

"Morning," I say, giving her a lingering sweep before tossing one of my shirts into the duffle bag.

"Morning." She stays put by the doors, leaning against the frame as though waiting for me to welcome her in.

Which I'd happily do if my mind wasn't still swirling over last night and if I might have...overstepped...or misread the situation.

Not ready to tackle the topic yet, I switch gears to professional. "I want to make sure you get at least one day off this weekend, so I've asked Angel to take Rory off your hands tomorrow."

She doesn't say anything so I glance over, tentatively. "I can ask her to stay the entire weekend if you need." Nicole is one of the sharpest tools in the shed. So I know she's reading between the lines when I'm offering her company for the weekend.

She cocks her head at me and gives me a knowing grin. "I have your travel schedule. I'm well prepared to take care of Rory for the weekend..." She glances away as if considering what I said. "But... I wouldn't mind if either Cora or Angel stay with me one night if you don't either."

I release a breath. "I would prefer it." I close some of the distance between us, stopping about a foot away and putting my hands in my pockets. "But not because I don't trust you." Neither of us had drawn attention to the fact that she would be alone the days I'm traveling—something Nick wouldn't allow knowing what happened. "But because I like the idea of you being surrounded by friends."

She nods understandingly then smiles and shrugs. "In that case, maybe I'll have them both over."

She's too fucking adorable in her flannel pajamas, her dark silky hair tied in a messy bun over her head. She's not wearing makeup, but her soft beautiful skin has an unmatched morning glow that I can't seem to look away from.

"Rory's first slumber party." I step back to my packing, needing the distraction before I do something stupid, like reach out and touch her for no apparent reason.

No other reason than the fact that one taste of her was not going to be enough. Nicole steps into the room and places something on top of the items in my bag. Something I hadn't noticed her holding. The box of the chocolates we shared last night. Or what remains of it.

"In case you..." she shrugs as though settling for a less-than-ideal choice of words, "miss me."

I frown and pick up the box. She pulls at her bottom lip with her teeth, no doubt picking up on my reluctance.

"Is the idea that I have one of these when I think of you?" I ask, holding up the box.

She shrugs again and it's cute as fuck.

"I'm going to need a bigger box."

Her radiant smile lights up my world. "I'll go get changed and start breakfast."

I catch her hand. "Are you sure? You...look very comfortable."

She glances back again. "Well, if it's 'wear what you slept in' day at the Collins residence, then I'd better let Rory know." She scans me. "It's a good thing you've got a plane to catch because I have a feeling you don't wear anything to bed."

I watch her leave and for the first time since Rory was a baby, I wonder how on earth I'm supposed to leave for two whole nights.

One night into my stay at the Regency Hotel in Seattle, my morals have gotten me nowhere. I should be coming up with ground rules for my arrangement with Nicole.

Rules that mostly apply to me.

Like keep your fucking hands and mouth off the nanny.

Off Nicole Kane.

The only rule I'd come up with for her was Stop being the woman I haven't been able to tear my eyes off of for the last two years. The woman who I've yearned to protect and shelter from the pointing and whispering. The woman I couldn't touch for too many reasons.

But instead of setting said rules, my mind wanders wickedly to every which way I would break them.

Every which way I would make her moan, make her come again and again and again. With my tongue, my fingers, my cock.

Fuck I'm in trouble.

After our win—a victory we desperately needed—I'm too in my own head to celebrate with the boys. I head down to see if I can catch anyone at the bar. The female bartender smiles at me the moment I sit and it makes me think of Nicole's easy smile every time I sat at her bar.

The drinks she'd create based on what mood it looked like I was in. Or whatever she was feeling that night. We'd spend the quieter hours of the night making fun of the patrons, taking bets on who's likely to pass out and who will be the first to leave.

My money was always on Nick and Cora. The team captain and his girl would rarely make it past one drink each before they made up some excuse about getting up early.

But those two were never the social butterflies.

"Shouldn't you be out celebrating?" she asks.

"Some things a coach should not bear witness."

She grins. "What are you drinking?"

"Whatever you have on tap is fine." I don't have it in me to order a scotch. I'd just hate it. It wouldn't have her special touch. Her cloves or burnt citrus or...carry the scent of her as she handed it to me.

Fuck, I'm doing it again.

"Hey, Coach. Night cap?"

I grunt. "Why is it when Jace has a beer after hours, you call it a drink. But when I have one, you call it a night cap? Is it because I'm a hundred?"

Nick laughs and slaps my back. "A hundred. Is that how you think we see you, Coach?"

Coach. I miss my first name from her lips. She's one of the few people who use it anymore and each time, it ignites me.

"Good game tonight." I slap him right back.

"How's it going with my sister?"

I stiffen. "Rory adores her," I say, because it's the truth.

Nick scoffs and drags a hand through his hair. "Who knew the answer to all your prayers was Nicole? She's certainly the last person I thought you'd consider but...I really appreciate you giving her a chance and trusting her." He swallows. "Not many in our town would have."

"Hank did," I offer quickly, diverting the attention away from myself.

"Yeah, well, I'm just glad that Nicole happens to have magic with children and not just beverages."

His food order arrives, and he thanks the bartender and pats my shoulder. "Going to give Cora a call, then head to bed."

"Isn't she with Nicole?"

"Oh no, the girls left this morning. Angel had to prep for her classes this week and Cora said something about needing one day to herself."

I knit my brows. Not loving the idea of Nicole being alone. I should probably call her. But I wouldn't be the father I pride myself to be if I didn't check on my little girl first.

I check my phone, swiping away a message from a *Veronica*. The name is familiar, but I disregard it until I check on Rory.

I click on the baby monitor app I never removed. It comes in handy for when I'm traveling. Checking on my little girl while she's safely tucked into her princess bed has been everything these past few years.

There's one installed in my bedroom and hers. A few years back one of the babysitters told me Rory preferred to sleep on my bed when I was away, so her camera became utterly useless to me. Until I updated the system.

A flash in the app tells me there's movement in my bedroom so I assume Rory chose to stay in my room again tonight.

But when the black-and-white video starts, it's not Rory moving about. It's Nicole.

My bedroom is dark and it's hard to see much. The only light comes from the open door to the master bath. But it's clear as day that Nicole is wrapped in a towel.

That's when it occurs to me. I never fixed the hot water in her shower.

Her hair is tied up in a clip and I stare at the back of her neck as she unhooks the towel, and lets it drop to the floor.

I swallow hard at the vision of her bare backside.

And when she bends to pick it up, I'm panting. I can't look away. Her glorious body is silhouetted in the night of my bedroom and I'm all kinds of fucked up.

I drop my phone down at the bar, disgusted at myself.

What are you, fifteen? Get a fucking grip.

When I pick up the phone again to shut off the app, I breathe a sigh of relief when I find her in a bathrobe.

My bathrobe.

She's naked under my bathrobe.

Forget being Buffalo's most eligible bachelor—I'm officially the luckiest bastard in town.

My phone rings and I stumble.

Veronica.

Who the hell is—

Ah yea. She's the reporter I had a date with a few weeks back. Before the season started. A date I planned to cancel until Angel made me go. Insisting I needed to get out more outside of work.

A call and a text?

Red flag.

Not that it matters. Veronica wasn't getting a callback. I vaguely remember making plans to see each other again but I can't think about that right now.

Not when thoughts of silhouette-naked nannies are running through my head.

After checking the right camera with my little girl safely tucked in bed with her bunny and blanket, I put my phone away and close my tab at the bar.

18

I<small>T'S</small> M<small>ONDAY</small> <small>NIGHT</small> <small>AND</small> I'm completely restless. I didn't want to ask either of my friends to stay with me another night since their men return late this evening and I'm sure they want to be home to welcome them back.

I've kept busy enough this weekend. The house is spotless. Rory and I finished two five-hundred-piece puzzles. And I've performed my facial routine twice today. Any more than that and I'd be at risk of losing healthy skin cells.

On the bright side, my face is positively glowing.

I'm in my shorts and an off-shoulder tunic in the dining area, staring at the glass-enclosed bar wall.

I'm not sure that restocking Coach's liquor cabinet was the step in the right direction—one that may very well get me fired. But it *felt* right. He shouldn't have to sacrifice a nice glass of wine or scotch because he was kind enough to offer a recovering addict a job in his home.

Besides—I'm not planning on drinking any of it—I don't want to. But just to be safe, I didn't buy any vodka.

Now that they're all lined up in front of me, I can't help but think this *is* a step in the right direction, and…it just might be the therapy I need.

Within a few minutes, I toss the kitchen rag over my shoulder and stare at six empty rocks glasses in front of me, a grin spreading as I plan out each one.

Flipping the bottle, I pour a finger of Jonnie Walker into three glasses and Jack Daniels into the other. I dip to check for even amounts. Satisfied, I start chopping lemons and oranges. I stir up homemade simple syrup since it's better than store-bought—and shake ingredients together, then pour out my first mix.

I don't need to taste it to know it's perfect and move on to the next glass.

I swipe my forehead and focus on the last cocktail, which I had to revise due to a lack of cocktail cherries in the fridge. Like anyone really has those sitting around. There is a better chance of him having some bitters in the house.

I twist back to the pantry and gasp, finding a figure standing at the entry of the kitchen.

Royce stands cross-legged and folded arms watching me. He shifts but doesn't say anything. He looks something between horrified and intrigued as his eyes dip from mine to the row of cocktails on the counter before me.

"This isn't what it looks like," I assure, humor and nerves in my voice.

"It looks like you're having trouble finding what you need." He steps in further, stopping across the counter from me and studying my creations.

I twist my fingers. "Um…you didn't have cherries so I couldn't make a Manhattan but if I had bitters, I could make this into an—"

Before I finish, he's moving to a low cabinet by the wine cooler. "Lemon or cherry?" he asks casually.

"Lemon."

He pulls out both and hands me the one with the yellow label.

I mumble a thank you, sparing him a glance, and finish off a perfect Old Fashioned, giving it a stir. With a sigh, I take a step back from the counter.

"Done."

Tearing his gaze off me, he scans the spread, then moves to his liquor cabinet, switching on the light behind the glass enclosure.

I hold my breath waiting for his reaction. *Any* reaction.

Is he assuming the worst? Or... satisfied with my selections for him.

Nothing. He's giving me nothing.

Should I start talking? Would explaining that I felt the need to keep busy to avoid an anxiety attack help my case?

"I was planning on cleaning this all up before—"

"Which one should I try first?" He strides back to stand across the counter from me.

"You're not disappointed?"

He lets out a soft chuckle. "I haven't tried them yet."

A breath puffs out of me. "Right. Okay." I move to my left and swipe my hand over the first set. "These three are a scotch mix. These are whiskey. All of which I think...you'd like."

His eyes flick back to mine. "You made these for me?"

"Well, they're certainly not for me. I was more of a vodka girl."

He nods and reaches for one. I hold up a hand. "Start with this one. It's less fragrant and won't overpower your tastebuds."

He grins. "Alright."

By the time he finishes the fourth, he steps around the counter. I'm still so on edge from being caught practicing the thing that calms me, that I worry he'll feel how much I'm still shaking.

But he doesn't seem to notice. Instead, he nudges my shoulder playfully. "You trying to get me drunk, Ms. Kane?"

"I think it would take a lot more than a few shots to get you to lose control around me."

"I've lost control around you on a lot less," he counters, gripping the edge of the counter.

"You're not mad?"

"Do I look it?"

I narrow my eyes, wishing that my sixth sense worked when it came to this man. "I don't know."

He smirks, pleased that I can't read him. "Fair enough. No, I'm not. But I don't like that this is the second week in a row that you've used part of your pay to buy something for either Rory and me."

I frown, then remember the pricey—yet totally cool—outfit I bought for Rory just to mess with her dad. And also because I thought she'd look adorable dressed like me.

I shrug carelessly. "I'm free to spend my money on whatever I choose." It's...the Nicole answer. The carefree, frivolous person I put out for the world. What I really wish I could say is that I don't want him changing his lifestyle because he was kind enough to give me work and a place to live.

"Besides," I add. "This...was more for me than it was for you. I'm a mixologist. This is my art."

He rubs his chin, observing my 'artwork'. "Do you *want* this to be your art?"

"I'm not tempted if that's what you're asking."

"It's not what I'm asking, but since you mentioned it, why not?"

"Because I'm working. Just like when I was at the bar."

He nods. "I have an art too, you know?" He moves to a cabinet over the counter, pulling at baking goods. Flower, jam, cookie cutters, and powdered sugar. I watch him with interest. "What are you doing? You just landed from a seven-hour flight, it's after ten, you are not going to bake right now."

"I'm a little tipsy. Might need some help," he calls back, ignoring me.

I cross my arms. He glances back and sees my protesting stance. "You need to go to sleep."

He turns and points a wooden spoon at me as he slowly closes the distance between us, grabbing an apron off the hook on his way. "This is your fault."

"Mine?"

"You and your art."

He puts the apron over my head and pulls my hair from under the neckline. Then takes the loose strings at the sides and ties them around my back.

The way he lets his body press gently against mine, the way he breathes me in when he leans close, is intoxicating. It sends millions of shivers down my spine, my arms, my thighs.

"Are we about to make a mess?" I ask, sounding a little hopeful.

"The biggest."

An hour later, Royce pulls a tray full of jam filled cookies from the oven.

At some point, the apron ended up on him instead of me, he'd finished off the last of the shots I'd prepared and I'm pretty sure is pretending to be more drunk than he is.

No. I *know* he's pretending. I've been serving the man drinks for over eight months. He *doesn't* lose control. He could likely walk a tightrope after a few shots of whisky.

While he's examining the baked goods to make sure they're done, I sneak another finger dip of powdered sugar. The one ingredient we're not supposed to use until the cookies have cooled.

Royce chooses that moment to glance back at me. I drop my hand.

"What are you doing?"

"Me? Nothing." I press my lips together to hide my smile.

His eyes dip to the tampered-with sugar bowl. "Let me see your fingers."

I narrow my eyes at him. "May I see your search warrant?"

He laughs. Like *really* laughs. And it draws out my smile.

"Ma'am. We can do this the easy way or the hard way."

My brows jump. "Hard way, please."

His smile fades and his eyes darken as he closes the distance. I'm convinced he's about to end our game and turn cold again.

But instead, he holds out his hand. "Don't get cute with me. I've got hard evidence."

I hide my hands behind my back. "You can't prove anything," I say, pulling my head back when he's a breath away. Toying with him as long as he'll let me.

He reaches around me and pulls my hand, holding it between us, assessing the dust of sugar on my fingers. "Are you sure about that?"

"That's flour," I say coyly.

He holds my hand in his, which is also laced with white powder. But admittedly, not as much as mine.

He grunts as he traces my powdery index finger. "I'm bringing this one in for questioning."

I bite my bottom lip with a grin before he slides my finger into his hot mouth.

I clench between my thighs. *How* can something like this be so stimulating? So... delicious.

My mouth waters as his tongue licks off every spec before pulling away. "Guilty," he rasps.

I stare at his lips. "Prove it," I breathe, sounding a little desperate.

With that, he crushes my lips with his. It's an intense, hungry kiss. It's so demanding, I moan, letting my body fall into his.

He supports me, one hand around my waist, the other at the base of my skull, keeping my head up for him. Without breaking our kiss, he lifts me onto the island—spreading my legs and stepping between them.

"Nicole," he says against my lips. We're both breathing heavily. Me because his kisses take my breath away. Him likely because he thinks we're getting carried away.

I send a small prayer that he's not about to tell me we need to stop, that it's getting late, that we can't keep this up.

Because of that, I don't answer. I don't want to know why he stopped. I just...stare at his chest waiting for the moment I knew would come if we ever finally kissed.

I can't get mixed up with someone like you...

He lifts my chin. "I need to make something clear. This... this isn't the alcohol. I've been wanting to kiss you again since the last time. And...I'm not ready to tell you how long I've wanted to kiss you before that."

I release a breath... an embarrassingly distinct *relieved* breath. "I know," I say with a small smile. It's all I say. I don't need to tell him how much I love that he wanted me to know that.

"How do you know?"

"What I meant was I know you're not a lightweight. Take it from someone who's been trying to loosen up our grumpy Coach for the past eight months. I may as well have been serving you water."

He strokes hair away from my face, then runs the back of his fingers along my jaw. "Is that so?" His hands travel down my bare arms and that's...okay. But when they land on my thighs and squeeze, I suck in a breath and tense. Hard.

In a single beat, his expression shifts from seduction to tenderness. "What is it, Nicole?"

I shake my head and drop it. *I can't tell him.* Not now. Not when he's finally letting go with me. Finally taking what we both know he wants. "Nothing. I'm fine. I promise." I wince at the lie.

He takes one step back and nods, briefly scanning the length of my body as I sit atop the counter. But it doesn't make me feel sick the way it does when others do it. He's not picturing me naked behind that look. He isn't thinking about all the dirty things he could do to me.

He's looking at me as if...he didn't think this through.

Reaching for me, he cups my face in his palms and kisses my forehead. "I'm so sorry." The words are so soft I want to cry.

Before I can say anything to backtrack, he quietly offers to clean up the mess and takes me upstairs to my room, then whispers a gentle goodnight.

Shutting the door to my room, I let out a sigh and slump down against the wall, wondering how I could have ruined such a perfect evening.

What *happened?*

I don't want to talk to my therapist about this. I know it would be the appropriate route, but right now, I just need a friend.

Since for obvious reasons, Angel is out of the question—I reach for my phone and call Cora.

I cringe when I realize something. She's not going to answer. Nick *just* got back—the last thing she wants to do is talk to me. They're probably...very busy.

"Hey girl," she answers cheerfully.

"Oh, hi. I didn't expect you to answer."

"Just finishing up my facial routine before bed. Hold on, I need to rinse off."

I wait as water runs in the background and it takes all of thirty seconds for me to realize how stupid I was for calling Cora at nearly midnight to talk about my ridiculous issues.

She once asked me—back when things between her and my brother were rocky—about my experience with men.

I never admitted it to anyone. Not even my therapist because that's a whole new level of discussion I don't want to approach. It would only trigger her bringing it up in future sessions and I don't need that.

The embarrassing truth is...I don't like being touched. And not just in an "I'm not much of a hugger" way. But something about physical—mostly male proximity—is off-limits for me. Except when I practically make out with Nick's dog, Max. Totally down for that.

"Ah, okay, done. What's up?"

"I just needed someone to talk to—but you sound busy—"

"Oh don't be silly, I always have time for you and I am so wired. What going o—" She cuts off briefly, then comes back. "Oh, yeah. I'd love to come by tomorrow. Early? Of course. I don't have to be at work until eleven. So, see you around nine?"

"Nick?" I ask dryly.

"Yep."

Somehow, my best friend knew this conversation was *not* meant for his ears.

19

IT'S OUT. ALL OF it. Before I can stop myself. I pour my heart out the
way it needed to be for *weeks*.

Cora and I are sipping coffee and wrapped in one big blanket on the
swing in the back porch. She was already waiting for me by the time I
returned from dropping off Rory at school.

Royce was gone before we woke up this morning—most likely out for
a run before heading to the arena.

I'm not afraid to tell her about my feelings for Coach. But I am
worried about what she'll do with the *other* bit of information I fed her.

Poor thing. Of course, I choose the youngest of our group of friends
to confide in.

To burden.

"Are you done?" she asks carefully.

"Yes. Of course. The whole thing was a mistake and I never want to
touch that stuff again."

"Nicole, Nicole." She touches my shoulder. "I meant with your story. Is that everything?"

I release a breath. "Oh. Yes."

"Good. Now I can hug you?" She wraps one arm around me and tugs me toward her. "Thank you for coming to me, you have no idea how glad I am you did."

"Yeah, but Cora—"

"Your secrets are safe with me—I'm not loyal to one Kane more than the other. But if I were—I always choose my bitches first."

I chuckle to hide the natural warmth spreading through me. "Thank you."

"I just want to say, that I was probably the first one to call it. This thing between you and Coach. And *of cooourrse* he wants you. You're Nicole Kane. You're the untouchable queen of Hollyville. But if anyone in this entire city is worthy of you—it's Coach Collins."

"Untouchable is right...I don't know where you're getting that queen nonsense from," I mutter.

She tugs my hand. "Nicole. You're my hero. You've been through some fucked up shit...only to come out stronger, brighter, and better on the other side. It's inspiring. And now you're caring for an adorable little girl who *only* seems to want you. You're as queen as this town gets." She pauses and gives me a sincere look. "But I think you do need to show all your cards."

I nod. "I have to tell him...about my issue...don't I?"

She winces. "If you want things to go anywhere without him wondering why you're freezing up—yeah, I think so."

"Easier said than done."

"Are you forgetting I practically stalked your brother and told him I wanted him to be my *first*?"

"Yeah, super smooth, babe." I laugh, then stare out into the peacefulness of his enormous backyard. "What if I get too intimidated?"

She nods once and follows my gaze. "If he intimidates you just by listening—then you probably want to rethink this whole thing."

She's got a point. It shouldn't be this hard. But nothing about me has ever been easy.

"Can I ask you something," she asks. "You told me you're not..."

"I'm not. His name was Christopher. Not as preppy as his name." I chuckle. "We were somewhat of a thing back when I was...around my old crowd. And we did it. Him because he was super into me. Me because well, I wanted to get it over with. I tried to hide that I was a virgin, and he was probably too messed up to even notice I...wasn't enjoying it."

"Oh my God, Nicole." She hugs me all over again and I tear up. But not from the memory, but relief.

Because it felt *so* good to get that out. To realize that I'm surrounded by better people now. People who see me, care for me, and make me laugh. Even when they're not trying to be funny.

She pulls back, searching my eyes. "It sounds like you're coming on a little strong with Coach. Are you sure you're ready for that?"

I nod. "Yes. I want him. If I didn't screw it all up last night."

She jerks. "Because you tensed when he touched you? I kissed another boy in front of your brother after he rejected me—you can't screw up more than that."

I laugh. "I remember that. It's a miracle you guys made it out alive."

We muse for a moment and then I look at her. "Thank you for keeping the part about what happened that night a secret for me. I'll tell Nick eventually. I promise."

She touches my hand. "I know. But if he kicks me out—I'm moving back into your apartment."

I laugh. Because the idea that my brother would ever let this girl out of his sight again is laughable.

Royce

It's not unusual for me to be out of the house at dawn—especially when things get hectic with game schedules and media. But I still can't help feeling like I snuck out of my own house to avoid Nicole.

I'm so...ashamed. How could I have so thoughtlessly put my hands on her like that knowing she doesn't like to be touched?

It's not something she—or anyone—ever shared with me, but I noticed. How could I not? Since I've known her, she's *visibly* reluctant to all kinds of physical affection. And there's a very clear vibe she gives off at parties to the male species to stay at least one yard away.

Except...with me.

And here I was, expecting to go from zero to fifty after one kiss.

The worst part of it is that *she* felt ashamed. Ashamed for needing to stop. For tensing up.

My whole body aches with regret...and a desire to fix what I'm afraid I broke last night.

There's a knock on my door and I'm grateful for the distraction.

"Come in."

"Royce." Grove Randall, the GM, nods as he walks into my office. He and Jeff Granger, one of the team owners, are the few who refer to me by my first name.

"Grove." I shake my head with relief as the next up in the chain of command strolls into my office and takes a seat across from me.

Grove shakes his head right back. "How the hell do we get rid of this guy?" he asks. He doesn't need to tell me he's referring to Hastings.

I lean back in my chair. "We can't. Regardless of his past reputation, he still has fans out there."

Fans that are louder than mine.

"You got to help me here, Coach," he starts, using my title deliberately. Reminding me this is still my job and I'm the only one who can keep it that way. "Who's our weakest link?"

"We don't have one. We're only a few weeks in. It's a rough start to the season but...we'll get where we need to be. I have no doubt."

Grove shrugs. "It's politics, Royce. When the economy is bad, people blame the people on top."

"I'm not on top," I say dryly.

"No. But you lead the team. And you're going to need to prove you're not growing soft."

"What does that mean?"

He twists his neck to ensure the door is closed but still lowers his voice. "The Blades Organization Kickoff Gala."

"The annual auction event? I go every year. The whole team does."

"You need to come with a plan. You're responsible for the team's on-ice performance. If you don't win seventy percent of the games between now and then, you'll need to announce plans for trades."

"That's your job," I remind him.

"In close discussion with my head coach," he practically shouts. "Just trust me on this. If the president and the owners see that you know where the problem is and plan to fix it, they'll dismiss any idea of replacing you as Head Coach."

I want to tell him that if that's an idea they're toying with, then Robbie can have the damn job. But this isn't just about me. My team is counting on me.

I shake my head. There has to be another way. Like to figure out what the fuck our problem is. But if I want to avoid having to hand pick them myself, I'll need to ensure we win at least five of the games over the next two weeks—until this gala.

"Maybe I can come up with one," I mutter quietly, mostly to appease him at the moment.

"Come on, there's got to be more than one. What about our alternate? Jace Knight. He had that injury last year."

"He's been on point even before the surgery. He's a hundred percent now."

Well, almost.

But he's certainly not the weakest link.

"Think about it." He stands and moves to the door. "Oh and bring a date. Jeffrey's wife is a chatter so if she's talkin' up a storm with someone, he's sure to stick around and hear you out."

I hate that he has a point.

Jeffrey isn't one to sit around and chat—especially if he's got his doubts about someone. But if I can have a few minutes with the guy, I can convince him that the team just needs time and motivation. That they'll—no—*we'll* get out of this rut and get back on track.

And that I have no intention of stepping down. Not before I prove what this team can do.

I swipe a hand across my face. "Not a bad idea."

He watches me carefully and takes his hand off the handle. "Talked to Claire the other day."

I grunt. "Weren't you just leaving?"

"She'd make a great choice. She works at the magazine. She used to be the face of the team. And she's one hell of a conversationalist."

"I'd rather cut off my arm than walk into a room with that woman on it," I mutter.

"Your ex-wife filled me in on the disaster you've got goin' on at home. An ex-con as your nanny? Really?"

I want to throw him against the wall. And I could. It would be easy. It would cost me my job—but it would be worth it.

"Her name is Nicole, and she was never a convict. Claire is being dramatic."

"I'm very much aware of her name. Everyone in this goddamn town is aware of her name and her reputation. Wasn't she just released from rehab?"

"That was two years ago and she's—" The lie gets caught in my throat until it no longer feels like one. "She's good now."

Grove waves a hand like it's just semantics. I know he doesn't care about the human behind who we're discussing. His only concern is keeping me in my position. And that means no filling the media up with extra fuel. "Fine. But you won't convince the organization or our local fans of that. Just keep her—hidden—at least until this whole thing with Hastings blows over and the Blades are back on track."

Keep her *hidden?*

I glare at him. "She's my daughter's nanny. She's expected to come to certain games as well as events I choose to bring Rory to. And are you forgetting she's the team captain's sister?"

He watches me as if I'm saying one thing, but he hears something entirely different. "Look, I'm not judging what you do behind closed doors. But if people hear you're involved with Nicole Kane while the team is on a losing streak, your credibility is toast."

"I need to get back to work. Can we catch up later?" It's my way of telling him to get out and he knows it.

It's after four o'clock when I get a phone call from a number I don't recognize. But the caller ID shows the area code is from town.

"Coach Collins," I say into the phone.

"Mr. Collins. I'm so glad we've reached you. This is Ms. Adams from Hammock Academy."

Rory's school.

"Oh, Ms. Adams, is everything alright?" My chest tightens.

"Rory is alright. Ms. Kane picked her up a little while ago." Her voice is tentative, and I wish she would just get to the point of the call.

"There was an incident this afternoon," she starts slowly. "Rory was playing in the yard with some children and the parents usually wait outside the fence until our staff brings each child out."

"Yes, I know how dismissal works, Ms. Adams."

"Well...and I'm not sure what happened. You see, I wasn't there, but apparently, there was some commotion and Ms. Kane jumped the fence, marched up to the children playing in the yard, and instructed Rory to push another child into the mulch."

I drop my head in my hand, pinching the bridge of my nose.

"Mr. Collins?"

"Yes, yes. So, you say you weren't there?" I ask calmly.

"That's right."

"Then why are you the one calling me?"

"Because I'm the headmaster."

"That's nice. But if you don't have a solid background as to what happened right before, then I can't take what you're telling me into any context. For all I know, there was a fire outside and Ms. Kane jumped in to help."

She laughs and I swallow down my anger. "Mr. Collins, I assure you there was no fire."

"Then I suggest you find out what happened. Especially the part where someone either touched or threatened my daughter because otherwise, I don't see how your version makes any sense, Ms. Adams."

"Of—of course. I'll be talking to some of the staff as well."

"Please do." I hang up.

My jaw clenches. The last thing I need is for Rory to be kicked out of private school.

Jesus, Nicole.

Practice is at seven and I've spent the last few hours coming up with drills and strategies. Something's been bothering me about the games lately and I can't put my finger on it.

I can't put my finger on *who*.

Needing the distraction, I take off and call Nicole the moment I get in the car. But there's no answer.

I don't want to yell at her. My frustration is misplaced because of what Grove has asked me to do, but she needs to know, she can't pull shit like this.

This is the kind of attention Grove reminded me I don't need.

I come home to an empty house and that makes my blood simmer. Calm down. Maybe she took her out for a donut or something.

Me: *Where are you?*

I'm pacing my living room, waiting for the response, which doesn't come through nearly fast enough.

Nicole responds with an address. That's it.

An address that's... *Downtown*?

Me: *Let me rephrase that. Why aren't you home??*

No response.

Okay. Maybe I could have asked better. I jump back in my Range and head downtown, checking the clock for when I need to be back at the arena.

Where the hell did you take her, Nicole?

Thirty minutes later, I pull up to the street and sigh when I see the emblem on the storefront of the address Nicole gave me.

A dojo?

I walk into the Taekwondo studio, reminding myself that I'm in public and need to keep my cool. And that there is a perfectly reasonable explanation for why my daughter was driven out of town on a school night without my permission.

I follow the oak wood floor down the long aisle until I reach the window of the front desk. It slides open as I approach, and a young woman greets me with a warm smile. "Hello. How can I help you?"

She catches the attention of a slender man behind her in the office. He's in a red uniform and black belt with all sorts of pins and badges.

He stalks over to the window. "You're Royce Collins."

I give him a tentative smile. "Yes."

"Welcome. We received your online consent forms. Thanks again for signing up. Rory will catch up to Nicole in no time."

I blink. *Consent?*

"Right this way." He comes around the side and opens the door for me. It's loud with combat grunts and bodies tumbling onto padded mats. He extends an arm to a seating area where a few people are tuned in, some on phones, some watching the action on the floor.

My eyes instantly land on the brunette in the white uniform and black belt and the curly-haired redhead next to her.

I nod a thank you. And he nods more profoundly...almost like a miniature bow.

"May I get a printed copy of the consents when you have a moment?"

"Of course. I'll get those ready for you."

My jaw is tight as I watch them from the glass wall. My arms folded across my chest.

"Daddy." The familiar little voice eases some of my tension and I watch my barefooted princess race to me. I kneel to greet her but glare at the woman who brought her here.

And she...doesn't look very sorry at all.

"Daddy, I learned to punch and kick today."

"Did you?" It's an absent response but I can't give any more right now.

Nicole finishes her routine with a man who also wears a black belt, and bows before reluctantly following Rory out to me.

I stand, leveling my gaze with Nicole's but keeping my hands on Rory's shoulders. "I know you're new at this, but this is the sort of thing you need to check with me first."

"No, it's not."

"Excuse me?"

"I said it's not," she snaps and her eyes glisten. She turns and grabs Rory's hand. "Come on. You need practice."

"Is there a problem, Mr. Collins?" The young woman from the front desk appears beside me, handing me the papers I'd supposedly completed online.

I take them. "No. No problem. How long is this session?"

"They should be done in another twenty minutes. Nicole prepaid for an extensive lesson today."

Of course she did.

"Thank you."

I sit back on the bench and watch Nicole expertly combat with a professional. A younger black belted girl—high school age—is with Rory, teaching her basics.

I could have taught her *that.* I grumble internally.

Next, the girl with Rory pairs her with a little boy maybe a year or two older and huskier. He's in a yellow belt.

What do they think they're doing? Pairing her up with a kid who probably can't control his own—

He bows to her, and she mimics. Then he stretches his leg briskly and in the blink of an eye, Rory falls on her side.

I'm on my feet and glance at Nicole, who watches them with a small smile—but the pain in her eyes is far from gone.

Rory stands and the boy tries the same move again. This time, Rory blocks him and twists his foot, making him fall harder on the matted floor.

Nicole jumps with a clap and races over, giving my girl a high five.

Running my hand over my face, I move to the far wall along the corridor, near the entrance and Nicole catches my eye. Bracing herself, she lifts her head and walks around the staff and children, reaching me in the corner.

My arms are crossed in front of me and my jaw is set. She takes me in tentatively. "So I *signed* a consent?"

"There wasn't enough time to reach you," she whispers.

"What's the urgency?" I ask but I've already pieced together this little puzzle.

"She needs to learn to defend herself."

"Nicole, playgrounds will always have bullies—in all sizes. You can't—"

"Of course, I can't. But she can protect herself." She nods as if reassuring herself.

"Nicole." I reach for her, and she snaps away.

"You weren't there. This kid tugged on her hair and then his friends laughed, and she looked so helpless..." She chokes and the tears fall. "She just...stood there, Royce."

She swipes at her tears and looks up at me defiantly. "It doesn't matter. Rory will learn to protect herself. And if I get to make any decisions as her nanny, then this is the *only* thing I want," she sobs, making heads turn.

I grip her shoulders and twist her away from the crowd. "Okay. Okay. We'll sign her up with a fast track if that's what she wants, okay?"

She nods vigorously. "Ok-ay."

"Oh, baby." I pull her against me, and she tenses before slowly calming under my touch.

She sniffles and turns her face against my chest. "I never want her to feel helpless if someone hurts her."

I turn her to face the floor of students. "Look at her. By the time she's in high school, she'll be able to take anyone out by just looking at them."

She laughs and swipes under her eyes. "She's going to be okay." She nods again, reassuring herself.

And I'm...done for.

20

I'VE CALMED DOWN SIGNIFICANTLY since this afternoon.

If only that girl learned to talk to playground bullies the way she speaks to her babysitters, we'd never have a problem.

Well, she'd never have a problem. Who knows how long I'll be around to protect her myself?

One thing's for sure, I'm not going anywhere until I teach that girl self-defense.

I may have gotten a little bit carried away this afternoon. Jumping the fence like I'm some superhero. Then hauling the six-year-old downtown to my dojo and drilling the skill of martial arts into her.

After her bath, Rory was out like a light an hour before her usual bedtime. She even finished all her vegetables, convinced it would make her big and strong overnight.

I'm sitting by the fireplace when I hear the lock turn on the front door and brace myself. He went easy on me because I was an emotional wreck earlier, but I know what's to come now that he's not faced with my tears.

Men can't stand seeing women cry.

I'm seated on the sofa and set the magazine down, letting him know he has my full attention. When he walks in, I wince.

He looks utterly drained. "Hey, how was practice?" I ask, somehow knowing this isn't about me.

He shakes his head and tosses his jacket on the chair, then steps further in. He sets down a small shopping bag at his feet and sits a cushion away on the sofa.

"There's a gala in a few weeks. With the team on a losing streak, Grove, the GM, wants me to show up with a few trade recommendations."

"Oh." I don't know what to say, but instantly, I understand why practice was so hard today. "You had to watch them with a different eye today. A critical one."

"It's the worst part of my job. Hell, it's not even my job. I'm supposed to make them better."

"I'm sorry," I say and it feels like deja vu. Because I'm sorry for making his day even more stressful than it needed to be because of my own issues.

But this isn't about me. This is about the relationship he's built with his team—and the choices he has to make.

He runs a hand down his face and looks me over. "How are you?"

I shrug and scrunch my nose. "Besides feeling like I may have crossed some lines today...I'm alright."

He grunts out a laugh. "It was the highlight of my day, Nicole."

My eyes flash. "It was?"

He rubs his forehead. "I'm always scared that no one is truly looking out for Rory when I'm not around—and I'm not around a lot. My...annoyance was...misplaced and the technicality of forgery is more my issue, not yours. You did what felt right. The truth is, while I was at practice today, dealing with what's going on there, I had some peace knowing that my little girl is safe. And *you're* making sure she stays that way."

I swallow the threat of fresh tears and offer a soft grateful smile.

He winks and touches my hand gently before standing. "I'm going to go check on her."

My stomach drops. He just got here and I want so much more of him. I'm not ready to say goodnight. I want to talk to him, open up to him the way I've longed to. *Thank* him for today.

And it can't wait.

I jump to my feet and call after him, a little too eagerly. "Royce."

He swings his head back.

"I...liked it when you held me today."

And when you called me baby.

He releases a breath, along with the tension in his shoulders. "I liked it too." Then his brows jump, and he bends to pick up the paper bag. "I got you something."

He hands it to me and I take a peek inside, only to see pink tissue paper wrapping.

"It's a bathing suit. You didn't bring one and I thought after the day you've had..."

I look up tentatively. "Like tonight?"

He nods toward the backyard. "It's all yours."

An hour later, alone in my room, I've dissected the hell out of what it means that the man of my dreams buys me a *bathing* suit. It's *practically* lingerie.

Is it...an invitation? Or just a thoughtful gift?

Finally, I try it on. It's a solid white one-piece with thick straps. And it's...*almost* perfect. A little snug around the bust, but I can make do.

I tie my hair back and throw on my bathrobe before heading downstairs. Soaking in his hot tub? It's an offer I can't refuse. But I don't want to do it alone. I'd rather...lurk in the hallway just in case I'd catch him. Or linger in the kitchen with a cup of tea in case he gets another chocolate craving.

Chocolate.

Maybe over confessions, I can open up to him. I can tell him why I turned to stone when he touched me.

And maybe...oh for the love of God, maybe...he'd do it again.

And I'll be ready for it. I'll welcome it.

I know that now.

Because this afternoon, in my most guarded of moments—when the only thing on my mind was protection—*his* touch, his arms around me, calmed me.

I have no doubt about it now. I *belong* in his arms.

And I'm not giving up without a fight. Even if it's a fight against my own demons.

Finding the downstairs completely shut down, I frown and check the time.

Dammit. I waited too long. He's gone to bed.

It's not like I can go knocking on his door. But then I hear something in the backyard. A gentle hum and the sound of water splashing.

I step out tentatively and find him in the hot tub. The sight of his bare chest again seizes my breath. His eyes are closed and I wonder if I should quietly step back into the house, given how downhill this went for us last time.

"You're up," he says as he opens his eyes. "Thought you'd gone to bed by now."

I don't say anything. This is the chance I'd been waiting for all night. And now that it's here—I can't speak.

He starts to get up. "I'll leave you alone."

"No, please. I'd much rather you stay." I glance around. "It's...dark," I point out, completely full of it. Nicole Kane might be afraid of a few things...the dark isn't one of them.

He raises a brow. "You're afraid of the dark." It's almost a question but comes off as more of a statement.

I scrunch my nose and shake my head, letting him in on my secret.

I want you to stay.

He smirks. "How does it fit?"

It's like he's asking me to strip for him, so I draw closer and untie my robe, letting it fall off my shoulders.

A low grunt comes from his throat and he shifts in his seat.

I settle a few feet from him, but closer than I was last time. "Are you feeling any better?"

"Getting there," he says, and moves a towel on the deck revealing a box of chocolates.

I smile. "Am I...interrupting your therapy session?"

"You're right on time. Although I'm cheating today. There are only sweet ones in this box."

"Are they any good?"

He looks up at me, daring me to play.

I sigh. "Coach...I have too many confessions and I don't think you have enough chocolates."

His eyes roam my body and he growls. "Certainly not enough for the both of us."

I inch closer. "Do you want to start?"

"That wouldn't be very gentlemanly."

"I don't want a gentleman," I say with confidence.

"Then I'll just be your...man. Because I'll never be un-gentleman with you."

My stomach flips. He's not closing the door on...whatever this is between us. He's just giving me time.

Then all at once, my stomach tightens. Because that fear is back. That what I'd tell him might be too much. I feel the shivers along my arms despite the heat lamp and hot water covering most of my body.

"Nicole." His eyes dip briefly, and he rattles the box. "I lied. There's more than enough and if there isn't, I'll fly to New York right now to get more if it means you'll open up to me."

I chuckle nervously and bite my lip as he reaches for my hand.

Taking it, I let him pull me beside him until our knees touch, barely. He pretends not to notice my tension as he plucks a piece of chocolate from the box. "This one is for me. Because I'm about to make a confession."

Silently, I huff out a relieved breath.

"I've always wanted your side of the story. But was never in the position to ask for it. Not because I felt sorry for you or because it intrigued me in some sick way or anything. But because I *despised* the things I was hearing. The level of judgement instead of compassion. And when I saw you again...that want became something much more powerful. I wanted to help. I wanted to make you smile. Then...you *actually* smiled. And I've been obsessed with it ever since."

"Making me smile?" I ask with a hopeful grin.

But he doesn't grin back when he answers. "Making everything right for you."

I swallow.

I pick a piece of chocolate from the box. "I've wanted to share my side of the story with you. Most people know that when I was sixteen, my mother left me with some men who she claimed were her friends."

He strokes my hair and nods.

"I never asked where she went to get it."

His eyes darken.

"Where the story changes... as it traveled through town, is what happened to me when I was there."

He touches my hand. "Only if you're ready."

I smile up at him, then focus on his hand in mine. "I was scared. I started to think that these weren't her friends. That maybe she wasn't coming back. They weren't touching me. These men, they're drug dealers, not rapists. I wasn't even restrained. But I was... somewhat of a bother to them because I was restless and freaking out. So they shot me up with something. It was two of them. One...had to hold me down."

He growls a curse, then brings my hand to his mouth, kissing it softly.

"The part that no one except Nick and Cora know is that...it wasn't just that one time. She left me with them four or five times over a few months. I kept going back because I was afraid of what they would do to her if I didn't. But every time one of them came near me, I tensed."

His jaw tightens and he turns away from me—I don't need to see his face to know he's cursing himself for last night.

I wrap my fingers around his arm, making him turn to me.

"Did they ever..."

I shake my head. "Nothing more than taunt me, make me think they were going to do something."

He looks like he wants to ask more but drops it and squeezes my hand, reassuring me that it's safe to continue if I need to.

I pop the chocolate I so deserve in my mouth and let it melt. "I've been with men, since. I didn't want to be a prude forever. When I was twenty-two, I met someone who agreed to no strings attached because I thought it was an easy thing to get over with."

"Was it?"

I shake my head like it's no big deal. "I didn't tell him I was a virgin so..."

Another low curse and he swipes a hand across his face like there was something he could have done about it. Then he looks at me. "How can I help?"

He doesn't realize this, but he's *been* helping me. For the last two years. The stolen glances, the coy grins, giving me permission to call him by his first name. The mundane small talk between us that felt both intimate and a little bit erotic.

I *craved* the times I'd see him.

But I'm *not* ready to tell him this. Craving is obsessing and that's borderline addiction.

But I want to answer his question—so I take the leap. "I wanted to share this with you because of my reaction last night. It was purely reflex—I didn't mean to push you away."

"Honey, you don't have to explain anything to me," he whispers, pulling my head against his lips and murmuring, "I'm so sorry."

I turn my head up with a smile. "Don't be. You broke my curse the moment you kissed me."

He searches my eyes in disbelief, like I've just given him the greatest gift.

I'm like a hawk. I watch his every move, testing the waters. He and I are not a forever deal—I'm way too messed up to be anyone's forever. But *right now*, he's the only one I ever want touching me.

My fears vanish when he's around. I can't pass up my chance to ask. "Is there any chance, we could—"

"Was that your only time?" he asks.

"No. But I didn't bother after the second. That was...five years ago."

He doesn't seem surprised by that at all. "Did either of them make you come?"

I almost laugh. "No."

He considers that for a moment. "What were you going to ask me?"

I blink. "I was going to ask if we could pick up where we left off. With your fingers in my hair and—"

Instantly, his fingers find their way into my hair. "I want you so bad, Nicole..." The words almost sound painful. "I don't want to hold what you shared with me against you but—I can't...I can't *touch* you."

"Then don't. Don't touch me. Let me touch *you*."

21

I stare at the most gorgeous woman I've ever seen. The one I've stolen plenty of glances with, but I will never stop being in aww of.

Just when I thought the hardest thing to do was keeping my hands and mind off places they shouldn't be—Nicole presents a new challenge.

Try to deny her the one thing she's begging me for.

Desire wins and my white flag goes up. "Fuck," I growl, digging my fingers back into her hair because I'm not strong enough to refuse her. But I want her to know she's in control of how we do this. "Come here. Sit on my lap."

With one swoosh in the hot tub, she's straddling me, eager for me and I don't need to think twice. I don't ask. I crush her lips with mine, loving the moan she releases each time I do.

Without fail.

She tastes like chocolate and heat. Hell, she tastes like there's no one else for her but me as she takes control of the kiss, her fingers digging into my hair and gripping the back of my neck.

She pulls back breathlessly. "Those last thirty seconds were better than anything I've experienced with anyone." Her eyes drop to my arms which are *firmly* disciplined at my sides.

When her face falls. I lift her chin. "I have another confession, sweetheart."

Her eyes lift with intrigue.

"When I was in Seattle...the other night, I checked Rory's bedroom camera as I always do when I'm away. I like to make sure she's asleep before I go to bed.

She smiles sweetly.

"But I accidentally got my bedroom instead. I have one in there for when she chooses to sleep in my bed instead of her own."

Her brows knit like she's trying to figure out why I'm telling her this and then she gasps. "Oh."

I wince. "I'm sorry, I should have said something—hell, I should have fixed your shower."

"Should I have used the one in Angel's room?"

"Maybe..." I admit.

When her face falls again, I add with a grin. "But from now on, you use no one's but mine."

She smiles. "It is a very nice shower," she admits coyly. "Did you see anything?"

"Mostly a silhouette."

She hooks her fingers under the shoulder straps of her bathing suit and I'm already in danger of violating her with my erection. Her exposed breasts would cross dangerous territory.

"Don't." I reach up and stop her, leaving the straps loose around her shoulders. Then swallow hard at the seductive beauty before me. "I won't be able to keep my mouth off them."

"Good."

"No. Not good." I shift to adjust under her and she gasps, gripping my shoulders and falling into me. The moan she releases by my ear is raw and primal.

Fuck.

"Nicole," I rasp into her hair, gloves thrown down, desire to make her come overpowering all my senses.

"Yes." It's breathless and I think I know what almost happened just now. Judging by her stillness and the burial of her head in my neck.

"Move your hips against me," I say, and it sounds too much like a command.

She hesitates and I whisper a few words of encouragement into her ear. Then slowly, she moves, shaking, holding onto me for dear life like she's going to explode any second.

"Keep going, baby. I've got you."

I refuse to put my hands on her hips to guide her, to grip her ass as she rides me...to touch her. Because *this* needs to be all her.

But I've still got her. I'll support her with my body—not my hands.

She's lifted her head at this point, her breathing harder, her speed increasing as she chases her pleasure. And the sight. The fucking sight of her. It's invigorating.

When my erection is at its peak, I lift her ass slightly for better friction—so it's not too much for her.

She jerks and gasps, her mouth falling open.

"Let it out. I want to hear you."

She screams and shakes, throwing her head back and all too soon, she's coming down from her orgasm.

"Keep going," I growl. I'm not ready for her to be done.

"I—can't," she pants, and I don't hold back. Yanking her straps down, I cover a hard nipple with my mouth, sucking and pulling as I thrust my tip against her center, both our suits between us, milking her orgasm as much as I can. Desperate to give her what no one's ever been able to.

Safely.

Secretly.

She wails and it's even better than before. It's a sound I would never tire of hearing. A sound made only for my ears.

"Holy shit," she breathes.

I rumble a laugh and hold her face. "You okay?"

She laughs. "I'm...incredible."

"Thank you," I whisper.

Her eyes are hazy with heat. "I didn't do anything."

"You let me be the one."

After a shower, I pace my bedroom, certain if I don't stop, I'll form a dent in the hardwood.

How the fuck am I supposed to sleep? Nicole is in the other room. She's safe. My house is under top-of-the-line security—minus visits from my ex-wife. Nothing is going to happen to her here.

But I'm still restless.

It's not enough. Anything less than having her in my bed every night for the rest of our lives is *not enough*.

I mutter a curse under my breath and reach for my phone. Screw the hour. This is important.

My friend answers after the second ring. "David, it's Collins."

"Dude it's almost midnight. This better be an emergency, for which I still highly recommend dialing 911. Not a police chief you happen to have in your contacts."

"I'm sorry it's late. I need a favor. Just to look something up."

"Text it to me, I'll check it in the morning."

"Just listen. Frank Lidowsky. Name ring a bell?"

I hear a grunt in the background and some shifting. Then his voice shifts more to the 'on duty' friend I know. "Course I know him; my team helped put him away for a long time after—wait a second. This about the Kane girl?"

My jaw tics, but I don't confirm or correct him. This is cop talk—he doesn't mean to disrespect her.

At least I hope not.

"Yes," I bite out. "Lidowsky was arrested little under two years ago when he showed up at Nicholas Kane's home here in town and then trialed for—"

"Countless crimes. I know. Don't worry, he's still locked up good."

"It's not him I'm worried about. It's his friends. You got that history? There were several associates, weren't there?"

"Royce, what's going on? Just tell me and I'll see what I can do."

I sigh, knowing I need to be upfront with the man. "One of the counts on his arrest was assaulting Nicole Kane."

"Yeah," he confirms, since putting your hands on someone—or a goddamn needle without their permission is assault.

"I need to know that every single person in that old warehouse of his has been put away."

Or dead.

He sighs and I know it's more complicated than that. "Call me after nine tomorrow."

I release a breath. "Thank you. I owe you."

I don't race out of the house in the morning. I wait downstairs for the girls to come down.

Rory skips down one step at a time, talking to the woman walking behind her. "What if he doesn't fall at first?"

"He will if you catch him off—" Nicole spots me in the kitchen and freezes as I raise my brow at her. "Of course you should *always* tell a grown-up first before doing anything." Then, like she can't help herself, she bends to my daughter's ear and whispers something not meant for my ears.

Rory giggles then, staying loyal to her nanny, nods back at Nicole, zipping her lips.

Straightening her features, Nicole clears her throat and approaches me as I hand her a cup of coffee. "Your poker face needs work," I tell her dryly.

"If I was trying to get one over on you, I would," she counters with a mischievous smirk.

God, she's sexy.

And I'm so relieved to see her so...relaxed. Comfortably flowing through my home, standing close as she sips her coffee.

Then I take out the single pill from the container and hold it out for her.

She shakes her head. "I'm good today, thank you."

"Are you sure?"

She nods. "It's supposed to be as needed. And I don't feel like I do."

I nod, satisfied and a little bit wistful that maybe I might be the reason. I put the pill back in the bottle. She's only taken two since it was prescribed and I like being the one taking care of her. For the days I'd left the house early, I'd leave one by the coffee counter and for the most part, come home to find it untouched.

"How'd you sleep?" I ask as Rory steps into the den to pack her backpack.

She sweeps her eyes over me. "Probably better than you did. Kept my bedroom door open and noticed your light on pretty late."

Running my fingers through my hair, I sigh. I'm not about to tell her that I had vengeance on my mind all night.

That's...not healthy and counterproductive.

"I was...going through strategies in my head for the next game and—" My gaze lands on my little girl playing in the other room and then back to Nicole. The woman who I'd asked for nothing but honesty while she was living here—and here I was lying to her face.

The same one that looks up at me with trusting eyes.

With a growl, I pull her against me. "I'm lying. I couldn't stop thinking about you. About what you shared with me. And all the ways I can make it better."

She smiles and presses a hand to my chest, her eyes dropping appreciatively to it. "God, you're so solid." Then her eyes flick back to mine. And I brace myself for an 'I don't need saving' defense. Or something about not needing a man to make it all better.

But she doesn't say any of that. Instead, she pushes up on her toes, grips my biceps, the way she does, the way I've come to love, and brushes her lips softly against mine. "You already have."

"What's going on, Coach?" Nick and Jace walk into my office after changing.

"I need another set of eyes," I say, glancing back at them from my office couch, facing the TV on the back wall. "Yours should count as one," I grumble.

"Hey, you're the one who needs help." Nick snips, joining me on the sofa. "What no popcorn?"

"Shut up," I say to one, then look at the other one—the one dating my daughter. "Sit down."

"I'm good," he says casually, leaning against the desk, arms crossed.

I roll my eyes. The guy is still traumatized from when I called him into my office last season threatening to expose the fact that he'd been hiding an injury—if he didn't break up with Angel.

Not my finest moment.

I've made amends—countless amends if you ask me. But the guy is still on edge every time he walks in here.

"I need you both to watch these playbacks from our last few games and tell me what you see."

"Coach, we've done this," Nick starts. "None of these are rookie mistakes, the other teams, they're just—"

"Don't say better."

"I wasn't going to. It's like—they know our next move before we make them."

"That's called research. And that's not it. I've changed it up. We're not predictable. The only ones who know our next move is *our* team."

Jace pushes off the desk. "What are you saying?"

I shake my head, refusing to believe that someone on the Blades is deliberately sabotaging the game.

I rub my forehead. "Nothing. It's nothing. I just need sleep."

My two captains exchange glances. "Is Rory sick? She been keeping you up?"

"Will you just watch the goddamn videos and let me know if anything looks off?"

I have three suspicions but I need to see if they come up with the same. And then, I have a plan.

But if I'm caught—and word gets out that I don't trust my team and have tested each one of them—I might as well retire today.

After the replays, I let my two trusted players in on my plan. And the room goes silent.

Jace's face twists. "Just for Friday's game?"

"No," I mutter. "Until my suspicions are confirmed."

Jace shakes his head, no doubt hating this plan. "Look, my methods, my research, my knowledge has never failed me before. Something is up and I have a feeling it has to do with Hastings being back in town."

"You think there's a connection?"

"I'm almost sure of it."

22

I T'S BEEN FOUR DAYS since our tryst in the hot tub and I just
feel...different. Opening up to Royce was liberating to say the least.
Weightlifting. My insecurities about my past and what people might feel
about me...washed away.

At least for now.

Not much has happened between us since that night and I'm disappointed...but patient. I can't get in his way. He needs to focus on the
team...he needs *sleep.*

He didn't make it home for dinner the last two nights but I see him
in the mornings. He's been up earlier than usual this week, handing me
my coffee, offering my meds—which I've been refusing—and whenever
we can, we steal a goodbye kiss before he leaves.

I don't ask what it means. I know it's just for now.

Maybe I'm just a distraction for him. The good kind. The kind he
needs to stay sane with everything going on at work.

And I'm alright with that.

Use me all you want, *Coach Collins*. Because I don't mind.

After all, one can only dream to be in his arms for longer than... right now.

It's Friday morning and I sip my coffee, trying to hold on to the memory of his scent when he brushed past me briefly this morning on his way out. Both of us sneaking a glance at Rory who was a mere three feet away. He'd turned back to me with a regretful gaze, and I nodded understandingly.

Of course. We can't show Rory anything. It would only confuse her when I leave eventually.

My phone dings with a text and I flip it over next to me on the porch swing.

Royce: *You smelled amazing this morning.*

Me: *I smelled like you—forgot to bring my own body wash when I used your shower while you were down in the gym.*

Royce: *I liked it.*

Me: *I should hope so. You use that bar of soap daily.*

Royce: *There's a game tonight. I want you to come. Bring Rory.*

Me: *Are you sure?*

Royce: *Yes. It's illegal to leave a child home alone.*

Me: *You're hilarious.*

Royce: *I'm being forced to attend the after party in the executive suite.*

Gah, the executive suite. I used to love going to those—before I started working at Bridges five nights a week, that is.

The suite is typically reserved for owners and their VIP guests so if you're lucky enough to get an invite—you take it.

But I can't tell if he's inviting me. So I dig a little.

Me: *Game sounds like fun. We'll see you when you get home.*

Royce: *You're coming to the after-party.*

A second later, he sends a quick follow up.

Royce: *If you're comfortable with it, of course. Don't worry about Rory. There's childcare at these events.*

I am definitely up for a social gathering with some of my close friends—and basically, anywhere *he* will be.

Me: *I'll see if Rory's up for it.*

He and I both know she will be. But it seems like an appropriate response. Plus, I don't want to appear too eager.

I am giddy with excitement. I actually squeal. I don't think I've ever squealed. I've done it for Cora's and Angel's benefit of course, but never in private.

Unable to sit still, I run upstairs and prep Rory's outfit first—I already have one in mind.

Pushing through hangers, I pull out a hot pink dress. It's a plain t-shirt cotton bodice with a pink tule skirt. Paired with her new leather jacket, it will be out of this world.

Since I'm staying for the afterparty, I ask Angel to give us a ride, hoping we can catch one back with a certain head coach.

As I say his title in my head, I wince.

While we wait for Angel to round the corner to the house, I send a silent prayer that tonight goes well for the Blades.

We need this win. *He* needs this win.

"Look at you." Angel beams at her little sister when I slide her into the back seat.

Rory doesn't flaunt her outfit or the yellow hairpiece I weaved into her curls. Instead, she looks appreciatively at me, calling attention to the fact that I look very much like she does. No, I'm not sporting a pink tule—although that would be awesome so perhaps another time—but I am in black jeans, a hot pink blouse, and my leather jacket. My long hair is down and over my shoulders, my typical look for nights I go out—minus the pink, that was for Rory's sake.

I did apply a teeny-weeny amount of pink eyeshadow on my girl because she saw me putting on my black one and wanted in on the fun.

"Aww, you've got a mini-me, Nicky. Then she side-eyes her little sister. "The only thing she ever wanted from *me* was my bigger bedroom."

I wink at Rory in the backseat.

"So do we have good seats tonight?" I ask, keeping the conversation light to deflect any possible questions about what it's like living with her father.

I can't tell her what happened between us—not yet and probably not ever if her dad has anything to say about it.

However this ends, I don't want things to be weird between Angel and me.

"Are you kidding? The best." Then she cocks her head to the side as she watches the road. "Just hope we get to see some good action tonight instead of a disaster." She glances at her rear-view mirror at the little one and then shakes her head knowing Rory isn't a threat. "Jace told me...there might be someone on the team that might not have our best interest at heart."

"What does that mean?"

"It means our losing...might not be because we suck this season."

"Like someone is screwing with their own team?" The question leaves my lips all too casually. Because unfortunately, this is familiar territory for me. I was *raised* by someone who set up her own team to fail...so to speak. Of course, I was the only team member who took the bait.

Angel glances between the road and me. "You don't seem surprised. Do you know something?"

I scoff. "Are you kidding? He's hardly been home this week." That's all I say. I suppose there's no harm in telling her he seemed super stressed this week, but nope—my lips are sealed. Whatever I witness living under his roof is no one's business.

"Can we stop by Dad's office?" Rory asks. "He always has popcorn for me."

"I don't think that's a good idea, sweet pea. I'll just buy you some." The last thing I want to do is walk into his office before a game asking for popcorn.

"Of course, sugar." Angel takes her sister's hand and then winks at me. "Come on, I know where he keeps it."

Reluctantly, I follow her through the long halls, where I'd rarely been allowed to follow in the past. Nick would typically send me to my reserved seat and then to the after-party suite.

When we approach his office, the door is pulled open from the inside and Nick and Jace step out. Immediately, I search their faces to see how they feel about tonight.

Surprisingly...confident.

The men exchange glances and there's a subtle nod before they spot us.

Royce steps out after them, wearing a crisp tailored suit and looking like the silver fox GQ model he could easily be.

Especially with that distant, stoic expression on his face.

Until he sees *us*.

"Daddy," Rory cries and races toward him. Poor girl's missed him this week.

He bends to catch her and lifts her. "Well, hello. Have you seen my little girl? She's about your height, messy hair, wears hoodies?" She giggles and he sets her down with a big smile and gives her another once over. "I love it."

His eyes trail up my body, starting at my ankle boots and casually making their way up until he meets my eyes. And by the looks of them...he loves my outfit too.

"Yeah, I'm diggin' it, kid. If you were just a wee bit taller, we probably wouldn't be able to tell you two apart," Nick jokes, pointing between Rory and me.

I sneer at my brother. "Isn't there some dumb ritual you should be doing right now?"

This time, the three men exchange glances, and the players briefly *and mysteriously* thank their Coach and head toward the locker room.

"Come on, let's go grab a few bags." Angel urges her little sister and pushes her into their Dad's office.

Coach's eyes are back on me and there's so much warmth in them now. Neither of us say anything since the door is open and anyone could hear but the way he's looking at me—and the way I can't tear my own eyes from him...we don't *need* to speak.

Suddenly, there's a face to go with the text messages from this morning. The ones that, if I were to summarize, read *I miss you and I won't survive tonight if you're not here.*

Now that I see it, it reminds me of our stolen glances over the last two years. The one that holds a secret.

That we're *crazy* for each other.

And just like that—I need another hit. I'm *addicted* to our chocolate escapes.

Instinctively, I lick my lips, like I could taste what we're no doubt going to do later.

His eyes drop to my lips. "Yes," he rasps like it's painful. Like he can't wait for it either.

"Okay," Angel emerges from the office. "Four bags. Jesus, you think it's enough?"

"Two plain and two caramel," Rory shrugs like it's no big deal.

"Caramel?" I feign shock "Looks like we'll be brushing those teeth a little bit longer tonight."

"Worth it," Rory calls as she races off with the bags.

Angel and I follow but I twist back and mouth *good luck.* He winks back and it's enough to get me through the evening.

23

I'M VAGUELY AWARE OF the Blades being ahead during the final period. I couldn't tell you how they got there, because I've had my eyes on my boss the entire night.

His eyes have been glued to the icy expanse, meticulously studying every trace of his team's performance. We're not seated too far behind the players bench, but we're at an angle where I can see his profile. And from what I can tell, he's not watching the team in the red and white tonight—the guest team. He's watching his own.

He's not taking notes either. His arms are folded across his chest, discerning eyes scrutinizing every player. Except for the two players in his office earlier, who I've noticed glance in his direction just before pulling an unexpected move that would take everyone by surprise. Making them score.

Each time, Coach gives subtle nods when things seem to go according to plan. His keen focus on his players, even during the celebration of each goal.

Our opponent's Coach, on the other hand, is a lot more active. Frantic, screaming out, directing his team.

But it's futile.

Because when the final buzzer goes off, we fly out of our seats in blistering roars.

Thank *God.*

Following the crowd out, I hold a tight grip on Rory as Angel and I leave in the other direction, toward the staff elevators. As instructed, I bring Rory to a large room with a handful of other children, some belonging to the players, and some to the staff.

Angel and I give our names at the door to the executive suite and step in. It's dark except for the lights coming from the windows to the ice rink, which are still very bright. The wall bar is lit up, showcasing top-shelf bottles. There are small floor lights in the black tiles which will be helpful when the room grows a little more crowded. And a balcony, which despite the cold weather, I'll likely be using often tonight just to get some air.

If only to avoid social anxiety.

There are too many people here already. Important people. People who probably know that Coach Collins hired me as his illegitimate daughter's nanny.

What if they can tell that I relapsed recently? Can you tell something like that by looking at someone?

Angel bends to my ear. "You okay?"

I nod.

"Ginger ale?" she offers, knowing my usual.

I shake my head. "Ice water to start," I say as casually as I can muster because I desperately need cold, unsweetened liquid to cool the heat of my cheeks.

"Be right back," Angel calls. She doesn't travel far. My tall friend steps between two male patrons leaning at the bar just a few feet from us and they step aside for the gorgeous blonde.

I scan the crowd—but I'm *not* looking for him. Coach is always the last one up after games. Sometime ago, when I used to...wait for him, I realized it's because he wants to spend the least amount of time at these things with the most amount of people witnessing his presence.

The team hasn't come up yet. I know it takes a bit for them to shower and change into their suits before they join us, but there are plenty of people here already. Including Grove Randall, the team's General Manager. I've met him once before, but he probably doesn't know me. He's with his wife, a beautiful woman, possibly in her forties, gracefully chatting with another couple.

He must feel my eyes on him because Grove turns briefly and catches my eye. Then does a double take, holding my gaze a bit longer, his expression a mix of curiosity and discomfort. He blinks away, as most do when they lock eyes with me.

The old Nicole would have walked right up to him and asked him what his problem was.

But I can't do that now. He's technically Coach's boss. Not to mention, I'm in no position to be proving myself to anyone.

Just stay out of sight, Nicky. You're five feet tall, it's not that difficult.

Cora emerges from the crowd, finding Angel and me. She's in a pencil skirt and white blouse, which tells me she came straight from work.

"Hey, you missed a great game," I say.

"I heard," she cries. "Thank goodness they won, I don't know if I can handle another loss, Nick's been so stressed."

"Welcome to the club," Angel grumbles and I realize, I'm *in* that club. I wonder if Angel meant welcome to *our* club, as in the one where Coach and Jace come home and burden us with the weight of their pent-up frustration.

"What are you having, Cor?" Angel asks.

"Oh, I drove here, so just a coke."

"I'll get it," Angel offers quickly, then returns to the bar.

Cora nudges me and already, I know I'm not going to be prepared to answer whatever she's about to ask. "How are things at home?" The question comes with a wiggle of her perfectly shaped brows.

I nudge her back. "Probably not as good as things will be for *you* tonight." Between you and me, I don't particularly like to make implications of my brother getting it on with his girlfriend. But anything to deflect my telling her about the mind-blowing orgasm Coach gave me in his hot tub.

Cora blushes and turns toward the double doors of the suite's entrance. "Where are they?"

I put a hand on my heart. "And here I thought you were looking forward to spending time with your very best friend," I state as Angel turns back with the soda.

"For the record, Cora loves us both equally. Don't you, dear?"

She takes the drink Angel offers. "Differently."

Angel narrows her eyes. "How differently?"

There's howling in the front of the large room as several players enter, and my senses are on alert. But it's not for me. They're working overtime for someone else.

If Coach is concerned about someone on the team he can't trust, it has to be someone who wouldn't particularly be happy about today's win.

Switching on my predator eyes, I search for the possible suspect.

Except...they all look happy. Or at least for the cameras.

If you're here, I'll find you. Just give me a minute.

Nick lifts his girlfriend in the air the moment he reaches us and she squeals.

"I'm sorry, I missed the game."

He doesn't seem the least bit fazed about it. God the way he looks at her. He's still enchanted. Bending down, he says something to her—or possibly asks. It's impossible to hear in this room.

Cora rolls her eyes. "Are you kidding? My day was not as exciting as your night. You won against the team that's in the lead. That must feel amazing."

He nods but looks solemn for some reason.

"Can we step outside for a minute?" he asks us and I completely get it. Nick isn't much for crowds either.

Once outside and alone, Nick wraps his jacket around Cora and turns to me. "You alright here?"

"I'm good. Are *you* alright?"

He glances around us. "Coach thinks we have someone on the team either tipping off our strategies ahead of the game or...sabotaging us—somehow."

"I heard. Is that confirmed?"

"Not yet. But a few hours ago—he called Jace and me into his office to share some revised strategies. It's not unusual to do, but adjustments are usually done *during* the game as needed. Anyway, he told me to fill in the team right before we get on the ice."

"And did you?"

He glances around again and nods.

My wheels are spinning. "So you won...because whoever it is...didn't have time to plan on how to intervene."

"Not without making it obvious," he adds.

Cora shakes her head in disbelief.

"All signs point to Coach being right. If the team—or someone in the team didn't know our strategy—our plan—our deliberate moves—until the last minute, we might have the benefit of surprise in our court."

I nod slowly. "Any of them...seem annoyed at the change-up?" I ask.

He levels my gaze. "Nicole, you're not doing this."

"It's a simple question."

"I don't need you getting into interrogation mode."

"Well, it's not Rielly," Cora says, ignoring our sibling quarrel. She narrows her eyes. "My money's on Garret."

Nick gives Cora a pointed look. "Not everything should be pinned on Garret just because you don't like him."

Cora folds her arms in front of her chest. "You don't know women very well, do you?"

"Like him or not, he's one of our best. He plays well," Nick argues.

"Doesn't make him trustworthy," Cora grumbles.

I smirk. Cora holds a personal grudge against Garret since he was the one who ratted out her relationship with Nick to her brother. Tipping him off he'd just seen Cora in the locker room—alone with Nick. It was two years ago, so I may have my story mixed up, but it was definitely Garret who pissed her off.

"So, if not Garret, do you have any suspects?"

Nick shakes his head, regrettably. "No. I can't...look at the team like that. Coach seems to, but I can't. I won't."

I nod and smirk at Cora. And I know we're sharing a thought.

But *we* can.

I pat his bicep. "Good game, bro. I'm gonna head back in." I leave the two of them to have their moment out on the balcony because obviously, living together isn't enough.

Angel is talking to one of the Ice Girls and waves me over the minute I step back in. Jace is behind her and watches me with knowing eyes. The same look he was giving me back at the house.

Oh fuck.

Does he think I'm an idiot? He knows. This isn't paranoia. Jace knows. Somehow, I know it wasn't Cora who told him about my setback. She wouldn't have been able to look me in the eye tonight.

Being the fight-fire-with-fire woman I am, I glare back at him. "Something you want to say, Knight?"

"Nope." He shakes his head. "All good."

"Good. Nice game. Nick filled me in on what the two of you had to do tonight."

He sighs. "With any luck, we won't have to play this way too long." He glances back at Angel, who's still chatting with enthusiasm—which means he can't pull her away. "You doing okay? I'm asking as your friend."

I roll my eyes, and I'm not sure what's come over me, but I soften my tone because I know he means well. "Yes. I'm good."

He shifts uncomfortably. "Will you call me if...you need anything?"

"You're not good at this, are you?"

"No."

I touch his arm. "I will. Thank you."

My spine tingles and a sense of warmth washes over me. *He's here.*

I turn and my heart flutters... because he's already found me. He's on the other side of the lofty space, surrounded by very important people and his eyes merely sweep over them, but keep landing back to where I'm standing.

My stomach flips at the attentiveness he's giving me in the middle of all this and I turn away reluctantly. I need to give him space here. This is his job.

I hear Angel sigh. "I'll be right back, guys. I need to say hello to some people."

Jace releases her hand and mumbles something about him not being paid enough to be nice to people.

"You're a real catch, you know that?" I grumble when Angel walks off. I never particularly liked the guy. The way he treated Angel last year after she did nothing but try to help him—he should be counting his blessings she gave him another chance.

Although my true angel of a friend would say he's the one who gave *her* another chance.

"Who told you?" I ask, finally.

Keeping a protective eye on his girlfriend, he answers, "The version Nick told us didn't add up. Plus, I don't believe Coach would bring you back to his place unless he was taking care of you. He's good like that. Always looking out. And then there's you—there's no way sober Nicole would just hide out somewhere because she was pissed. You'd sooner drop kick each one of us and tell us to stay out of your business."

"That's pretty insightful. I'm impressed."

He scoffs. "Great. You're finally impressed with me, and I can't brag about it to my girlfriend."

That makes me laugh for the first time in hours and a familiar voice cuts in. The voice I'd been waiting to hear all night.

"Nicole."

"Hey, Coach," I say, breathily.

He tears his gaze off me and turns to Jace. "If it helps, you can brag that *I* was impressed with you tonight."

Jace nods appreciatively at his coach. "I'll take it. Now if you'll both excuse me, I think I'll go do that right now."

I follow his gaze and understand the urgency. Angel is caught up in a conversation with two very handsome men in suits.

"Coach?" he asks, feigning disappointment.

I smirk and raise a playful brow. It's an entirely different world now that we can talk to each other at these things in a way we couldn't before. Have this secret language where we're both saying what we're feeling.

And no one is the wiser.

After a moment of watching the crowd with me, he nudges my shoulder. "I haven't done this in a while so forgive me if it's forward, but...you want to go back to my place tonight?"

I laugh. "I should tell you, I've got a kid with me."

"A kid? Forget it then. I'm not tryin' to be anybody's daddy."

I keep my expression blank, but my tone playful as we continue to stand side by side, watching the crowd like we're looking for someone more interesting to talk to.

I kink a brow. "Hmm. Too bad."

An audible breath escapes his lips. "Fuck, you're way better at this than I am."

"You should go," I murmur as Angel starts heading back in our direction.

With a nod, Royce excuses himself and steps away. I can almost *feel* how much it pains him.

Sometime later, I find Garret and Rielly lounging by a red sofa on the other side of the room. Without a second thought, I b-line toward them. I know Nick told me to stay out of it, but if anyone can catch a liar, it's me.

But I'm stopped by someone. Someone who grips my arm not too tightly, but not very friendly either.

"Nicole, right?" the team's GM asks before he spins me around to face him.

I see red as I stare at the unwelcome hand around my arm. I don't answer him but my brow turns up. The one that says you have two point five seconds to get your hands off me.

He does as soon as he has my attention. "Grove Randall, a pleasure to meet you."

My jaw clenches with the fact that I can't react the way I want to.

"Are you having a nice time?" he asks as if this is *his* event.

"Not at the moment."

He chuckles. "In that case, I'll cut right to the chase. Do him a favor, when you're out in public, *be* the nanny."

"I don't know what you're talking about."

He watches me. "My mistake, thought you could read between the lines." He steps closer if it were possible. "It's not good for him to be seen with you—as anything more than *the nanny*."

"Still having trouble reading between those lines," I say curtly.

"I don't care what happens in his home. But not here. His job is on the line right now. Today's win means nothing. Don't feed the media with something that will only hurt him. Do you understand?"

I swallow. "Thanks for the tip."

He touches my arm again and I lean in close. "Put a hand on me again, and I'll cut off your dick with my pocketknife and hand it to your wife as a souvenir."

He blinks and drops his hand.

"See how easy it is to speak plain English?" I whisper, then turn and weave through the crowd until I reach the balcony, desperate for the cool air to touch my burning skin. For the cold to freeze my tears in their tracks.

I'm not alone for long. Behind me, I hear the door slide open and someone stepping beside me.

"Can I tell you a secret?" Royce's voice soothes me, and for the moment, I forget the last five minutes.

I nod in response.

"I've waited two years to say these words to you." He holds his elbow out for me. "You wanna get out of here?"

24

R ORY IS STILL FAST asleep in her daddy's arms as he heads up the stairs with her.

I move in front of him and turn down her bed. Then help change her into pajamas. She barely lifts an eyelid the entire time.

"How was your night?" he asks when we step out into the hall.

Better when I walked out with you.

"It was nice being out with everyone again. Thanks for inviting me."

"It was for selfish reasons."

"Was it? How?"

"I like these things a lot better when you're there. They're almost unbearable without you."

My heart slams against my chest. "Well, then you're welcome."

He chuckles then puts his hands in his pocket and I sense hesitation.

"What?"

"This is the part where I'm supposed to be a gentleman and walk you to your door before saying goodnight."

"Still don't want a gentleman," I say, inching closer.

"What do you want, Nicole?"

"Right now?" I bite my lip and give him an honest answer. "A shower."

He takes my hand. "Perfect."

He wastes no time pulling me into his bedroom and I tingle all over. It smells like him in here. I could *live* in this room—so long as it always smelled like this. Like that clean, forest musk.

Leaving me in the middle of the room, he instructs me to undress while he starts the shower.

I strip off my jeans and fold them neatly on his bench. I'm about to pull off my blouse but hesitate. It's not like he hasn't already seen me topless, but this feels...so much more intimate. And I don't know why, but I *don't* want to be the one taking off my clothes.

Stepping into his bathroom, I'm surprised to see steam come through the shower, fogging up the glass doors.

"Looks hot," I observe.

"Thanks. The shower is pretty warm too." He winks, then scans me, noticing I'm still half dressed. "Need some help with that?"

I nod.

Stepping over to me, he pulls my arms up, his hands grazing my skin deliberately, sensually. Then lifts my hot pink blouse over my head, revealing my white silk bra.

He swallows. "The rest is all you. If I take anything else off...you won't make it into that shower...alone."

I'm about to tell him that I'm okay with that, but he covers my lips with a feathery kiss. "I'll be right outside."

I nod and watch him close the door behind him before removing my underwear. I never have to worry about privacy or respect with this man. He wants me to know I'll always have it no matter how intimate we get. And it's beyond comforting.

Thirty minutes later, I find him sitting on his bed with a book and the sexiest pair of black-rimmed reading glasses. He's in plaid pajama pants and no shirt.

I grip the knot of the towel around my bust and smile wickedly at the sexy sight of him. I feel like I'll *always* smile at the sight of him.

He takes off his glasses and scans me the way he always does. Protectively and possessively. I move to his dresser and pull it open, picking up a vintage-looking tee with the name of an old band on it.

He watches me with what I think is appreciation. "I saw Grove talking to you earlier. Do I need to break his arms for putting his hands on you?"

"You wouldn't do that," I challenge playfully.

"True. My signature move is a broken nose."

I don't let on that Grove upset me tonight. I know Royce will feel the need to defend me and it's not worth his job. Much less add to his stress. "Well, if that's the case, I've got you covered."

"Oh yeah?" He scratches his chin and sits up on the edge of the bed, intrigued. "Come here. Let me see what you got."

I hold his shirt up to my nose coyly and step between his spread knees. I let his hands roam up my forearms, squeezing my solid biceps gently. "Damn girl," he whispers. "Let me guess, you don't need a big strong man to defend you."

"Oh, nothing like that. I'm just willing to take this one for you." I wink.

He laughs and pulls me in for a languid kiss, tasting me, breathing me in.

"What, no chocolates?" I tease.

"No. Just us." It's a throaty response and I'm like putty.

"I like just us."

"What's the shirt for?" he asks, his eyes never leaving mine.

"It's *not* for you," I say, admiring his chest shamelessly.

"Are you cold?"

"No," I breathe.

He pulls on the knot of the towel, letting it fall between us on his lap.

His eyes drop to my breasts, and he swallows hard. I know he's trying to control himself.

"You smell like me."

Lust shoots through my body. Why are those words so arousing? "Do you like it?"

His lips graze under my collarbone. "I...love it."

I'm shaking with lust and heat and a need I don't know how to communicate.

"Tell me what you want, Nicky," he murmurs against my skin.

"I want to know how to please *you*. What do you want, Coach?"

"What I want isn't fair."

"Try me."

"I want you to sleep in my bed tonight. I want to torture you with infinite pleasure." He brushes my lips with his. "And I really, really want to fucking taste you."

I shudder with a desire I've never known. "You're right." The words are almost a whimper. "That's not fair. Because I want that too."

"Nicole." It's a warning but I don't want to hear it.

"No. Please don't think twice," I beg. "I promise I'll tell you if we need to slow down."

He nods and stands. Twisting me and sitting me on his bed, then cupping my face. "I'm glad. But I was going to say that I don't just want you here tonight. This is where I want you every night. In. My. Bed."

I gasp softly and he strokes my hair tenderly. "The other night after you shared your past with me, I couldn't sleep knowing you were alone in the dark in another room. I know it doesn't make sense, but I want you here. I'll sleep on the floor if that's what it takes, but never in a separate room—"

"Yes." Oh hell, the answer will always be yes for this man.

"Thank you." He picks up the shirt that fell on the floor and puts it over my head. "What are you doing?" I ask with a frown, sliding my arms through.

"You're going to need it. The walls are cold." He twists me presses me against the wall by the bed and kisses me ferociously. "How wet are you?"

"How—what?"

"Tell me how wet you are," he repeats.

"I...don't know," I say, somewhat in a trance.

"Push your fingers inside your pussy and tell me."

"Isn't...that something you can do."

"It will be. Later. But the first time I feel you bare, it's going to be with my tongue."

My mind spins. I'm delirious for this man. For everything he plans to do with me.

I sweep my hand between us. Over his magnificent torso, tracing down each perfectly cut muscle before I push my fingers inside my heat.

Holy shit, I'm so fucking wet.

But I keep my poker face on and pull them out. "Hmm."

He gives me a naughty grin. "Give me those fingers."

I shake my head slowly.

He lifts a brow.

I lift one right back. "You're going to have to find out for yourself."

His tongue shifts in his mouth and he spreads my legs before kneeling in front of me. "Fine."

I tremble as he kisses my inner thigh. Softly, tenderly, smoothly until he gets closer and closer. I clench and he grips under my ass.

He lifts his face to me. "You're beautiful."

Then he pauses. Like he's giving me a minute to adjust to the invasion.

I run my fingers into his hair, gazing back at him as I live through the most erotic and heart-melting moment of my life.

I breathe out and offer a quick nod.

I yelp as he jerks my legs over his shoulders and lifts me, positioning his face at my entrance.

Jolts of pleasure shoot through my body and I feel like I can come just from his hot breath on me.

"Oh fuck."

He gazes at me with fire and hunger before he twists his head and kisses along my inner thigh on both sides. Teasing me with his sexy stubbled jaw around where I want him the most.

I gasp when his tongue finds my clit. It's followed by a not-very-nanny-like moan coming from my boss's bedroom.

I arch my back against the wall as he devours me, lacing my fingers into his hair reverently. My moans and whimpers grow louder with each thrust of his long, skillful tongue.

Pleasure radiates through my bones and my entire body singes when he sucks on my clit. I cry out, coming hard against his mouth.

He grips my ass. His kisses grow deeper, more possessive. And I'm one hundred percent on board with that. I'm his.

Eternally and timelessly his. I never want him to stop owning me the way he is right at this moment.

"Get naked with me." I pout, lying on top of him, coming down from my third—or maybe fourth orgasm.

"You're tired. Close your eyes and sleep with me." His voice is so tender, it's deceiving because I feel tortured. I was expecting him to fuck me tonight. For there to be no clothes between us.

But the bastard is denying me. My top has been covered with his t-shirt but my pussy has been bare for him all night. I should at least get the same respect.

"Coach, I've got this."

His stomach rumbles, his laugh contagious. He pinches my chin. "Baby, I'm not going anywhere. You asked me what I wanted tonight. I wanted this. To taste you, to make you come over and over again...and to have you in my bed."

My eyes grow heavy. "You tricked me." I yawn. "I didn't do anything for you."

When my eyes are closed, he rolls me onto a pillow next to his. "I'll finally get a good night's sleep with you in my arms."

Giving in—for now, I slip into those arms and feel an unparalleled warmth. The kind that touches my heart and reaches my toes. The kind of warmth I never knew existed.

The kind I'm suddenly wildly afraid of losing.

25

"WHY DON'T WE GO out?" I suggest when Nicole tries to slide out of bed, insisting Rory will be up soon. This morning she plans on making my famous Mickey Mouse pancakes.

Or attempt to.

Nicole's smile—which has been plastered since we fell asleep last night—fades and she glances back tentatively. "Oh. You two...should go out without me." My shirt falls over her bare ass as she stands.

I yank her back and kiss her neck. "Why?"

"You two never spend time together and I could use some me time..."

She's bullshitting me again. And I'm determined to get to the bottom of whatever it is. "Hmm...what will you do?"

She raises a temptress brow at me. "Wouldn't you like to know?"

I pull on her waist. "Fine. We can do this the hard way." I pull her on top of me, making her squirm and wriggle. "Tell me what's really going on," I urge, playfully, my fingers poking at her sides.

"Jokes on you, I'm not ticklish...not there at least."

I growl and lower my fingers to her thigh and she tenses but the squeal from her throat and the grin on her lips tells me I've found her weakness.

"Alright, alright." I pause as she takes a breath. "It's... just...probably best...that you're not—"

"Don't say it."

"Seen with me."

My jaw hardens but I don't loosen my grip on her. Her eyes are glued to my chest, which means who ever fucking told her this made her feel ashamed of who she is. "Who'd you talk to?"

Her fingers trace the lines across my stomach, my muscles tightening as a shield not to melt at her touch. I won't be derailed. I *need* to know who she talked to.

"I don't want to make things worse for you right now."

"Grove," I answer for her, almost factually. Because I had eyes on her the moment I stepped foot in the room. The only people she spoke to were her friends—and Grove.

She doesn't deny it. Her eyes drift shamefully to the side.

I lift her chin. "Promise me something. If you hear anything like that again, come to me."

She hesitates and pouts. I hate that I've ruined her mood this morning. With a sigh, I twist her on top of me, so she feels in control. "Better?"

She giggles. "You sure know a way to my heart."

I grip her hips. "Are you always going to be this stubborn?"

There's a question in the way she's looking at me, but she doesn't get a chance to ask because there's a knock on my door.

"Daddy?"

Nicole squeals and drops onto the mattress, pulling the quilt over her head.

"Coming, Squigs." I lower my head to Nicole's. "Don't move from this bed."

I pull the door open halfway and bend to greet my girl. "What are you doing up so early?"

"I can't find Nicole."

"Hmm...did you look downstairs?"

"No."

"Okay, why don't you get dressed and we can go look for her together."

She bobs her curly head. "Okay. But I don't smell any coffee so probably not." Sighing, she stalks back to her bedroom like I'd just given her a chore.

"Coach Collins, did you just *lie* to your own daughter?"

I wince and join her back on the bed.

"I think that qualifies you as a hypocrite, sir."

I drop my head. "You're right. Let me call her back in here." I stand and she yanks me back with impressive strength. "Jesus, woman."

"Aww, did I hurt you?"

"No. But I'll consider myself warned to never cross you," I mumble against her lips. "Now get dressed. I'm taking you and Rory out to breakfast."

By the look on her face, I know she's still uncertain but doesn't want to argue. And that's not how I want to win this.

"Look, it's the weekend. You're off. I can't *make* you come with us as Rory's nanny. But I would really like it if you did."

"I forgot I'm off today. Do you and Rory have plans? We have Taekwondo at three. And I was going to make those Mickey Mouse pancakes."

It amazes me that this woman doesn't tire of my daughter. And I give in. "Tell you what. I'll start the batter and make coffee while you *take your time* getting dressed and meet us downstairs. Then we can all decide what we do."

She nods like that's a plan she can work with. "Okay."

I watch my spirited little girl take her stance in the crisp white uniform on the dojo floor. Her small frame is playful but serious as she tries to mimic the taller version of her a few feet away.

Nicole shoots tiny glares at Rory urging her focus, but silently giggling along with her.

I'm utterly enchanted with her. Unlike her little apprentice, Nicole expresses respect and self-control, bowing gracefully and moving at a pace appropriate to her opponents in this world of kicks and punches.

Nicole is yet to be knocked down, but Rory has landed on her little behind at least four times.

Frustrated, Nicky gives a warm smile to Rory's student teacher and asks if she can step in. With intense determination and focus, Nicole goes through each one of the basic moves.

"Roundhouse kick," I hear Nicole say through the glass windows as she lifts her foot high in a circular motion to an imaginary opponent, aiming it at his head.

"Damn." I don't realize I muttered the word out loud until a nearby parent turns his head.

Rory mimics the move, her foot only rising about halfway to the opponent's chest. Nicole nods and then sits her down on the mat with her. "Can you do a split?"

I'm in awe. In all the time I've known this woman, I never imagined how she might fit into the absent piece in our lives.

A piece I'm not even sure Rory and I knew was missing.

After their session, I don't tell Nicole I'm taking them both to dinner. We drive back to town quietly since Rory fell asleep in the backseat.

"What are you thinking?" she asks.

I glance at her. "I know the history of how you got into karate—from your brother. But what I'm curious about is why you stuck it out all these years."

"I wanted to kick some butt, I guess. And not only is it allowed. It's encouraged." She laughs.

I nod. "Why did you really stick it out?"

She lowers her head. "You're asking if I was afraid of being violated?"

"Self-defense is an obvious answer. But...so is pepper spray," I point out.

She gazes out the window. "Aggression mostly. This place helped me control it physically, while my therapist helped me control it mentally. But the discipline and respect that goes along with martial arts is a big part of it too."

"Yeah, because you're so damn respectful," I joke.

She chuckles. "Yeah, well, I skipped a few classes."

I laugh.

"Want me to sign up for a refresher?" she asks.

I shake my head. "I wouldn't want you any other way."

"There were four of 'em," David tells me.

I'm in my bedroom returning a missed call from the police chief while Nicole reads Rory her bedtime story.

"Okay?"

"Three in prison. The last one never trialed, by the name of Kyle Johnson. Tried to start fresh—we're keeping an eye on him.

"Keeping an eye? So, you know where he is?"

"We didn't have enough to bring him in. Similar to Nicole's story. Been brought in a few times, but nothing stuck. And hanging out with Frank Lidowski doesn't count. At least not to a judge."

"Whereabouts?" I ask, testing my luck.

"Downtown."

"Can you tell me where Johnson was seen specifically?" I need to make sure Nicole never sees any of these men again.

Even if they're currently considered harmless.

A little under two years ago, when Nicole came face to face with Frank at his poor attempt at an apology, she suffered a severe anxiety attack. Luckily, she was under the care of her brother who made sure she was alright, but we didn't see her again for some time.

I can't let that happen again.

I want to make sure she never has to face her past unexpectedly again.

"Let's see." I hear typing in the background and thank him again for pulling this information for me on a Saturday night. "Mike's Ale House. Dicky's Tavern. Oh, what do you know, Sylvie's Bikers and Babes."

"Those are all downtown. Does he live around there?"

"Like I said, we're keeping an eye on him, but that's all I can tell you."

"I appreciate it."

"Why do I get the feeling, this is more than just looking out for your daughter's new nanny?"

"I never told you she's Rory's new nanny."

"Oh. Did you think your ex-wife could know something and not tell the universe?"

I grunt. "Good point."

"See you at the game Monday?" he asks, hopeful.

"I'll get you a sweatshirt."

"My kid wears a medium."

I smile. "See you soon, Dave."

"Hey." The voice comes from my bedroom door and I turn, my heart in my throat.

"Hey," I say, my usual calm voice abandoning me.

"Who was that?"

"A friend." Jesus, could I sound any more guilty?

When she playfully approaches me and tugs on my shirt, the tension in my shoulders releases. *Was my door open? Did she hear any of that?*

"You know"—she swipes her fingers across my collar—"I have a Royce Collins sweatshirt."

I chuckle. "I remember. You purchased it at the fundraiser last year. Your brother teased you about not picking his...since it had your last name on the back."

"I'm glad you didn't mind when I chose it."

Mind? Fuck, I was ready to *make* it her last name if that was the only issue.

She's quiet as she strokes my arm and I feel myself tense again. I don't want to be overbearing and controlling her life—but I won't risk her coming face to face with anyone from her past again.

I break the silence. "How's Rory?"

"Out like a light. Told you you'd be thanking me for these lessons."

"I am thanking you. But not just for the lessons, but for loving her enough to do anything to protect her."

Her eyes lift to mine. "I do love her. Do you think she can feel it?"

"I'm sure she does," I say. But if I know my daughter, she won't let on to knowing how much she's loved. "But her walls are concrete, it'll be a while before she shows it."

There's a knowing grin that touches her lips. "I'll just have to break them with my steel ones."

I frown and wrap my arms around her waist, pulling her against me. "Walls of steel, huh?"

She bends her head to the side, giving me access to her neck and I wonder how I got so lucky.

"Nicole," I start. "I told you I want you in my bed every night. But I don't want you to think I expect anything."

Her eyes gleam with question.

"I just want you close. I want you in my arms."

With a cold glare, she drops her hands. Then turns and walks out of my bedroom quietly.

What the hell?

I run a hand down my face and am about to follow her when she returns seconds later with a pink stuffed bunny. She throws Rory's toy at me and I catch it.

"If you're looking for something to cuddle with, that's all I've got," she snaps, her tone icy and her eyes piercing. "I'd rather sleep alone for the rest of my life than with someone who thinks I'll break if he fucks me."

Jesus, I need a moment to process but I know she won't give me one. "I know you're not going to break," I rasp. "I'm just taking it—"

"Slow. I know." She lifts her eyes, her sharp glassy eyes. "I'm getting tired of throwing myself at you. Enjoy your night."

I catch her arm and twist her back. "What do you want?" I growl.

She hesitates. "You're only going to stop me."

I swallow. "Try me."

She searches my eyes briefly before dropping to her knees. Then lifts her chin shamelessly. This isn't a tease. It's a test. There's no passion in the way she's looking at me. No warmth. It's a challenge.

Because I upset her.

And I'll be damned if I do it again.

"Get up," I say through clenched teeth.

She releases a disappointed breath and stands. The minute she does, I tear off her shirt, making her gasp, then push down her bra. "I want you topless when you suck me off." I dip to suck one nipple into my mouth, swirling and pulling hard, making her cry out as I undo my belt and zipper. I can feel her quivering with need.

Wrapping my hand around her throat, I bring my lips to the side of her face. "Now get on your knees and take me to the back of your throat."

Her breath catches and I feel her gulp under my hand.

I don't backtrack. I don't add 'but only if you're comfortable with it'. Clearly, that's a sure way of making her walk out this door.

I even hesitate asking if she's ever done this before. *But God, I fucking hope not.*

My cock springs out hard and aching for her mouth. She got me there the minute she dropped to her knees seconds ago.

I mutter a swear when her fingers wrap around the base, stroking me gently. Her eyes flash at my length and I want to tell her that's not all of it.

But she'll find out soon enough.

My sexy woman licks her lips before pulling me into her hot mouth.

I suck in a breath as her tongue circles my tip, tasting me decadently. *Fuck.*

A fiery burst of pleasure shoots down my spine and I fight the urge to pump into her. Feeling the need to get a fucking grip, I take a breath and look down at the beauty kneeling before me. I throw one hand to the wall while the other rakes through her silky hair, fisting it.

She moans, moving her head at a luscious pace, taking as much of me as she can.

It's getting harder not to fuck her mouth as my dick grows, hardens, pulses. I tighten my grip on her hair and growl.

"Open wider, honey."

She does and draws me deeper, licking teasingly and sucking powerfully, growing more confident with every stroke.

I bite back a praise.

Heat rushes through my body and I hold her face with both my hands. "Nicky, baby..." I tug gently, but her fingers tighten around my ass, holding me in place.

The earth spirals around me and I don't fight her as pure ecstasy surges and my release shoots down her throat.

Through silent panting, I offer her a hand and she takes it, rising to her feet. She wipes at her bottom lip and looks up at me, her eyes wholly satisfied despite it being me on the receiving end just now.

She lifts on her toes but her lips still only reach my chin. "Now we can cuddle."

She turns toward the bathroom, and I catch her hand and whisper to the back of her neck. "But I'm going to need a shower first." *Because in about three minutes I'm going to want to fuck you from behind and that's not ideal.*

Nicole might want me ungentlemanly but I'm only ready to unleash so much of it at once.

Her eyes drop before they meet mine again. "Did I do something wrong?"

"No," I rasp, pulling myself to her and cupping her jaw. "It's because you did everything so fucking right that I need to cool off before I get in bed with you tonight."

Her eyes drift thoughtfully, and I bring her mouth to mine. "Get comfortable and naked in my bed, honey. I'll be quick."

But the minute I reach my bathroom door, I freeze. I'm not taking any chances with her.

26

I SAW THE LOOK in his eyes. He wanted to throw me up against the wall again. And this time—it wasn't to eat me out. His self-control is appreciated but frustrating as fuck.

I unhook my bra and place it gently on the end of his bed. Then push down my shorts but keep my panties on. He might be taking care of himself in the shower to ease his eagerness, but I'll be ready for him when he comes out.

"You're gorgeous."

I gasp and turn. He's standing at the bathroom door stripped down to nothing. His body, his defined muscles, abs, legs, cock...just *chiseled everywhere*.

"What happened to your shower?"

"We'll take one later together."

I try not to stare below his belly button as he walks back toward me. He's so thick. And I'm suddenly terrified.

I'm having a serious *be careful what you wish for* moment right now.

"Tell me again, sweetheart. How I intimidate you."

I grin up at him. "Aren't you getting a little cocky?"

He laughs. "Maybe." His eyes drop to my panties. "You missed one." Lying me back on his bed, he pulls them off me. "Now you're ready for me."

"Ready for what, exactly?" I prod.

He joins me on the bed and drops his mouth to mine. Kissing me slowly, sensually. He rolls one nipple between his fingers and I squirm and moan. Then he slides that hand down my stomach and presses his palm against my mound. I jolt when his fingers push into me. I'm so hot for him. So wet.

He strokes me slowly, in sync with the way he's kissing me. He's not trying to get me off this way. It's too graceful. Too languid.

But here I am...close to coming apart.

I whimper and lift my hips, needing more.

But he pulls them out.

I groan. "Did you have other plans for tonight?"

"As a matter of fact, no. But...since you're here." He positions himself at my entrance and strokes me with the tip.

"Fuck." He stops and reaches for what I assume is a condom at his nightstand. He tears it open, and I grasp his hands.

"I'm clean. I wouldn't lie to you about that."

"I believe you honey, but—"

"And it's a safe time of the month for me. I don't want anything between us. At least, not the first time we do this."

He whispers words of endearment and bends to kiss me. When I open my eyes, the condom is gone and his hands are on my hips as he slowly pushes inside me.

I freeze.

I know he's not fully in, but I feel so full already.

It hurts. But not in a painful way. I feel an unfamiliar ache in my chest, in my stomach.

It feels remarkably good, but it also makes me want to cry.

"Nicole."

I meet his gaze. The tender way he's watching me.

"What is it, baby?"

I reach up and cup his cheeks. "Make me yours tonight. Own me. Own my body." If I ever wanted to be possessed by anyone, it would be by this man and this man only.

He gives me another slow thrust. "Then I'm yours," he counters, moving slowly until I have every last inch of him.

It's intense. And it doesn't even feel like an invasion. It feels like he belongs.

I'm so aroused that I lift my hips for him, urging him on.

He drops his palms on either side of me and watches me as he thrusts faster, deeper, his cock pulsing inside me, making me clench.

He groans when I do and pumps furiously until we're both breathless. I cry out and moan low, shaking beneath him, feeling like I'm literally coming apart at the seams.

"Squeeze my cock again," he growls.

I comply and with another deep thrust, he roars beautifully, meeting me there.

I return from the bathroom a few minutes later, feeling much cleaner than I did when he tried to gently wipe me with a washcloth.

He breathes me in when I slip back into his strong arms. "Do you like flowers?"

"Um...I don't know," I answer honestly.

"You don't know if you like flowers?"

"I mean, they look pretty in gardens. But I don't have a favorite or anything. We never had fresh flowers in my house growing up. Wh—why do you ask?"

He strokes my neck. "The perfume you're wearing. It smells like lilac and vanilla."

"Really? Well, I guess I like lilac then. But I'm not vanilla. Is there a chocolate perfume?"

He laughs. "Maybe. But wait, let's back up. If you're not sure you like it, then why do you wear it?"

"I felt bad for the perfume lady."

"What perfume lady?"

"The one that sprays you when you walk into the department store. I was shopping with Cora last week and it smelled pretty enough, so I bought one."

"Hmm."

I turn to him, intrigued. "Do I have to have a favorite flower or scent just because I'm a woman?"

"No. I suppose not." He drops the subject and I snuggle deeper into his chest. Loving that this is where he *insists* I be every night.

"Who's ready for a slumber party?"

I'm half asleep after putting Rory to bed on Sunday night and stare blurry-eyed at my friends at the front door. "What are you guys doing here?"

Cora's round face jerks. "What do you mean?" The boys are out of town so we're here with sparkling cider and junk food and we're going to watch *The Lake House*.

I pull the door open and step aside for them. "Okay but be quiet. I just put Rory to bed, and I'm exhausted."

"Oh yeah, Dad told me you signed her up to your dojo." Angel rolls her eyes.

Cora gasps. "You did? Good for you. Teach that girl some discipline."

"And respect," Angel adds, clearly in agreement for Rory's need to shape up her attitude.

I smile. "I don't know, I kinda like her the way she is."

Angel cocks her head. "Of course you do. It's why you two hit it off. She may as well be your kid."

Cora side eyes me and I catch it.

Unfortunately, Angel does too. "Oh, please I know all about Nicole's crush on my dad. It's weird, but who am I to judge? I'm living with a guy who hated me for five years." She shoots me a glare as she repeats my words.

"It's not weird," Cora argues on my behalf as I unbag junk food onto the counter. "It's sweet and kind of perfect. Nicole is way too good to be with anyone her age. Only a real man can handle all of this." She waves a hand in front of me as if I'm some canvas painting she's showcasing.

I dip my toes into the conversation. "I'm sorry, so what is my brother to you exactly? Not a real man?"

"Your brother is still in his twenties and laughs anytime someone says *balls*. I love the guy but the snickering is not quite 'man' material."

"You have a point," I mutter, stepping back out of the conversation.

"I think Nicole can do better," Angel mutters like I'm not in the room.

"Wait, what?" I blink up. She thinks *I* can do better? Not the other way around?

She sighs and digs into a carton of ice cream. "My dad is a complicated man. He's private, grumpy, moody, and does this thing where he stares at you until you come clean about something that was probably not your fault, and—" She looks up at us, then focuses on me. "Actually, I think you two might work..."

"Really?"

She shrugs. "Sure. Just be careful, my mother is competitive."

"Your mother?"

"Well, she might be out of his life, but I get a sense that she's subconsciously living with the idea that if she can't have him, no one can." She rolls her eyes, and it's clear that Angel has tried to convince her mother otherwise. "She's sweet though, once you get to know her," she adds, defensively.

"I haven't been that obvious, this whole time, have I? I thought I was *pretty* discreet about it."

"Not to us," Angel admits. "You don't think we notice when your eyes linger on anything?"

"And you don't linger," Cora agrees. "Unless you're pinning your next target with your death glare."

"I don't have a death glare."

"You're right. You don't," Cora admits. "It's more of a *I know you know who I am so don't fuck with me* glare."

I think about it for a moment. "Okay. Maybe that's accurate."

"Oh, and for what it's worth, I think it's totally reciprocated," Angel says, wiggling her brows.

Cora and I exchange glances, since she knows about the kissing. But only the kissing. I'm not quite ready to share... the other stuff.

"Aww, you're blushing," Angel chirps. "Don't tell me you didn't notice? I mean I know my dad can be cold as ice sometimes, but I feel like he holds you to a whole different level."

I'm not sure what that means—but I think I like it.

"Nicole?" The little voice comes from the top of the stairs and I race to a sleepy Rory before she comes tumbling down.

Reaching her, I grab her waist. "Hey, sweetie, what is it? Did you have a bad dream?"

"I heard Angel."

Angel hops off the counter. "Hey, Squigs. Yeah, sorry, my voice carries. We're having a slumber party, want in?"

Rory's eyes light up.

I bag up the junk food and leave the microwave popcorn on the counter.

"Yeah, we were just going to pop this in the microwave and watch...*The Swan Princess.*"

"We were?" Cora groans.

I shoot my friend her very own death glare. "Yes, we were."

Royce: *Why aren't you in my bed?*

Nicole: *I think you just answered your own question.*

Royce: *Because I'm not in it?*

Nicole: *Sure. Let's go with that.*

Royce: *I like knowing you're in my bed. Are you at least wearing one of my shirts?*

Nicole: *I don't know how I'll explain that one to your daughter.*

Royce: *Angel?*

Nicole: *And Cora. It's a slumber party.*

Royce: *Good. I'm glad you're not alone.*

Nicole: *Not only am I not alone, I'm crowded. Rory is in my bed with me and Angel and Cora are sleeping on the floor. Even though Angel has her own room here, but whatever.*

Royce: *Figures, that girl spends half her day on a hard surface.*

Nicole: *Goodnight.*

Royce: *Kiss Rory for me.*

Nicole: *Done. Slobbery, this one.*

Royce: *What?*

Nicole: *Oh, I read that wrong. Thought you said Rover. Well, I just made out with your dog.*

Royce: *Lucky dog.*

27

A NGEL GRACIOUSLY OFFERS TO take Rory to school for me on Monday morning. After all the girls are gone, I scurry into the master bedroom bath for a long hot shower. I can't help myself. It's glorious, with a big square shower head on the ceiling that makes it feel like I'm in a tropical rainforest. He's got a standalone tub in here too, but maybe some other time.

I lather the bar over my arms and think about what Royce said to me the other night. About my favorite scent. Is it weird that *he's* my favorite scent? That I don't mind using his cedar and sage soap because it makes me feel like he's close?

I thought it might be a little weird, so didn't say anything when he asked.

When I step out of the steamy bathroom with a towel draped around my waist, I swear, I pick up a faint aroma of coffee.

And I know, he's home.

I slip on my underwear. The sexy kind I never bothered with before. And then...because I know how much he loves it, I pull on one of his sweatshirts, which hangs mid-thigh over my heather grey leggings.

"It's yours."

I turn to the sound of his voice at the door.

Grinning, he sets down two glass mugs of coffee and approaches me. Reaching under the collar, he pulls my long, wet hair out from under the sweater, then bends to kiss my cheek. "How was the rest of your weekend?"

I shrug. "Rory kept me pretty busy yesterday. Angel took her to school this morning."

"Well, I should hope so, since I asked her to."

"You asked her to? Why?"

"It's your day off."

"Will you quit it with that?" I roll my eyes and walk around him to grab one of the coffees, not bothering to ask which is mine.

He catches my waist. "I don't have to be at the arena today. So, I want to take you out. We can leave the city. We'll drive out to the falls."

"Canada?"

"Well no, the traffic is insane crossing borders, we'll never make it back in time to pick up Rory. I meant the American side of the falls."

"Sounds dangerous."

He smirks. "Should be right up your alley then."

I scoff and adjust his tie, which is all disheveled from the overnight flight. "I can't. I have a therapy session this morning."

"Oh." He steps back. "I'll drive you. And then we'll get lunch, and...go someplace...*almost* as cool."

I open my mouth to apologize, but I know he won't like that so, I accept. "Okay."

"Pamela seemed nice," Royce tells me on the ride to lunch. To ease my anxiety, he offered to still take us out of town for lunch where we're unlikely to be spotted together. But then told me I'll need to get over that soon because he doesn't plan to drive forty-five minutes every time he plans to take me out.

I agree because I don't want to argue about something that's likely a moot point.

I smile. "Yeah. I tend to like her too. She kind of adopted my language so when I talk to her, it's like I'm talking to my own conscience, you know?"

"Hmm. She's good at her job. Think she'll train me?"

I laugh. "You don't want to be inside my head, trust me."

He glances at me while watching the road. "What would I see there?"

Fear.

Doubt.

Too many fucked up emotions muddled together.

"Dirty things I want to do to my boss."

"I'm not your boss, Nicole."

"Well, the weekly fund transfers would say otherwise."

"Technically, Rory is your boss."

I gasp. "We have to stop at the mall later. I need to pick something up."

He sighs. "It's for Rory, isn't it?"

"I saw this super cute shirt that says *Boss Lady* on it. I can totally get it in pink."

After a quiet lunch by the water, Royce drives us further down the highway in the opposite direction.

"You know we don't have time to go to the American Falls, right?"

"I know. But there is a close second on the way."

I gaze out the window, drawn by the overcast blanketing the road ahead. Despite the gloomy sky, the drive expands like a canvas painted with fall colors. My eyes zoom in on the mountains in the distance and the rolling hills that lead toward it.

"It's so beautiful here...so peaceful."

Quietly, he takes my hand but doesn't say anything to my comment as he drives. So I keep the rest of my comments, like how much I'm loving today...to myself.

When we begin our trail along the water with a couple of hot chocolates, I finally speak again.

"Did I say something, or...are you worried we won't be back in time?"

"No. It's not you." He grips the guardrail along the walkway and looks out into the water. "Nicole, inside and out, you are the most beautiful woman I've ever met." He turns to me, regret in his eyes which don't make any sense. "You're a real fucking treasure."

I blink.

He looks at our surroundings like it's just his backyard. "I want to show you so much more than this. A hidden escape a few miles from town is not even a fraction of what you deserve."

"Where is this coming from?" I ask, but he doesn't need to answer. I think I might know.

"Have you ever been outside the city?"

Yep. Bingo. I swallow the tears stinging my bottom lids.

Because no. I haven't. And this man must have seen the world. Unimaginable beauty while I'm captivated with the simple view in front of us.

I do feel like I've missed out on a lot because of my issues, but traveling and sightseeing isn't one of them. "I think all of this looks and feels beautiful and peaceful to me because I'm looking at it with you. Because you make me feel those things."

He tugs me close, raking my hair back to kiss me softly. Then he holds me. And it's almost like I can feel him tell me that he's never letting me go.

"I don't want to stop what we're doing. I don't want to just be your right now."

I frown and smile a little. "Do you want to be my later?"

He laughs once. "Yes. Your right now...and your later." He lifts my chin. "I want you to be my date to the gala this Saturday night."

"What? No, I can't."

"I was asked to bring a date. And I want to bring you."

I blink up at him. I want to say yes, but there's something I need to know first. "Tell me what happened with Claire."

He nods as if acknowledging that it's fair to tell me at this point. "This doesn't...you can't tell Angel."

I shake my head. "I would never betray your trust."

He strokes my cheek, then drops his hand, stepping back. "She cheated on me. Repeatedly. In our own home."

"Oh no."

"Funny thing is I thought our bickering was funny. But after she had Angel and her modeling career slowed down, our fights weren't so lighthearted and quirky. Suddenly, they became bitter and hurtful. I thought it might be a mid-thirties crisis, and not just for her, I was looking at myself too. But it didn't pass. It just got worse."

He struggles with the next words.

"I came home early from an away game to surprise her. Angel was scheduled to be at her friend's for the rest of the weekend. And I wanted to rekindle our romance. John was there. In my house. Claiming he came to see me. But an idiot could tell they were just fucking like rabbits on every surface of the house."

"Oh my gosh, I'm so sorry."

"It's why I don't have friends anymore really. Hard to trust anyone after that."

"John was..."

"My best friend."

"That's horrible," I whisper. "I'm so sorry."

"I left and put the house on the market the next day."

I debate on the personal question I'm about to ask. But after watching my brother pay our mother's way just to get her to leave, I can't help it. "Did you... have to give her anything?"

"No. She was a successful model. She did just fine on her own. She's broke now, but we had a prenup. Before I found out, we were fighting so often, there were times I thought a divorce might be what she wanted, but that she was avoiding it because of the prenup. I was willing to settle a reasonable sum if it was what she wanted. That day I came home early was my last try to make it work."

"Angel should know." It's anger talking because of the relationship Angel has with her mother. And all the times she'd claimed to me *Dad stopped being romantic.*

He nods solemnly. "The truth has a way of coming out, but I don't want it to. Angel loves her mother. They have a good relationship. I can't take that away."

"You didn't deserve that."

He nods. "Thank you. So..." He takes my hand again. "It's why I was so harsh when you first moved in. I couldn't put up with the lying. I lived with it for months from the two people I trusted the most. I wasn't about to live with someone doing it again."

I lower my head. "I understand."

He lifts my face. "It's all I'll ever ask of you, Nicole. To trust and be honest with me."

I smile and lift to kiss the corner of his lips. "You have my word."

He clears his throat and swallows. "There's something else. I need you to promise me something."

"Anything." The minute I say it, I feel like I'm going to regret it.

"Promise me you'll never go back to Sylvie's again. Or any of those places downtown."

Confusion touches my brows. "I wasn't planning on it..."

"I know. It's not that I don't trust you. It's that...I don't want you...unprotected."

That's not the word he wanted to use. He's filtering. There's something else he's afraid of. But I don't push. I get that he just wants me safe. And I'm alright with this promise. I smile and nod. "I promise."

He pushes my hair behind my ear and kisses me gently. "So...have I earned that yes?"

"The gala?" I shake my head regretfully. "Royce, I'd rather not. People will know me—"

"You can't hide forever."

"Can too. Been doing it half my life."

"You're part of mine now. And I want you out in the open."

28

I COULD WATCH HER sleep every day for the rest of my life. I stroke
Nicole's dark silky hair across the pillow. It's barely dawn but I've
been up for hours. It was a mistake—telling her about Claire.

But how could I not? It's not fair to demand honesty if I'm not
completely upfront with her.

Finding out about Claire's affair was an eye-opening kind of pain.
Not because of how much I loved her. Our love was fading. But because
I had tunnel vision. All I saw was fixing something that was once my
everything. I didn't see the signs. The red flags.

I'll never be that blind again.

I'm in my office on Tuesday night after practice. I'm no closer to finding out what's going on during our games than I was last week.

There's a knock on my door just as I'm putting on my jacket.

Angel pokes her head in. "Hey, Dad, you in a good mood?"

"Probably not. What do you want?"

She steps in and closes the door. "I was thinking about Thanksgiving. I want to cook."

I raise a brow.

"Okay, so maybe it's Jace doing most of the cooking, but it's our first Thanksgiving and I want it to be special with a full house."

"Sounds good. We'll bring desert."

"Awesome. Oh and...I mentioned it to mom, and she invited herself. Is that okay?"

I stare up at her from across the room. "She invited herself?"

She sighs. "Okay, I invited her. Jesus, how do you do that?"

"It's a gift," I mutter, flipping through papers on my desk.

"Does it work on Nicole?"

I look up, setting my glasses down. "What do you mean?"

"Well, let's be honest. Nicole is a born pathological liar. And she's good at it...but they're harmless fibs really. Oh no. You don't give her the stare-down, do you? Dad, it's so embarrassing, please don't."

"Nicole isn't a liar. She's just..." *Afraid to be herself.* I sigh. "Don't worry. I *won't* embarrass you."

She mumbles something under her breath like she doesn't believe me, but I let it go. She pulls my door open. "See you at the gala Saturday night."

Shit.

"Angel," I call out.

She pauses and turns.

"I asked Nicole to...be my date to the gala."

With a smirk, she steps back in and closes the door. "Tell me more." Then quickly shoots up a hand. "But not too much. It's still weird."

My eyes narrow. "What do you mean, *still* weird?"

"Dad, she's my best friend, and I'm not blind—I see the way she looks at you."

"How does she look at me?"

"Oh no—I'm not going there. It's...a look."

I nod and stand, rounding my desk. "And...you don't mind?"

She shakes her head. "Dad. I love you both. And...I accepted the idea of it some time ago." She strolls over and pats my shoulder. "Just don't go wearing your reading glasses and telling dad jokes."

I smile at my very grown-up daughter.

If only everyone else's reaction—including a certain member of my team—would be just as supportive.

Friday night's game is the last chance I have to win before I'm forced to recommend a trade for next season.

I huddle my team in the locker room and do the only thing I can at this point. Give them my all.

"Look guys, I know we've faced our fair share of setbacks on the ice so far this season. But I don't dwell on losses. And you shouldn't be either. Every game is a new game. Not a continuation of the last. Start seeing a turning point. Start seeing the win. It's the only way to keep the head in the game."

I get several nods.

"You have a choice –yield to despair or to rise above it." I watch them carefully, unable to keep my own head in the game and feeling like a complete hypocrite.

"The scoreboard hasn't been in our favor lately, but our commitment to each other will not be measured in numbers. Stay focused and communicate. Most importantly...trust your teammates."

Garret's jaw tics and he glances to the side.

His head is either somewhere else or...he heard every word I said.

Either way—I'm not happy.

With a nod to my team captain, I step out and get on the ice.

Nicole and Rory are here again tonight. And I'm taking them both to dinner later. We'll likely get a booth so that Rory can spread out on my lap and fall asleep after a bowl of mac and cheese.

And Nicole and I can spend some time together. She's been nervous all week about tomorrow night—which means I have one night to make her realize she belongs on my arm.

"Lay it on a little thick tonight, don't you think?" I ask Nicole on the drive home from Bridges, trying to keep my tone neutral because while I was planning dinner in town after the game—a game we lost—Nicole made plans of her own.

Meet up with the team at Bridges. Insisting that as head coach, I needed to be there to show support and keep spirits up. She had a point, but I still didn't like the idea of being around anyone but her and my little girl tonight.

"I don't know what you mean." There is zero innocence in the way she claims it.

Which ticks me off even more.

"I mean you avoiding me all night by talking to literally every player on the team," I snap.

She smirks. "You kept track?"

"Shamelessly," I admit, glancing back at Rory in the backseat, sound asleep. "I thought I made it clear, you're not my dirty little secret. You didn't need to talk to guys tonight just to prove there's nothing going on between us."

She blinks, staring out the window. The wheels in her head spinning and I'm not even sure she hears me.

"Nicole."

"Hmm?"

Glancing in my rearview mirror, I pull the car to a stop on the side of the road and zoom in on her. "What's going on?"

"What's Carter's deal? He's a little quiet, no? Has he always been quiet?"

I take a moment to answer. My insecurities—the ones I refused to feel ever again when it came to women—spiking. "Carter?" I ask sharply.

Carter Hayes *is* quiet. He's also the newest in the team. A rookie last year but not someone I would ever think to be Nicole's type. "He's like nineteen."

"He's twenty-three, was born in Brooklyn, has two sisters, and just moved in with his high school sweetheart."

My brows shoot up. "You know all this from one conversation?"

Her eyes shift down and to the side. "Or was it Peters who has the two sisters?"

"What?"

"Oh and did you know Garret grew up without a father? Or that he had one close by but left and started a new family or something..." She scratches her chin, trying to remember.

I did know that. I know a lot about the team's family background. It's how I knew about *her*. But I'm not in the mood for life stories. "Nicole."

"But he's hoping to rekindle that relationship—tell ya, that guy is a talker once—" She glances at me as if snapping out of it. "Why are we stopped? Shit. Did we get pulled over? Let me do the talking."

"No, I pulled us over, Nicole. And you've got five seconds to catch me up to where your head is before I snap."

Biting her lip, she waits just about six seconds—because of the spiteful little minx she is—then takes a breath to explain. "The guys told me that you suspect someone on the team may be sabotaging the games."

My head falls back in the seat and I pinch the bridge of my nose.

"Anyway...when I found out the whole team was going to Bridges, I knew it could be a good opportunity to get to know the players on a more personal level. I tried to at the executive suite last week, but everyone was too stiff there. No one was drinking because of the VIPs attending. But today, whoever it was, should be in a visibly different mood than everyone else. I have a skill in reading people. I can help you find out who it is...and why."

I blow a breath into my fist. "So you're not interested in a younger man?"

Understanding settles in and her lips spread into a grin. "You're the *only* man I'll ever want."

The way I burn for this woman.

"I'm still angry with you," I tease, pulling her in for a soft kiss as she rides me slowly.

She nibbles on the corner of her lip, her forehead still pressed to mine. "I think I like angry Coach in bed."

I jerk her harder onto my cock and glide my hands over her bare ass. "I didn't take you for a girl who likes to be spanked."

"Neither did I...but apparently..."

A nod with satisfaction. "Apparently, you do. Very much." It's only our second time tonight, but it's been a long day for both of us and I need Nicole to rest.

She's too invested in helping me solve this mystery with the team and I don't want that kind of pressure on her.

I want to savor the heat of her body. I glide in and out of her slowly, and deeply. But I feel her growing hot and urgent as she grips my biceps, rocking her hips. "Harder. *Please.*"

I give my woman everything she asks. Slow, deep, hard, tender, demanding. I crave her pleasure.

And I will deliver.

But there's one thing I'll never do.

Flipping her on her back, I pin her down, giving her one hard thrust before I pause and gaze into her sparkling green eyes. "You never have to beg with me."

I pump into her until her thighs shake. Until I fill her with the mind-blowing orgasm she shouldn't have to chase. Until she's screaming loud enough to throw me over the edge beside her.

There's nothing like it. The way she gives herself to me. The way I'll always give myself to her. The way she *fits* right here.

There will never be anything like it.

29

"AND YOU HAVEN'T HEARD from your father either?" Pamela asks on Saturday morning. I had told her about the gala today and she insisted on seeing me before to ease my mindset.

"No. He contacts Nick every once in a while, but he hasn't reached out to me. Probably afraid to. I know he cares about me and he worries, but probably feels responsible for some of the things that happened."

"Did he ever admit to that?"

"Not to me," I say honestly and a little bitterly. Because he doesn't open up to me the way he does to my brother.

Pamela nods and makes notes. "Okay. Well, if he does, just make sure whatever it is he wants to talk to you about, you're mentally ready for."

Not likely.

"Let's move on to current relationships. Tell me about Royce. You mentioned on the phone he finally opened up about his ex-wife."

I sit up, fueled by the subject. "I can't believe after what she'd done, he won't tell Angel. Did you know he had to listen to his daughter blame *him* for the marriage ending? That he was too busy for her? That he stopped making her feel beautiful after she lost her career? And he didn't say a word."

Pamela nods. "It sounds right. Children blaming their parents. But Royce probably won't budge on this one. When it comes to family, people are willing to take all the hits as long as you can save a relationship that depends on it."

"I don't get it."

"Like say if Claire were a long lost parent who abandoned Angel and now wants to get to know her—Royce would probably feel like she has no right, but for his daughter's sake, he's willing to do it."

"Long lost parent?"

She shakes her head. "It's just an example. What I'm trying to explain is, people would go to great lengths in order to protect or maintain a relationship."

I blink as something hits me. "I'm sorry, can we cut this short? I...really need to get ready for this gala."

"Of course. Call me Monday. I want to hear all about it."

The partition in the town car is up as the car heads east on the way to the gala. After waiting forty-five minutes for my vehicle from the valet at last year's event, I'm not taking any chances. Because, tonight, the minute I'm ready to take my girl home, we're off.

It's just us in the backseat. We dropped off Rory with Cora, who graciously offered to babysit tonight since she isn't going. I heard her tell Nicole that there are only a handful of fake smiles per calendar year she's willing to dish out and—it being November—she's running short.

Nicole is leaning toward the window, visibly anxious. Her long silky hair, which is usually straight, is wavy tonight and elegantly pinned at the sides. Her makeup is modest, and her luscious lips glossy and tinged in berry.

It's rare that I get the wind knocked out of me—and hasn't happened since my hockey-playing days.

But when I walked into her bedroom tonight after getting dressed myself, that's exactly what happened. Nicole took my breath away, looking sinfully beautiful in a deep lilac dress, showing off her curves beneath an iridescent tulle that just barely sweeps the floor.

She's wearing a new scent tonight. I'm not sure what it is but it reminds me of a purple flower. I wonder if she chose it because she liked it, or because she thinks it goes with the dress.

I put my hand over hers on the leather seat. Beautiful green eyes meet mine. Her berry lips turning at the sides. "I'm okay," she reassures, knowingly.

"We can leave whenever you want," I reassure right back.

"No, we can't. You have business to take care of tonight. Impressions to make to keep your title. I'm a brave girl and...I can adapt to my surroundings."

"Okay. Just give me a signal if you've had enough."

She turns away and I'm wondering if she's upset with me because I blew off her theory about Garret. Earlier she tried to convince me that Garret Garrison, one of my most valuable players, is the culprit.

Just because he mentioned he's trying to reconnect with the father who abandoned him. Her notion is that there is a connection somewhere but there's no way of knowing without doing some more digging.

I told her—maybe a little too distinctly—to drop it.

"Nicole, you know I'm just looking out for you. This could go on for months, I don't want you obsessing over it. And I don't want anyone finding out that you're investigating. We don't know who's involved."

She shrugs. "I do. It's Garret."

I sigh. "Would it make you feel better if I looked into it?"

She glances back at me haughtily. "It's the least you could do."

"Done. Will you hold my hand now?"

She glances at it. "For now."

We don't hold hands when we walk through the front doors of the large venue. This year, it's at the Golden Terrace, usually reserved for weddings and corporate gatherings. The grand entrance to the lobby is very ornate. Too ornate for hockey, but I digress. Immediately, I look for an escape. Someplace I can take Nicole if she gets overwhelmed.

Or intimidated.

But it won't get to that. I'm making sure of it.

It feels unnatural not to hold her hand or wrap an arm around her waist, keeping her at my side all night, but Nicole is right. Tonight is about appearances and talking to the owners about the team. Not flaunting whatever is developing between my nanny and me.

I find the *Coach Collins and Guest* place card on an entry table, which isn't hard considering we're fashionably late, and extend an elbow for her. With a curt nod—which is new and un-Nicole-like—she takes it and follows me in.

Her eyes scan the crowd and I do the same. She's likely searching for a friendly face, while I search for the ones I'd like to stay away from.

Nick and Jace find us almost instantly. Jace already has his suit jacket off, which doesn't surprise me. The guy raised his kid sister practically on his own, but you'd never tell by the level of cockiness on this guy. It's disturbing that I may very well be looking at my future son-in-law.

"Coach," Nick greets us, his tone clipped when he addresses me. He glances at his sister. "Isn't this kind of counterproductive for hiring a nanny?"

"Nick, could we not do this now?" Nicole asks quietly.

"Did you run out of numbers in your little black book? Because I could lend you mine. I haven't used it in a while, but the age group should be about right," he offers, glancing at his twin.

"You are so lucky my sister isn't here right now," Jace mutters to his friend.

Nicole starts to pull her hand out of my arm and I tighten it. "Nicole is my date. If you have an issue with it, you're free to stop by the house tomorrow. But we're not discussing it now."

Nick turns to his sister, scanning her briefly. "You look good."

She glares at him and he rolls his eyes, forfeiting—the guy never could argue with his sister. "Thanks," she says dryly.

Jace intervenes. "So, what table are you sitting at?"

"Ten," I murmur.

"Super," Jace beams and I notice him grip Nick's stiff arm. "We'll see you there." He tugs his friend. "Come on. Help me find my girlfriend."

When they leave, I turn to Nicole—her expression is sharp but blank. "You alright? You're usually very vocal with your brother."

"I didn't want to make a scene," she says evenly, keeping her eyes focused on some of the couples in the room.

I nod and search the crowd, finding the man I'm mostly here for tonight. "There's Jeff Granger. The woman next to him is his wife, Sandy. She hates these things almost as much as I do, so she likely won't leave his side. Want to come over with me?"

She swallows but nods once, as if I'm sending her into battle.

Bringing Nicole tonight is part of a bigger plan I have for her to come out of hiding. To stop feeling like the whole town still thinks of her as the outcast, the unfortunate Kane twin, the one who belongs downtown with the drug addicts rather than in the suburbs.

Hundreds of people are here tonight. Important people. People who could easily spread the word.

I want tonight to be her golden hour. "Nicole, look at me."

Her eyes linger on my chest before lifting to mine.

"You *belong* here with me. Maybe even more than most people here tonight. Just...be yourself. Don't worry about what anyone thinks."

She blinks up. "Easy for you to say."

"Honey, relax. Just breathe. And be yourself."

She nods, but I know my words fall on deaf ears.

It pains me to tear my eyes off her when I still have so much to reassure her, but I'm forced to when my name is called from a few feet away.

"Grove," I acknowledge, curtly. A part of me still ticked off that Nicky wouldn't let me confront him. Saying something about how it would discredit her threats if he knew she told on him.

Clapping my shoulder, he says, "Let's chat privately when you have a moment."

Before I have a chance to tell him we can speak in my office later, he turns to Nicole. His eyes scanning her in a way that makes me want to tear his eyeballs out of their sockets.

"You look absolutely lovely. Nicole, is it?"

She grins wickedly. "You know it is."

I cover my mouth and clear my throat to hide my smile because this is what I admire most about my girl. The way she calls people out when they're practically asking for it.

But the moment I do, Nicole's eyes flash and she backtracks. "I mean, thank you, it's...nice to see you again," she says softly.

"My wife is around here somewhere. Let me go grab her."

I touch her elbow. "I'm sorry about that, I meant—"

"No," she hisses at me. Her eyes glistening. "You don't have to apologize. I do. I'm here for you. I need to keep myself in check."

I tug her arm gently and growl into her ear. "*Enough* of that."

Gove and his wife, Jessica, a middle-aged woman with short dark hair, high cheekbones and too much makeup, approach us, and the little chat I was about to have with Nicole is cut short.

"Oh goodness, you finally brought a date that isn't a tall blonde. They always intimidated me." Jessica scans Nicole like she's someone she can handle, and it makes my chest simmer. She extends her hand. "Jessica Randall."

My date returns the pleasantry. "Nicole Kane. And you're beautiful. You should never feel intimidated by anyone."

My jaw tics and I swallow hard. Nicole shouldn't have to suck up to anyone—especially not for my benefit.

"Oh, I like you." She waves her arm at nearby servers. "Let's get some champagne. Yoohoo."

Nicole's eyes widen and she stretches a hand. "Here, let me." She finds one with the flutes and catches his eye, then smiles brightly, holding up two fingers.

The waiter holds out the tray to Nicole but she shakes her head. "Oh, I'm alright. Thank you." Then extends a hand at the couple across us.

Jessica scoffs. "Not drinking? Jesus, why bother going out?"

Grove attempts to discreetly shake his head at his wife.

My woman doesn't miss a beat. "For the pretty dresses, of course."

"We'll see you two around," I say to the couple, then slip my arm around Nicole's waist, leading her a few feet away.

I glance around us before dipping my head slightly. "You want to explain to me why a fucking nobody like Grove's wife just insulted you and you bent over backwards for her?"

"I'm just...being the type of woman you're expected to be with. I don't want to embarrass you."

"I brought the real Nicole Kane out with me tonight. Don't make me have to fuck her out of you."

30

MY PULSE SPIKES AND my stomach flips all at once at his tempting threat. I blink up at him. He can't possibly be serious. My expression must give away my thoughts because his blue eyes shine wickedly.

"You heard me," he whispers.

I lick my lips and swallow. "Alright."

I'm about to ask him what the hell he expects me to do or act like when someone else calls his name.

"Royce."

I plaster a smile and we turn. A very good-looking man I know I've seen before with a woman I likely haven't, approach us.

"Jeffrey," Royce acknowledges with a sincere charm which tells me he respects the man.

Of course. This is Jeff Granger, one of the owners of the Blades. And I'm supposed to act myself *now?* Is he for real?

Royce tilts his head to the man's date. A stunning woman with a blonde bob, slender figure and poised in a way that just screams rich. "Marisa, you look lovely, as always."

She smiles appreciatively. "You never seem to have a bad day, yourself." She winks playfully then glances at me.

Royce puts his hand on my back. "You might remember Nicole Kane, she's our team captain's twin sister."

Marisa scans me subtly. "I've heard the name."

Jeff extends his hand. "Nicole, a pleasure. Your brother has some serious skill on the ice."

I scoff, dryly. "If he did, he wouldn't have broken his nose three times last season."

Jeff and Marisa laugh, and Coach squeezes my waist, tossing me a smirk.

Marisa catches it. "Are you two here together?"

"Yes, Nicole is my date tonight."

Tonight? He makes it sound like I'm an escort.

Is that what he needs them to believe? Did Marisa's mention that she heard my name before make him rethink this whole, *I want you to just be you*?

But I don't have time to dwell on the hurt and rejection I'm feeling over that one little word that makes all this an *entirely* different scenario for me. Because I'm reminded of the reason I'm here when Royce starts his pitch to Jeff.

I'm to "*distract*" the wife.

"You've been tough to get a hold of lately, Jeff. I was hoping we could catch up this evening on some thoughts I have on the team."

When I see Jeff hesitate and search for an escape, I take my cue.

"That really is a lovely dress, Marisa. Blue is definitely your color."

Instantly, she releases her husband's arm and turns to me. "Ugh, thank you, Jeffrey insists I wear team colors to these things."

"Well, it's a good thing we're not orange."

I chat her up, laying on the charm, which she seems to appreciate. My bartending ears are trained to hear multiple conversations, so I wait for Royce to deliver his thoughts to Jeffrey before I even consider wrapping up awkwardly with Marisa.

Just when I start to relax standing at his side, I catch sight of Claire Collins as she tosses a hug to her equally tall daughter, Angel, across the room.

I stiffen. My stomach churns and I'm reminded of the permanent fixture in his life.

While I'm...just his date tonight.

"Are you alright? You look pale," Marisa asks.

Royce allows Jeff to finish his thought before turning to me. His brows twitch and he glances around us, pausing when he looks in the direction his ex-wife is standing.

"It might be time for that drink and some food. Would you excuse us?" Royce says to the couple.

"Certainly." Jeff nods. "But I'm interested in what we were discussing. I'll stop by this week."

"Look forward to it." He lets them stroll away before zeroing in on me. "Are you alright?"

Is he seriously playing dumb? "Your ex-wife just walked in."

His eyes stay on mine, like he's waiting for more. So I give it to him. "Maybe you should let *her* know that I'm only your date for tonight too. Wouldn't want to give anyone the wrong idea."

I spin and quietly walk toward one of the many double-door entrances, hoping one of them leads to the ladies room.

Or, you know...any black hole I can crawl into.

He doesn't follow me—at least not in a way that I can tell. When I exit one of the doors, I scan the halls both ways, looking for the lesser of the crowd, and head in that direction.

This whole thing was foolish of me.

Foolish to think we could be more than physical, more than just tonight, or last night, or the past few weeks.

I find a quiet carpeted corridor around the back of the main hall. It must be close to the staff rooms since I only see full uniform personnel bustling through doors and moving about at top speed.

"Hi, is there a restroom I can use here?"

"Third door on the left, dear," a woman calls back, barely looking at me as she rushes toward one of the halls, carrying a tray of cocktails.

I'm about to push through that last wooden door in the dark, narrow hallway when a hand catches my arm and spins me.

Royce gazes at me with fire in his eyes. Not anger, not embarrassment for running off on him. But with pure heat.

And the tiniest hint of a smirk, like he's just won a game he hoped I'd lose.

Without a word, he flips me around to face the wall and I gasp.

His breath is on my neck. "I'm sorry I added that word when I said you were my date."

Despite his dominating actions, there's enough regret in his voice that I believe it.

"It was unnecessary," he adds, his fingers lifting the tulle of my skirt. "I don't know why I said it." He reaches the hem of the dress and lifts slowly, stroking my inner thigh, making me shudder. "But I am so fucking glad I did."

I turn my head to the side and he meets me there. "Because now I know you want this too."

"Royce," I whine, panic in my voice when I hear a door swinging in the distance and footsteps. But then they fade out.

He shushes me. "Tell you what. If you're not wet for me right now, then I'll fix your skirt, fluff out your hair, and walk you right back into that ballroom."

I swallow.

"But if you are..." He licks my earlobe. "Then I'm holding onto my promise and we're going to walk back in there and you're going to be the woman I'm fucking falling for. Got it?"

I nod.

"Good. Because I don't only want you as my date tonight. Starting with your brother tomorrow, I'm telling people the truth about us."

"About us?"

"That I'm crazy about you."

"You don't know what you're talking about," I cry softly. "I'm a mess."

He slides his fingers around my waist and dips under my soaked panties. Swiping one finger between my thighs, he hisses. "No. You're wet. Put your palms against the wall, honey."

I gasp out. "We can't."

"The longer you wait, the more likely we'll get caught. Now do it."

I press against the wall with the fancy ornate paper as he slides my panties down my legs. "Step out of them." I do and he picks them up, shoving them in his pocket. "Good girl."

I hear him undo his buckle before lifting my dress from behind and yanking my hips up for better access.

I push out shamelessly.

Bringing his hand back around, he rubs tantalizing circles on my clit, making me wetter, getting me ready to take *all of him*.

ROXANNE TULLY

I writhe with anticipation. With a need, I didn't know I was capable of.

"You're dynamite. A goddess that no one in this fucking building will ever live up to. You're the treasure I was lucky enough to find first."

He dusts a kiss over my neck and positions the head of his cock at my entrance. "You're mine. You've been mine since the moment I laid eyes on you. It's why no one else came close to pleasuring you in the past. You've always belonged to me."

With one hard thrust, he's inside me, sliding his hand over my mouth and letting me bite down on his index finger. "And I'm yours," he grits. "I'm yours in every way."

Holy shit. He's tearing me apart in the most delicious way with every thrust, every word and I'm already so close, I'm going to scream.

"Not yet," he growls.

"But I'm so close."

"I'm not letting you come until you say it. Claim me the way I'm claiming you."

"You're—you're mine," I whimper out.

Another hard thrust. "And you're going to go back in there and make sure everyone knows it."

"Yes. God, yes." I chant as pleasure coils in my belly.

He orders me to clench around his cock as he lowers his fingers back to my clit. I silence a scream inside my throat as he muffles a groan against my neck and empties inside me.

A few minutes later, when I step out of the bathroom, Royce scans me and gives me a soft grin, offering me his elbow. "Ready, beautiful?"

296

I give him a wicked grin right back. "If I say no, am I looking at a round two?"

He chuckles. "There's my girl. Come on."

My hand is still in his when we walk in and take our seats at the round table. Nick is across from us, pretending not to notice. He knows better than to fuck with either of us here. There's also a huge centerpiece between us, thankfully so we don't engage in conversation. There's no sign of Jace or Angel and our table is mostly empty.

When the auction starts, I lean in and whisper. "I heard bits and pieces, how'd it go with Jeff?"

"I told him enough to make him want to stop by my office this week. Hopefully, there's time to verify your suspicions."

The corner of my lip perks. "You're so sexy when you're serious."

"I was serious back in that hallway," he murmurs in a new mischievous tone I think I adore.

I play aloof and fold the napkin on my lap. "We can discuss labeling what this is later. I think you're just trying to prove a point and I'm not—"

He tosses his napkin down and sits up, holding his hand out to me. "That does it. Get up."

He can't be serious, so I laugh him off. "No."

He slumps back into his seat. "Shit."

I giggle. He looks like a kid who just had his video game taken away. "What, that's it?"

He tosses his hands up in defeat. "You said no."

"So?"

He raises a brow. "Nicole. No means no."

I slump next to him. "Noted."

"Hey, you two," Garret calls, taking a seat a few chairs down from us. A leggy blonde at his side.

I stiffen, but Royce doesn't even flinch. His smile doesn't fade. He doesn't give anything away. "Hey, Garret. And I thought I was fashionably late."

Garret wraps an arm around his date. "Melinda and I...got caught up."

Royce turns to me with a smile. "Should go say hello to a few more people. Take a walk with me?"

I shake my head. "I'm good."

He pins me with a warning glare. "Okay well... try not to have too much fun without me."

I smile right back, challenging him to trust me.

With a very subtle head shake, he strolls away. I gather my thoughts on how to approach this...discreetly.

I come up blank.

I'm not used to being cautious or tactful. I *plunge* into dangerous situations, never worrying about consequences or having to filter my words.

But it wouldn't matter, because I don't have my target's attention. He keeps looking away uncomfortably.

I follow his gaze.

He's looking at Coach?

Or the person Coach is talking to. A man I don't recognize.

"Who's that?" I ask. *Shit*. Was that too obvious?

Garret shrugs and turns away.

But Nick heard me and tears his eyes off his phone. Following my gaze, he says, "That's Robbie Hastings," he mutters.

My brother and I lock eyes briefly.

As a matter of fact, maybe I will join my date as he makes his rounds.

I stand and make my way across the room when my blonde friend pops in front of me.

"There you are." She beams as she scans me appreciatively. Then licks her finger and brushes under my bottom lip. "Here you got something under—" She jerks back her hand like my mouth is on fire. "Oh my God, was that...lipstick smudge from my *Dad* kissing you? Please say no."

"Um...no?"

"Ewww," she groans. She takes a deep breath, calming herself. "Okay, new rule. Only tell me things on a need-to-know basis, okay? For example. Hey Angel, can't hang out—I've got plans Saturday night. Or hey, I'm Christmas shopping. Is your dad more of a solid or stripe tie kind of guy?"

I give her a thumbs up. "That works for me." It's a lie. It doesn't work for me because I'm dying to tell someone about what Royce said to me by the staff rooms earlier.

Be the woman I'm fucking falling for.

It had to be the heat of the moment. Or hell, the heat of the last few weeks. Because I'm *not* the type of girl you fall for.

"By the way...this dress is magical...and here I thought you'd come wearing black."

"It would be more suitable."

The comment comes from behind me, and I turn.

Claire Collins, Angel's mom, looking dangerously gorgeous in a fire-engine red dress with matching heels and lipstick.

She steps up to us, her eyes scanning me.

"Mom, that wasn't very nice."

She glances at her only daughter. "Angel, why don't you go get me a glass of champagne."

"Why don't you go get it yourself?" Jace snaps, coming up behind his girlfriend, who immediately shushes him.

I always did like Jace.

Claire keeps her glare pinned on me. At five foot ten, the woman towers over me. But she doesn't say a word to me. Like I'm not worth them. Looking over my shoulder, she shakes her head. "You can't be serious."

A familiar voice sighs behind me and touches my shoulder. "What is it now, Claire?" Royce asks.

"Someone needs to look out for you since you've clearly given up. Hiring her as your nanny is one thing, but bringing her out with you—in front of all your bosses? The media? If you wanted to retire, there's a much simpler way of doing so."

From the corner of my eye, I see Nick approach cautiously and stand next to Jace, who puts a hand in front of his friend's chest.

"Good God, woman, enough. And you're disrespecting my date, so I would appreciate it if you stopped."

"Fine. You're right. This isn't the place. I'll stop by tomorrow." She turns on her heel.

"No, you won't!" That comes from me.

She turns a hard glare in my direction. "*Excuse* me?"

I push Royce away so I can face my own opponent. "My boyfriend made it very clear that he doesn't want to speak to you. And while we're at it, stop barging into his house and move on."

Claire scoffs and looks at me like I'm some joke. "Is there anything else?"

I cross my arms. "Yes. I think you owe me an apology."
Okay, that one might be extra.

She laughs and I honestly think it's real when she wipes at the corner of her eye. "Good one." She turns to walk away again.

There's a distinct difference between Royce and *Coach*. Because the man squeezing my shoulders behind me is not the man who takes me to bed. He's the man who gives his team hell on the ice at practice. He's the man I hear behind me when he growls at his ex.

"Claire!"

She twists and stares back at him. I can't see his expression behind me or the warning he might be giving her.

But when her fearful eyes travel to Angel, my heart stops.

He *wouldn't*.

She swallows. "I—I'm sorry, Nicole. You look lovely. Enjoy your evening." With that, she walks off, disappearing through a crowd of people.

I turn slowly, my eyes blazing. "You didn't have to do that," I hiss.

He lifts his gaze to his daughter. We both watch as Jace leads a stunned Angel away and toward our table.

Nick lightly nudges my arm. "You okay?"

I nod. "Yeah—" I sigh. "No. Do you think Angel is mad at me?"

"No." They both say simultaneously.

"But I'll go make sure," Nick reassures, probably picking up on the tension between his coach and me.

Royce pulls me aside and grips my hands. "I had to. She was out of line. And I don't think that was about you."

I snatch my hands away. "Fine. But please let me deal with her myself next time?"

He smirks. "Deal. I'm going to love watching you fight for me." Then...he bends down and kisses me. Right here in the ballroom. "*Girlfriend*."

31

I T'S BEEN TEN DAYS since the gala and as promised, Claire has stayed away. There's been no sound of her. Even Angel claims to have not spoken to her mother.

My friend has been fairly quiet about the whole thing and my guess is she was mortified and shocked.

I don't know how to tell her that I'd never make her choose between us.

Claire will always be her mother.

And as long as she'll have me, I'll always be her best friend.

"Uno!" Rory cries gleefully. "Nicky, it's your turn."

"Hmm? Oh right." I jerk back to life and press my cards to my chest. "Did you peek?"

She shakes her head innocently.

"Alright." I study my cards and set one down, then lift my eyes to Royce, who still holds several cards...and appears to be lost in thought as well. I clear my throat loudly.

"Oh, my turn, okay umm..." He flips through his cards and sets one down.

"That's not yellow or a seven," I point out.

"Daddy, don't you know how to play?"

"I do, I do." He rearranges his cards as if it will help, then sets one down. "Does this count?"

Rory's eyes widen—because since she's next and close to winning, she'd be drawing *two* cards from the stack, which would set her back.

"No. Pick something else."

"Rory!"

Coach blinks like he's coming out of a deep thought. "What? What's wrong?"

I exchange devilish glances with my mini-me and she gives me a look that I swear says *It would be so easy.*

I give her a wry grin then turn back to her father. "Umm...no you can't use that."

He crosses his arms and leans forward. Suddenly very interested in the game—and me. "Why not?"

I press my lips together. "Because...I...saw your cards. When your head was *somewhere else,*" I say pointedly. "So it's not fair. You need to collect a new stack."

He studies me comically. "Hmm..."

I *not-so-subtly* slide the rules card away from his side of the table.

"Fine," he grits. "New cards."

Rory breathes a sigh of relief and her dad and I exchange a knowing smile.

He sets a card down and Rory follows with her last one. "I win!"

"Awesome." He folds down his cards. "Time for bed."

"But now you have to play against Nicole."

He winks at me. "If it's between the two of us, Nicky will always win."

Rory pouts. "That's not fair."

"When you're older you'll disagree," he teases, for my benefit.

I love his timeless charm. It's one of the perks of dating an older man. Dating.

Are we *dating*?

I watch as he lifts her off the chair and positions her into an airplane.

"Arms out. Ready for take-off?"

"Ready." She giggles.

Then he dips her downward to me and she kisses my cheek. "Night, Nicky."

"Night, sweetie."

He winks again. "Be right back."

I push off the table and start cleaning while he tucks her into bed. When I'm done, I sit in the living room, wrapping a fleece throw blanket around my shoulders. It's a cold night and I'm looking forward to slipping into his arms later.

Come to think of it, I don't know how I survived winters without his arms around me.

He returns and quickly moves to the fireplace, starting it up.

"A fire. Are we hanging out for a while?"

He tosses me a smirk. "Did you have other plans?"

I sigh. "I guess not.

He joins me and pulls me into the crook of his arm.

"You going to tell me what had you distracted during our game?" I ask.

"Nope."

"Hmm. Is it a secret?"

"It's none of your business. Ow." He winces away, gripping his side.

"Sorry, what was that?" I ask naively, shifting my head back.

He groans. "Okay, there is definitely a disadvantage to having a girl-friend made of steel."

I grin and cozy up beside him again.

He releases a breath and relents. "You might have had a point. About Garret."

"I knew it. What did you find out?"

"I didn't. That's why I didn't want to tell you, it's still speculation." He sighs. "After you told me that Garret was suspiciously interested in my conversation with Robbie Hastings at the gala, it triggered a memory of him mentioning something in passing when he first came to town. About having more than one ex-wife. So...I took a page out of your book and...poked around. Had a few beers with him and...asked a few questions to connect the dots."

I shift to face him. "And?"

"And nothing. All I know is that he has two ex-wives here in Buffalo. One he's rekindling with. They have a kid going to college up north. So, I talked a little bit about Angel and casually asked if *all* his children went to school here and he said *no*. But then—he paused. Like he caught himself. Like he almost slipped."

I beam. "That's amazing."

"That's *nothing*. Maybe he's just private about his past."

"Couldn't we find out if he and Garret are related?"

"My buddy Dave is good. But not that good."

"So, what do we do now?"

"You do nothing. I will figure something out." He pulls me back and rubs my arms. We're quiet for a few minutes, watching the fire. Then he kisses the top of my head. "Nicole."

I lift my chin.

"I want to tell Rory about us."

"What...will you tell her?"

That you're madly in love with me? That you want us to be a family?

Is this where I can finally tell him how my feelings have grown to something that feels...permanent?

"That we're together. That you'll be staying a while. That we may have another sitter some nights because I want to take you out."

My heart breaks a little. I blink down and shift back to resting my head on his shoulder. "I don't think so."

"Why not?"

"Because...it's not a good idea. Let's just not. Not yet." I try not to sound disappointed. It's okay that he doesn't use words of promise and forever the way I only dream of.

I'm not his forever.

But maybe...I can be.

Maybe after I prove I can be a better person. Prove I can be normal.

Pamela keeps dropping the word *closure* at our sessions. That if I find a way to do that with everyone who has wronged me...it can set me free.

Silently, I make a decision. I'll build up the courage to find that closure soon. Then maybe after I do, I'll feel confident enough to tell him...I want more.

He bends to kiss me again. "Okay. We'll wait."

32

"Rory, you're going to be late. Come on." I call the girl down for the third time this morning. It's the first day of December, which means Christmas shopping is underway.

This never used to be a happy holiday for me.

Or Nick for that matter. But we've somehow always made it special for each other. Either with a dollar store card and a chocolate-shaped Santa or just spending Christmas Eve at Jace and Cora's house, since their dad was always welcoming.

Cora was a kid then. One a troubled teen like myself wanted nothing to do with—but I'm so grateful for her now. And sure...even Jace.

Now I feel like I have a real home. I'm still not sure where this is going with Royce, but for now, we're happy not knowing.

I love him.

So much that it hurts.

Since telling me he's falling for me at the gala, which I'm still convinced was out of the heat of the moment, he hasn't said anything like that again.

But he's made me *feel* his affection.

When we're alone, when we're in public, when he never lets me slip into sleep without holding me. The constant text messaging throughout the day.

The stolen glances that brought us to where we are.

I love *us*.

I want to tell him. There's nothing wrong with being the first one to say it, is there?

"I guess we'll find out," I tell Rover as I kneel to pet my newest best friend.

"Okay, I'm ready." Rory shows up, fully dressed with her backpack on.

"Finally. Okay, I've packed your breakfast to go, you'll eat in the car. Let's move."

I offer Mrs. Matthews a friendly smile and let her know I'll pick Rory up at three. The woman has warmed up to me. Sort of. If you can call no longer acting like one of her students was walked to school by Cruella de Vil, progress, well then, we've made progress.

I'm fidgety when I get home. Which is odd because I didn't have any of the coffee I made earlier since I screwed it up twice and didn't bother with a third time.

I settle for lemon water and sit on the back porch in Coach's sweatshirt. Letting my mind daydream the way it has been for the last few days.

I want to be a part of this new world I'd somehow been pulled into. I want it so badly.

It's pure and filled with love, laughter, games...honesty.

Being here for Rory has been everything. Loving her and treating her as my own has been a gift I never want to take for granted.

But my mind keeps going back to what Pamela keeps telling me I need so I can truly let go and enjoy this.

Closure.

I know she means my mother, and possibly my father if he ever comes out of whatever rock he's hiding under. But there's no way I'm ready to confront my mother. She doesn't deserve it.

There are *other* people who hurt me. People who were toxic but loved me in their own special way.

Like Sylvie.

The last time I saw Sylvie, the night Coach found me a few blocks away on the ground, I stole one of her bottles, left my car keys, and took off.

That's not how I wanted to end that relationship. I want to let her know that I'm better now. Yes, I'm technically still in recovery and might always be, but I'm happy.

No matter what happens with Royce and Rory, I know what I want. What I'm worth.

And maybe I can convince her that it's not too late for her.

My chest tightens. I *can't* go back there. I made a promise to never set foot in that place again.

My leg twitches and I consider the stakes. And then...the reward. I *have* to do this.

Perhaps Sylvie is a good place to start. Then my brother...with the whole truth. Then Angel and maybe three or four years from now...my parents.

I check the time on my phone.

Sylvie's opens early for the afternoon crowd. If I get there at one, I can have a quick chat with my old friend, have my closure, offer my advice and get back in time to pick up Rory.

It'll be fine.

Royce: *I'm thinking roast chicken for dinner.*

Nicole: *Sure. I might have eggplant. I'm not really feeling chicken.*

Royce: *Whatever you want. I'll pick it up. What are you up to? Want to come by my office and...hang out?*

Nicole: *I can't. I'm going to therapy.*

Royce: *Didn't you just go on Friday?*

Nicole: *I feel like sneaking one in today.*

Royce: *Okay. Is everything alright?*

Nicole: *It will be.*

I groan. "Why did you have to ask me what I'm doing?"

I hate lying to him. But I know if I tell him I need to do this, he'll only stop me. Or insist on coming with me—and that's not happening. He may be a fairly large man, but they will eat him alive at this place.

Still, when I do eventually tell him about this, that lie is going to make it worse.

That faithful bell rings when I push the heavy door open and step inside.

"Sorry, we don't open to the public until—" Sylvie stops in her tracks. A large ice bucket in her hands. She doesn't smirk. She doesn't even flinch. "You alone?"

"Of course."

"Come on in."

I settle on a bar stool and set my keys down. Sylvie reaches for a vodka bottle on the top shelf and settles it in front of me.

My eyes widen in horror and I twist the bottle. "Who put orange peels in here?"

Sylvie rolls her eyes. "New guy."

"Did he make it out of here alive?"

"Just barely."

I scoff and push it back toward her. The place reeks and I don't want to be here long. "Can we talk?"

"Am I taking those keys?"

"No."

She sighs. "Yeah, I guess." Sylvie's no dummy. She knows what this is. But she wouldn't be who she is without offering me a glass. "Just one?"

"*None*. And I'm serious, Sylvie, just sit with me so we can—" My voice trails off when my eyes land on a familiar face sitting at the far end of the bar. He's got dark hair, light scruff, and a worn suit. The only familiar feature about him is his eyes. They're a very distinct grey, almost cat-like, and there's a small scar on his left eye. "Do I know you?"

The guy looks up and grunts, turning back to his drink.

Then—he does a double take.

And it hits me like a pound of bricks. I've seen this man before. In one of the worst memories of my life. I jump out of my stool and move toward him. "You're one of the assholes from the warehouse."

He twitches uncomfortably. "You don't know what you're talking about."

"Oh, I do. I never forget a face."

He glances back. "Look, just go about your business and I'll go about mine."

I assess the guy. He's scrawny, weak and his reflexes are probably shot. Bottom line—easy to take down.

"Nickles, Kyle's a regular," Sylvie warns.

"Yeah, well, I'm irrational." Swinging my foot, I hook his leg and knock him off his stool, watching him drop to the floor.

He groans. "What the fuck are you doing?"

I put my foot on his chest and bend down, whacking his nose, making him cry out. "You still terrorizing innocent young girls?"

"Shit," Sylvie hisses behind me.

"Look I've got nothing to do with those guys anymore, alright?"

I whack him again. The sting in my knuckles sharp and welcome. "Oh that's okay," I reassure, gripping his shirt just to lift him off the floor an inch. "I don't care if you're the new town Mayor and settled down with a wife and kids. We've got a score to settle."

"Nicole, enough," Sylvie calls tiredly from behind the bar. She's used to brawls in her bar. No one calls it in—not usually. But she's not exactly a fan of them either.

Two men pull me off him successfully somehow. The smaller of the two spills the contents of his pint glass on me. While the other seems very uncomfortable with having to touch me.

I pull on my soiled shirt. "Oh, come on."

I'm dizzy suddenly. Which makes sense since I barely ate anything today other than blueberries and water. The scent repulses me more than usual.

I straighten my spine, feeling achy. Which is not unusual after a fight.

"Fuck," I hiss, looking at my bloody knuckles.

Sylvie tosses me a wet rag. "Here. Now sit down before you mess up your pretty hair."

I watch the two patrons take Kyle to a booth in the back since sitting on a stool is no longer manageable.

Shit. Could he press charges against me now?

"How long has he been a regular here?"

She shrugs. "Stopped in sometime last year. Will you calm down and sit? The guy is harmless, I have all my regulars checked out."

I feel woozy. "So you knew he used to hang out with Frank?"

She spins and pulls out another glass, pushing it toward me, then hovering the tip of the vodka bottle over it. "How about that drink now?"

I'm in my car when I wake up. But in the passenger's seat. It's daylight and my eyes sting as I blink them open.

"The fuck is in my eye?"

"Sorry, that was me," Sylvie says behind the steering wheel. "I tried to snap you to consciousness with some sink water. Not exactly the cleanest."

"What happened?"

"Don't worry, you didn't hit the ground. Chuck was nearby and caught ya."

Oh no. How much did I have?

"Usually takes you at least four glasses before you knock out. So I don't know what *that* was about."

"Sylvie. Where are we going?"

"I'm taking you home. I'm assuming it's somewhere in the suburbs. So I'm heading north."

"Thanks."

A nap. I need a nap. That sounds so good right now.

I rattle off an address and curl up in the passenger's seat.

Sometime later, Sylvie wakes me up. "Hey, Sleeping Beauty. We're here."

I sit up groggily and look up at Coach's big, beautiful house. The one he's opened up to me because he trusted me.

"Hey, Nickles?"

I turn, wondering how my plan for closure backfired and now I'm back to where I always was with this woman.

Delirious and confused.

"I'll get there someday," she says, reassuringly. "I guess I just don't have as much to live for as you do."

My eyes well and I reach for her. She meets me halfway and wraps me in her strong arms.

"You and my cat are the only living creatures I'll ever hug."

"Thanks, Sylvie. You know I was hoping today would be some kind of closure for us."

She shrugs. "It was. In our own special way."

"Take care."

"You too. I'm going to park this thing here and call myself an Uber. You need me to come inside or you good?"

"I'll be alright. Thanks for driving."

I'm nauseous when I get in the house. I head up to my bedroom, vomit a whole lot of nothing and lie down.

33

I MISSED THREE CALLS from Rory's school since practice ran long. The last thing I need is for Mrs. Matthews to complain about another inappropriate thing that Rory or her nanny did after school.

It would be the fourth time since Nicole started that this woman has called me with a complaint.

As soon as Grove leaves my office, I'll call her back as a courtesy. But maybe I'll call Nicky first just to see what I'm in for.

"What's this about, Collins?" Grove asks.

"Jeff is coming to my office Friday. I need to confirm something before he does."

Grove stares back at me and waits.

"I need your word that you won't repeat what I'm about to tell you."

He shrugs. "Something tells me you have no choice."

I stand and start round my desk. "I have suspicions that Robbie Hastings is behind our bad luck lately."

Grove scoffs. "Oh yeah? Think he'll let us borrow his magic wand and reverse the spell?"

I glare at him. His mockery pissing me off. "I think he might have a relative on the team. A very *close* relative."

He doesn't respond and sits back in his chair, waiting for more on my assessment.

So I give it all. I don't hold back. The only thing I leave out is that Nicole had planted this seed in my head. I won't get her involved in the slightest.

Grove glares at me. "That's all you got, huh?"

My jaw tightens. "That's all. I don't have proof. I just know that we're losing and we shouldn't be. My strategies are solid. They always have been."

He sighs. "Yeah. I agree." He stands and paces my office for a minute. "Without proof, our hands are tied. You got a plan?"

"I do."

I'm pacing my office when the door finally opens and Garret walks in, eyes full of question. And maybe a little fear? Grove is behind him.

"Have a seat on the couch, Garret," Grove starts, sounding a little too cheerful. He doesn't sit beside him. Instead, Grove leans against the wall next to me, rubbing his chin. "Great practice today. Really giving it your all out there. You always were one we can count on."

"Thanks, I'm happy to—"

"I think it's interesting...this losing streak we found ourselves in this season, right? I mean—it just doesn't add up." Grove cocks his head.

He wanted to be the one to do this because of rank.

Garret's voice drops when he attempts to speak and he clears his throat. "No, I agree, we're doing everything—"

"You said you never knew your father, right?" Grove asks outright, his voice even.

Garret's face pales. Visibly pales. I can almost feel his heart slamming against his chest.

After a deep swallow, he answers. "That's right."

Grove's head bobs. "Yeah, that's too bad. He would have been so proud." He walks up to him and touches his shoulder. "If he could just see you now."

Garret rubs his hands together, his right leg shaking. "Is uh...is there something else?" He stands.

Grove shrugs and looks at me. I follow his notion and shake my head casually and add. "Nope. Just wanted to thank you for your loyalty to the team."

Garret nods vigorously and heads for the door.

"Oh Garret," Grove calls, making him turn.

"Got a big game tomorrow. Keep up the great work. You never know who's keeping their eye on you."

Garret's brows twitch and he exits my office.

Grove settles onto the couch and looks up at me. "How long have you known about this?"

"Since the gala."

He nods. "You should have come to me sooner." Then with a shake of his head, he stands. "Well, see you at the game tomorrow. I've got a feeling our luck's about to change."

It's after five when I get home.

Emotionally drained. This whole thing with Garret and finally putting a plan into action should be a relief. But it's anything but.

Garret's a good player. And a good man. Nicole was right. He's likely trying to prove himself. Or under his father's influence to win his affection.

The house lights are off and it's too quiet.

Rover races up to me, whining. I follow him to his bowl. It's empty. That's odd. "I'm sorry, boy. You see the girls?" I ask, filling his water and then checking the taekwondo schedule on the bulletin.

No lessons today. Where are they?

"Nicole? Rory?"

I'm about to head upstairs when my doorbell rings. I answer with a sigh. "Whatever it is, I don't have time for it, Claire. And I thought I made it clear—"

Her expression is too smug to ignore. When my little girl steps out from behind her, I drop to my knees.

"Hey, baby. What's going on, are you okay?"

Rory nods, but sadly.

"Looks like your nanny never made it to pick her up. Gee if only you had someone in your life to warn you about that."

I frown. "Get inside sweetheart and wash your hands."

Claire tries to follow her in and I hold up my hand. "How did you know to pick her up?"

She blinks. "The...school called. You know they still have my number from when Angel attended."

"It doesn't add up."

"Can you at least let me in the house so I'm not freezing my ass off out here? I did just bring your daughter home, you're welcome."

I growl and step back, letting her in. "Don't get comfortable."

I follow her into my living room and try to remember if Nicole mentioned anything about her plans today. Did something happen at her therapy session?

I whip out my phone to call her when the stairs begin to creak with footsteps.

Claire sees her before I do and throws her hands up in the air. "Oh, great. She looks like hell, too. Nice, Royce. Really, you sure know how to pick 'em."

"Shut up, Claire."

But when I see her, my chest tightens with dreadful concern. She really does look like hell. She's in black jeans and a black crop top. There's a shawl around her shoulders as she descends the stairs, watching us with utter confusion. Her hair is down and untamed, like she'd been sleeping. Her eyes wary and the strong scent of ale and something unpleasant reeks from her clothes.

"Where's... Rory?" she croaks.

34

C LAIRE LAUGHS UNCOMICALLY AT my question and turns, her fingers pinching the bridge of her nose—Royce's signature move. "Oh my God," she scoffs.

"What time is it?" I ask in a whisper.

Royce is at my side the minute I reach the bottom step and stumble. He catches me and leads me to the living room at a slow and sturdy pace, holding my forearms. "You can go now, Claire," he mutters sharply.

"Why don't you ask her where she was today," she drills, loudly.

My hand goes to my head the moment he sits me down on the sofa. "Can you please use your inside voice?" I ask, shutting my eyes so I don't see her roll her eyes at me.

"I know where she was today," Royce grits with an edge to his voice. "She *told* me."

"So, you're not going to ask her, then?"

My head is spinning. Why is my head spinning? I feel so tired. I never get like this after I drink. Never.

No.

I'm not drunk. This is something else. Stomach bug?

Holy shit, was I drugged?

Royce smooths a hand over my head. "Hey, don't worry about Rory, okay? It happens. I'm guilty of forgetting to pick up Angel once or twice from school when she was little."

"Four times, but who's counting?" Claire mutters.

"What's going on? Did something happen at your... doctor's?"

My bottom lip trembles and I hear little footsteps enter the room. "Is Nicky alright?"

"Rory, go upstairs." His voice turns sharp, urgent.

I recognize it. He's growing impatient.

He kneels back in front of me. "Nicole, talk to me." But his tone isn't warm. It's not soft. It's demanding.

"She's obviously piss drunk, *look* at her," Claire says in the background.

I manage to look at him and he searches my eyes. I know he sees me. He sees my pain. I'm not afraid of anything. But I'm afraid of whatever is going on through his head.

I'm just too weak to argue right now. If only he'd give me time, I could explain.

"Nicole?" he urges. "You went to see Pamela today, right?"

My heart hurts as I nod. Stupidly nod.

"Is that all? Did you...go anywhere else?"

I don't answer. I just...let him stare at me.

Finally, he gives me a soft smile, strokes the side of my face, and stands to face his ex-wife. "She's not drunk."

"Of, course she is—"

"Not that it's any of your business, but Nicole doesn't drink *beer*. She prefers vodka," he snaps.

Claire laughs diabolically. "Then how do you explain her passing out at Sylvie's earlier this afternoon?"

I turn a hard glare at the woman standing with her arms crossed a few feet from me. *How...could she know that?*

Royce follows my eyes. Waiting for an explanation—from her.

She scoffs and rolls her eyes. "I was concerned for your wellbeing after you banned me from your life, clearly under her influence, so... I had her followed."

"What?" My voice is so strained I'm not even sure she heard me. "You...can't do that."

She raises her voice just to fuck with me. "You're close to people I care about. You spend time with my only daughter. I can do what I damn well please." She turns to Royce. "I have *every* right to want to look into who she associates herself with."

Royce blinks, and tilts his head toward me, his jaw working.

"Go ahead. *Deny* you were there," she shouts and I really wish she would just leave. "By the way, you owe me two grand for the services from this P.I. He came highly recommended."

Royce drags his gaze from me and looks at Claire. "Send me his bill. I'll take care of it right now." His voice is strained, and I know he's hurt. Angry.

She pulls her phone from her pocketbook. "With pleasure."

I scrunch my face, feeling ill again, and shiver.

Royce puts his hand on the back of my head, then lifts my feet. "Lie down," he says softly, helping me on the pillow and securing my shawl over my shoulders.

He walks away from me and picks up his phone from the coffee table.

"The photos are attached," she says in a hushed voice like they're engaged in a private conversation.

I swallow hard.

He murmurs something to his ex-wife that sounds like confirmation and then scans the images. He shakes his head and curses under his breath.

Then puts his phone to his ear.

I can't watch this anymore. I just want this couch to swallow me whole.

What did I do to deserve this?

Oh. Right. I broke a promise.

"David hi, it's me. Listen, I need a quick favor. Yes. I'll hold."

The chief of police?

Claire nods. "Good call, get the police involved. Her arrest is long overdue."

My throat clogs up and I fight to breathe.

His eyes are filled with rage as he waits and I have to close mine just to keep myself from crying out. Begging to let me explain first.

But he doesn't want to hear it. He's done.

"Yes, I'm still here. I'm sorry to call but this is urgent." He glances at his ex. "I need a restraining order against Claire Collins, maiden name Bennet." He pauses. "Yes, my ex-wife. She's been storming into my house uninvited for years now and I just found out she's stalking and harassing my family. Including picking up my daughter from school without my consent."

"What the hell?" she screeches. "You can't be serious."

"Yes, she just handed over the proof, I'll email it as soon as I hang up. Take a look and we'll talk later? I appreciate it, David."

He hangs up and for the first time, he reacts. His voice lethal, as he advances at his ex. "Don't you dare go near Rory again. My next call is to the school for releasing her to you. And for the last time, get *the fuck* out of my house. And if you come around here again or anyone I care about—including Nicole, I will tell Angel what really happened between us. Now *that's* long overdue."

She shakes her head in disbelief. "You're out of your mind."

"Four seconds, Claire."

She storms off and I wince as the door slams. I keep my eyes closed, letting the tears finally fall.

In no time, he's kneeling before me again. "Baby. It's just us now. She'll never come near you again—not if I can help it."

I sniffle. "You shouldn't have done that. I'm not worth it."

Without a word, he lifts me off the couch and brings me upstairs. To his bedroom. There, he lays me on his side of the bed, which is closer to the bathroom, and strips me of my soiled clothes. The next thing I hear is the water running in the tub. A moment later, he's beside me, lifting me into his arms.

"I *forgot* about Rory," I say absently.

"It's okay. She's safe."

Gently, he sets me in the rising warm soapy water and I cry out, jerking my right hand out. My knuckles are bruised and colored with dried blood.

He growls and I wince, looking up at him. "I won."

With a shake of his head, he lowers it back into the water gently. "I'll clean that later. Did you eat anything today?"

He picks up his phone, his eyes still avoiding mine. "I'm ordering you soup. Extra broth. You need fluids."

After ordering, he tells me to stay put while he checks on Rory.

I think I'm going to be sick again. I pull myself up and grab the towel he'd prepared for me. After heaving, I brush my teeth, wrap myself up in his bathrobe, and lie down.

Maybe this is all a dream and I just need to wait to wake up from it.

Sometime later, I'm up again. It's dark outside and the lights are dimmed. There's a bowl of soup beside me and a can of ginger ale.

I reach for the soup and find my hand bandaged up. I rub the covered knuckles.

The broth has cooled, but the salty liquid helps.

I want desperately to see him. To talk to him. The number of times he'd looked me in the eye all evening hurts, because up until I screwed up, he couldn't tear his eyes off me.

His tone has been soft, but I could hear the undertone. It's clipped and distant.

After Rory is asleep, I hear him downstairs. On the phone. *Several* phone calls.

I wonder if any of them are to Nick. *Please come pick up your sister.*

But that doesn't sound like him.

The door creaks open and he steps in, but not too far in. "You're awake. Can I heat up the soup for you?"

I shake my head. "I just had the broth. Thank you. I really needed that."

He keeps his distance and watches me.

I wait for the questions to start. I wait for anything that's not the mundane, just taking care of me, clipped dialogue.

I wait for him to show me how badly I disappointed him today.

"Did you know you were going to Sylvie's when we were texting earlier?"

I nod.

He drags a hand through his hair, then scans me. "You have a stomach bug or something?"

"Royce, I didn't drink. I promise. I didn't."

"And what kind of promise is this, Nicole? Should I believe it the way I did a few weeks ago when you promised not to set foot in that place again?"

"I fell. I was talking to Sylvie and then...I don't know I just fell."

"Are you hurt?"

"A guy named Chuck caught me," I grumble.

He scoffs as if this is just getting better and better. "What was it, Nicole? What set you off this time?"

I pull myself up, feeling strength returning to my bones. "Nothing. No one. Royce, this isn't like last time. I'm done. Yes, it's always a fight but I swear, I have no reason to. I'm happy. You and Rory make me happy. I *love* you."

He doesn't even blink. "So happy that you lied?"

I swallow the pain. "Royce."

"Lie down. We'll straighten this all out tomorrow, okay? You need to sleep off whatever this is."

I nod. "I'll go to my room—"

"You're staying here," he snaps. "I'm just going to lock up downstairs and I'll be up soon."

I wait for him for some time, but he doesn't come.

Finally, I fall asleep on his side of the bed. Next to the bathroom, just in case.

I'm cold when I wake up in the middle of the night.

331

Royce is beside me, but I can't tell if he's asleep. Something feels heavy and I realize there's an extra blanket over me. But it doesn't replace his arms around me because I'm still shivering.

Why didn't I just go to my room? And why the hell did I tell him I love him?

Having slept all day, I'm up way into the night. I wake up warm and find myself flush against his body. My back to his front. His arm around me and the extra blanket pushed aside.

I manage to slip out from under his arms and tiptoe into my bedroom. I pack a few of my things into a duffle bag. Stuffed into one of the pockets is an opaque pink beaded bracelet. Given to me by my first taekwondo instructor. If you think I'm badass, you should have seen Jane.

She gave it to me when I earned my blackbelt, knowing I was still a frightened girl no matter how hard I fought. She told me this bracelet would keep me safe.

I knew it was more of a mind thing. But it's been ten years and I still keep it close.

I slip into Rory's room and set it on her nightstand with a little note, hoping it does the same for her.

I lean in to kiss her cheek softly. "I love you." Smiling, I brush her hair back. "And you don't have to say it back."

I'm sitting in my car in the driveway of Nick's house, waiting for the sun to come up. My phone has rung twice with Royce on the screen and I haven't looked at the texts. I don't need to.

When the text I've been waiting for finally comes through, I swipe to read.

Angel: *Hey hun, got your message. No worries, I'll take Rory to school today. Hope you feel better soon. Xoxo*

I knock on his door, somehow knowing that this is what I needed to do from the start. Instead of hiding behind a man I thought would change my world.

My brother answers almost instantly. "Nicky. You alright? What's going on?" His panic voice is in full force but I don't back down.

"Can I come in?"

"Get in here." He pulls me in from out of the cold. "What happened? Is it Coach? Rory?"

Cora comes down the stairs, wearing sleep shorts and one of my brother's t-shirt's. One look at my face and her smile fades. She presses her lips together and turns to her boyfriend.

Unfortunately, Cora's poker face needs work, so when Nick turns back, he shuts the door and addresses us both. "Someone start talking."

I start from the beginning. Right there in his foyer, I spill my guts about where I ended up the night I left Bridges two months ago. How his coach found me, the lies I've been telling ever since, and then finally...about yesterday.

My tears are spilling out of me. "Look, it's true. I don't remember what happened before I passed out, but I didn't drink. I couldn't have. I care too much about them to risk it all."

"I believe you," Nick says abruptly.

I blink up at him. "You do?" It comes out more of a statement than a question.

"I'll go make you some tea," Cora offers, leaving us alone.

"Of course, I believe you," he breathes softly and that tone is so, so needed right now. I throw my arms around him. "Oh, Nicky. I'm so sorry."

I sob. "I knew you would blame yourself."

He nods, like he totally gets me, and pushes hair away from my face. "You were protecting me."

I roll my eyes. "And...a little scared."

His green eyes flash with regret. "What can I do? Please tell me. I don't want to control your life. It's done nothing but upset you. I just want to help."

"Can I... borrow your girlfriend this morning?"

"Yes." But the response comes from the petite brunette across the hall as she saunters over to me with tea and sets it on the table. "What do you need?"

"Can you take me to the hospital? I want a blood test. I need proof. For myself," I add, so there's no mistake on who I'm doing this for.

I know I'm on my own now.

She exchanges glances with my brother. "Of course."

Nick takes my hand, grabbing my attention. "If they *do* find it in your system, it doesn't change anything. We'll figure out a way that works best for you—not me."

With a kiss on the top of my head and a sweet kiss on Cora's lips, he walks us to the door. "Call me and let me know."

"I will," she assures.

Nick doesn't appear to be home when we return from the hospital and I'm grateful for it.

Cora takes me to the sofa in the den. It's darker here, which is fitting to my mood. The living room gets too much daylight. It's like my bestie can feel exactly what I need right now.

"Can I make you more tea?"

I shake my head.

"Should I...leave you alone?"

I shake my head again and look up at her through my watery eyes. "I didn't drink, Cora. There was zero alcohol in my blood."

"I know...but...you *are* having a baby."

I swallow. It appears that what I went through yesterday were common side effects of early pregnancy. Fatigue, nausea, headache, dizziness, food aversion. And fainting.

It all hit me at once. And not eating makes all the symptoms worse.

"I'm pregnant. There is a difference."

She sits beside me and rubs my back.

I'm overjoyed and I want to believe that it's because I have proof that I didn't drink, that I chose not to when everything in me was screaming to just have one after seeing Kyle.

But the truth I'm going to avoid as long as I can, is that the idea of having his baby fills my heart in a way I never thought possible.

"You're going to tell him, aren't you?"

I shake my head. "Not today."

"Okay, I'm going to be brutally honest, okay?"

I throw an arm up, giving her the floor. "I wouldn't expect anything less for a therapist in training."

"You've been nothing but two-word answers for the past five hours. I'm worried. That means you probably have way more in your head than you can think to make sense of. Or that you're super confused."

I glare at her. "That's literally the same thing."

"Right. Well. I'm here to help. Tell me how you feel about this baby, Nicole."

I nod and consider it *for her sake*. "It makes me feel like I'm nothing but trouble. I upended his life when he found me drunk out of my mind and wanted to take care of me. I made him lie for me. I stressed him out with all my drama when he had enough to worry about. I embarrassed him in front of his ex-wife and now...drumroll please. I'm fucking pregnant."

It's at this moment that my brother decides to walk into the room.

35

"I'm happy. You and Rory make me happy. I love you."
"So happy that you lied?"

It was the worst response in the history of responses when someone confesses their love for you.

I hate that it's what I picture every time I think of her. The steep pain in her eyes. The shattering in her heart.

The same one I feel every time I replay my words.

She's been gone three days, and I haven't slept more than a few hours each night. By now, it's clear that she's not *missing* my calls.

She's ignoring them. And I refuse to show up at her brother's door insisting on seeing her. I won't put that kind of pressure on her.

The only thing giving me some peace now is the restraining order I have on my ex-wife and the guarantee I set in place that she'll never utter another word about Nicole Kane again.

Or she'll lose her daughter.

And I won't feel a tinge of regret.

"Daddy, when is Nicole coming back?" Rory asks as I tie up her hair.

"I don't know, Squigs, but we need to head down soon. I'm going to take you to school this morning and then head to work."

"Can Nicky pick me up?"

I sigh. "Angel will pick you up and bring you to the arena later, okay?"

A look of sadness falls on my little girl's face. And I know what she's thinking. That Nicole isn't coming back.

I drop her backpack and bend on one knee, scooting her over my other one. "Sorry baby. Daddy's had a lot going on this week at work. But I promise you'll see her soon, okay?"

She nods and reaches up to fix her hair. That's when I notice a familiar beaded bracelet on her wrist. One I feel like I've seen before.

"What's this?"

"She left it for me on my lamp table with a piece of paper." She reaches over and hands it to me.

There was a note from her this whole time? My heart sinks as I read it out loud.

I should have been the one to make you feel safe, Nicky. Not a piece of jewelry.

And now she's left with neither.

"How about...we make one that looks just like it for her? So she always feels safe too?"

Rory nods vigorously. "Can we go to the craft store together later? I need a few things."

I laugh. "I'm sure you do."

After a quick huddle with the team in the locker room before tonight's game, I ask Nick to stay while the team warms up on the ice.

He's in full gear and I envy him right now. I wish I could get on the ice, move like I'm unstoppable, get into a fight, serve my time, and then do it all again.

I drag a hand over my face and pull the pills out of my pocket. "Her anxiety meds. You just have to—"

"Yeah, I know the drill, thanks." He takes them from me and moves to his locker.

"Can you tell me if she's alright? Is she *feeling* better?"

He nods into space. His jaw works like there's something he needs to say but he's holding back. "Yeah. She'll be fine."

My chest aches and I lose an internal argument. "Do you know if she...do you know what it was that made her sick?"

He nods. "Yep." He meets my eyes finally and asks, "Can I go now?"

"Yeah. Go get 'em," I say dryly.

I try my luck with another text.

Royce: *Coming to the game tonight? Rory misses you.*

It's not until after first period that I find a message on my phone. From her.

My heart leaps.

Nicole: *I miss her too. I'll catch the next one. Hope she understands.*

I do.

I understand that I did something terribly wrong.

"Where are your friends?" I ask Angel when I find her in my kitchen. I assumed she'd be out celebrating with the team on their win tonight.

It's the third win in a row since Grove had that chat with Garret in my office. But we're still feeling things out in that department. Especially since Hastings mysteriously skipped town again. Which almost confirms our suspicions.

"If you're talking about Cora and Nicole, I don't know. They're avoiding me."

I tread with caution. "Why do you think that?"

My daughter turns a hard glare at me.

I sigh. It's been a long week. "Angel, can we talk about this another time?"

She pushes up from the counter chair. "Why doesn't anyone want to tell me what happened? My best friend is avoiding me. I cheered her on to go after what she wants"—she motions to me—"and now she can barely look at me."

"I'm sorry, Angel."

She shakes her head. "Will you at least tell me what happened with Mom? Is it true you put a restraining order on her?"

This one, I can't avoid. "She crossed some lines."

"You sure have a way with women," she mutters.

I lean against the back wall of my kitchen and watch my daughter. Hating that it's my fault she's feeling left out.

And in the dark.

I move to stand across from her on the island and rest on my elbows. "We had a fight and... now she's not taking my calls."

"Obviously." She pouts stubbornly. "What did you do?"

"Based on your rule of need-to-know only..." I sigh. "I think...I got mad at the wrong person."

She sucks her teeth. "You and your stupid complex with lies."

This girl knows me so well.

"It's not a complex. And it isn't a lot to ask."

We're both quiet for a moment and Angel twiddles her thumbs. "You know...when Cora wasn't answering Nick's calls, he sat outside her door every night for a week and poured his cold little heart out."

I scratch my chin. "I guess I could do that...but someone's going to have to pick me up."

She laughs. "You're not *that* old."

"Thanks." I shake my head, relieved to see her smiling at me again.

"Ugh. Fine. I'll just keep badgering Nicole until she comes out of her shell again."

My gut twists because I'm the one who put her there.

She grabs her car keys off the counter. "Need help with Rory this weekend?

"I suppose it wouldn't hurt if you stopped by on Sunday. We've got a game Monday so I might schedule a late practice."

"Noticed you're out of chocolates," she points out. Since I usually bribe her with expensive treats even her boyfriend couldn't find.

"I'll get you a box. I'm due for another shipment."

"Then you've got a deal. See you Sunday."

I walk her out and head upstairs.

As usual, my stomach sinks when I walk into my bedroom. Because I still see her in it.

Waiting for me the way she was that last night she was here. Shivering because I was so heartless.

I don't know what the fuck came over me. All I know is that the moment I saw those photos of her, I was outraged. I couldn't see straight. I couldn't think.

I thought I was angry with *her*.

But I'm the only one to blame for her being followed.

It's three days before I hear from her again. I've been good and given her space. She doesn't need the guilt of not answering my calls.

And it pays off.

Nicole: *Will she be at the game tonight?*

Royce: *Yes. And she has a gift for you.*

36

Tears. I drove her to tears. Can I not do anything right?

I let my best friend embrace me for as long as she needs to after I finally open up to her about everything. Everything *except* the pregnancy.

That one just needs to wait.

And she's taking it...well, as expected...with tears. Lots of them.

"I'm sorry, Angel."

"I'm not mad at you." She sobs. "I feel responsible."

I rub her back. "Oh honey, you know no one is to blame but my brother."

She coughs a laugh. "You have a point."

We're standing a few yards away from Coach's office by the locker room before tonight's game. I told him I'd be here tonight, and he'd arranged for me to sit with Angel and Rory.

But there was no pressure in coming to see him. He's been painfully sweet, giving me space.

She follows my gaze to his office door. "Yeah, he's in there."

I bite my lip.

Angel perks with interest. "Would you mind...grabbing Rory for me? She's in there getting her popcorn."

I start to hesitate but she gives me a little push. "Just go." Then she catches my arm. "But, whatever happens...I don't want it to affect us. I want to be part of your life always—no matter what."

My shoulders relax. "Oh, sweetie. Being friends with me is like being in the mob. There's only one way out..."

"You're going to beat me up?"

"No. Death."

She scrunches her nose. "I forget how dark you are."

I'm wearing black leggings and a Blades jersey tonight. The one with Nick's number and the Kane name on the back. Not *his*.

I knock on the door and inhale sharply.

My heart lurches when I hear a sharp, "What is it?"

I push the door lightly and step in. Coach's hard features soften instantly, and he freezes mid-stride. By the looks of it, he'd been pacing his office.

He looks amazing. Sharp suit, gleaming blue eyes, and a heart-melting grin that spreads at the sight of me.

"Nicole!" Rory races up to me dropping several bags of caramel popcorn.

"Hi, sweetie." I embrace her, fighting tears. "You look so pretty." I smooth her hair and stand. "Come on, Angel is right outside. I think we're interrupting," I add in a whisper.

"You're not," Royce blurts. "Perry, we'll catch up later. Would you mind taking Rory outside to her sister?"

That's when I notice the tall thin pretty-looking boy seated with a notepad at the desk. He nods dutifully and stands.

"Are...are you Nicole Kane?"

"Um...yes."

He huffs out an excited breath. "Is it true you can do a jumping sidekick, like they do in movies?"

I laugh. "No. It's just a sidekick. I don't jump for anyone."

Rory picks up the last of the popcorn bags and hands them to Perry.

"Wait, Nicky, we have a present for you." She lifts her sleeve revealing two beaded bracelets. The light pink one I gave her. And another one.

She pulls the bright yellow one off her hand and stretches it over mine. "Daddy and I made this one. So you could always feel safe too."

I feel him watching me as I run a finger over it. "It's so pretty. Thank you." I hug her once more since I don't know when I'll get to do this again.

"Can we be bracelet buddies?"

"I'm not supposed to make promises anymore, but I promise we're buddies forever," I whisper.

Rory smiles back at me. "I know. Will you come spend Christmas with us?"

I shake my head. "I don't think so, sweetheart. I'm moving back to my apartment in a few days and might need some time to settle in."

Rory looks at her father as if he might have told her something different. Poor thing must have so many questions.

I turn her back to me. "But I'll come hang out with you soon." Then I hold up my bracelet, clinking it with hers.

She wraps her arms around me. "I love you."

I choke. My words are caught in my throat, but thankfully, she doesn't wait for it before she skips to the door.

"Come on, Perry. I can do the sidekick too. I'll show you outside."

Perry takes her hand and waves to us before shutting the door, leaving us alone.

It *smells* like him in here and I realize how much I miss it.

With my arms wrapped around myself, I step further into this space he calls his office. It looks more like a living room. I stop somewhere between the sofa and coffee table.

"I know the feeling," he says, coming up behind me. "You're so caught off guard that you can't tell her you feel the same."

I don't turn around. I swipe at a tear that falls loose. "She knows I do."

"Does she?"

I turn abruptly, in a 'can we get this over with' manner. "I'm sorry I lied to yo—"

"I forgive you," he responds just as rushed—for my sake. Then grins as he inches closer. "That part's easy." He takes my shaky hands and settles me on the sofa. "What happened?"

I focus on his fingers around mine. "Pamela told me that I needed closure with people who were toxic in my life if I wanted to move on and let go." I lift my eyes to his. "And I really wanted to...so *we* could have a chance. I started with Sylvie. I knew you wouldn't—"

"But you didn't drink there," he says so matter of factly.

I shake my head.

"Then what *happened*? What was that?"

The words come out in a whisper. "I'm pregnant."

Just like I expected, his features fall, and he drops my hands.

"That's why I was so sick."

I can see the wheels in his head turning as he blinks and stands.

"It's why I couldn't eat, why I was so emotional and tired."

He kneels in front of me again, touching me as if checking for broken bones. "But...you were in a fight. You fell."

"Everything is fine." I can't help my smile and he beams with a sigh of relief. I swallow. "I umm...basically turned Hulk on a guy named Kyle Johnson. He was one of—" I pause when I see him pale. "What is it?"

"I know who he is. A few weeks ago...I found out he was a regular there. It's why I asked you to stay away." He sighs. "I should have told you."

I smile and rub my knuckles, which have faint scars now. "I'm glad you didn't."

He shakes his head and stands again. I see him planning. I see him working out a way to do the right thing by me and I can't have that. I won't make a mockery out of him in this town. The minute Claire finds out, she'll ruin us. I'm already done for. But he is still respected and admired.

They consider him a legend. And me, a legendary loser.

"I still need some time," I whisper.

He drops again. "What? Nicky. Honey, I'm not letting you go again. I *love* you. You know that."

I nod and my tears fall. "I think I do. But it's all so overwhelming. I need more time to process." It's another lie, but a necessary one. Because I need to give *him* time to think. And he'll never admit to needing it.

His jaw works and he stands. "I promised myself I'd never pressure you to do anything." He runs a hand down his face. "I guess that has to include this."

It's my first week back in my apartment and between the Christmas carols I've been blasting, the presents I've been wrapping and meals for one I've been prepping, there's very little room for loneliness and regret.

It's been ten days since I was in his office. Asking him for more time. But truthfully, I've always known what I want.

I'm just waiting for him. For him to prove that I'm not an obligation at this point. But the woman he's madly in love with and can't live without.

He's been paying me weekly regardless of my walking out on the job. I texted him to stop but he's ignored it.

Well, that one.

We do still text once or twice a day. Usually, it's a picture of Rory or the dog. And I'll text him a picture of my tea, muffin, and blueberries in the morning since he's worried about my diet.

I realized the baby doesn't like coffee. It's why it tasted so off to me when I made it that Monday I went to see Sylvie.

Nick and Cora drop by at least once a day but I'm refusing my anxiety meds until I check with my doctor. Something *else* I've been avoiding since I found out.

Dropping my shopping bags, I remove my hat, scarf, and coat and wonder if Rory is staying warm enough with the weather growing brutally cold.

I turn on the oven and dig out the recipe book for the winter bisque I'm making tonight. When my doorbell rings, I glance at the clock.

Yep. Right on time.

I pull the door open, finding a beautiful flower arrangement. "Oh, what are these?" I ask the young man, stepping back to let him in.

"Gardenia's," he says as he sets them on my counter. Then looks at all the other flower arrangements I have spread around my living room. "Are...you getting married or something?"

I laugh. "No. Why?"

"Usually when we send different flower arrangements on a daily basis, it's when bride-to-be's are trying to decide the perfect flower for their wedding."

"Something like that. Someone is just trying to help me figure out what my favorite flower scent is."

He nods awkwardly but doesn't question it.

I offer a quick thanks and tip him. It's his fifth time delivering flowers to me and he's already told me the delivery includes a generous tip, but I refuse to let him leave without one from me.

I'm so tempted to read this note tucked inside. What he'll tell me this time, how these flowers compare to me, but my stomach is growling so...I opt for delayed gratification and start my soup instead.

Nicky,

What about these? The gardenia has a sweet, heady scent. It's stimulating with a somewhat tangy aroma. It's an intoxicating flower... I think we have a winner.

Love always,

Royce

I inhale the aromatic flower arrangement. They really are lovely and smell amazing. But still not quite drawn to it.

I find a spot for them and stand in the center of my living room, which is looking more like the Botanical Gardens every day.

Sitting on my couch, I reach for the box of chocolates he sent along with my first delivery and let one melt in my mouth.

I shouldn't read them all again. It doesn't help me think straight. It only makes me fall more in love with him.

But I'm my own boss now and I say, fuck it.

In no particular order, I pluck at one of the notes.

Nicky,

Red roses. A classic. I'm not a fan because of it's popularity. It's cliché and to be quite honest, not the most exotic smell. Which means, it's probably not meant for you. Why did I send them then? It's considered a timeless flower, with a soft and smooth texture. So yeah, it reminds me of you. But you're too unique for this to be your favorite scent.

Let's keep looking.

Love always,
Royce

Nicky,

These remind me of the night we claimed each other to the world. Okay, maybe it was just to a handful of people at the gala and some cocktail servers in that back hallway. But I loved the smell of lilac on you. It's sweet, powdery, delicate, yet quite distinct. There's no mistaking it.

They may not be your favorite, but maybe it will remind you how deeply I've fallen under your spell and nothing you can ever do will change that.

Love always,
Royce

The other day, I sent Angel over to the house with Rory's Christmas presents. It's just a few days away and I want her as excited as a six-year-old should be.

It's been three days since my last bouquet and my heart sinks at the idea he might be giving up.

Especially after my last message. I probably sounded so ungrateful.

Nicole: *They're all beautiful. And smell incredible. But not quite for me.*

At exactly eight p.m. my doorbell rings. My heart leaps. It's another delivery. It has to be. Maybe he was just waiting until the aroma in my apartment subsided before sending more.

But it's not Josh the delivery boy.

It's Royce standing on the other side of the door.

His beard has grown in a bit...more salt than pepper. His eyes are warm but tired. His expression—full of hope.

He's holding another gift for me but not a flower arrangement. It's a basket with an assortment of green and white boxes and a mistletoe stuffed in the middle.

He stretches it out for me. "What about these?"

I reach out and lift the bar of soap and it smells... *like him*. That cedar and earthy musk with a hint of sage.

My eyes water. "Yes," I breathe. "This is it." I push my door open for him.

He steps in and sets down the basket of soaps and lotions. I hold my breath as he releases his and removes his shoes and jacket, then steps into my living room. His hair is wet from the snow. His cheeks flushed. His eyes as blue as ever.

His voice is rough when he speaks. "I was never angry with you. I was angry, yes, but..." His jaw tightens. "It was at Claire for violating your privacy. At myself for driving her to it. The idea that you were *followed* and fucking photographed all because"—he swallows—"because of the threat I made at the gala...about Angel." He closes the distance and takes my hands. "I *put* you in that situation and I'm so sorry for taking it out on you. You didn't need soup—you needed me, you needed reassurance. Deep down I knew that and I denied you of it."

I release a breath that feels weeks old. It's everything I didn't know I needed to hear. *Except*... I scrunch my nose. "I did need that soup."

"I know you needed the soup, but I rehearsed it *with* the soup, and not saying it would have thrown me off."

I huddle over in laughter and look back at him with tears. "You rehearsed for me?"

"And I'd do it again in a heartbeat." He chuckles.

I shrug coyly. "I never thanked you for standing up for me."

"You never have to." He strokes my cheek. "My loyalty and trust will always be with you. I love you, Nicole." He kneels in front of me, wrapping his arms around my waist. "Have this baby with me. Let me be your husband and give you the life you were always meant to have."

My eyes blink fast and burn with tears.

I exhale a whimper and fall into his arms, lifting my chin, and letting his mouth find mine. He lifts my shirt and pulls it over my head. "I want you, Nicole. An eternity with you."

"Show me. *Please* show me how much you want me."

He doesn't need to be asked twice. Lifting me, he carries me to the sofa that's already covered in blankets I've been using to stay warm.

He strips for me. Not slowly, but also not fast enough. He's *so* sexy.

I unhook my bra and push off my panties, growing impatient for him. His hungry eyes scan me. "You didn't wait for me."

"And I won't wait for you for the rest of it either if you don't get on top of me."

I yelp as he lifts me and straddles me on top of him. He pulls me into an all-consuming kiss as he lifts my hips and lowers me onto his cock.

I gasp as I settle and then moan. He grabs my face and looks into my eyes as we rock in a slow rhythm. "Marry me, Nicky. Marry me." He brings my forehead to his as I grind against him, practically shaking from the intensity.

I'm already so close but I can't say a word. It all just comes out as a moan.

"Don't come yet." He brings his hands between us and holds up a radiant yellow diamond ring.

I gasp at it's beauty. Before I can scream my answer, he rubs his thumb over my clit. "Now," he rasps.

"Yes. Yes, I'll marry you," I scream out, coming hard, gripping his shoulders, and kissing him hard as he groans and jerks through his orgasm, emptying inside me. "I love you," I whisper against the side of his face.

Breathlessly, he slips the ring on my finger. "I love you more. No one. I mean no one, will ever hurt you again. You're mine to protect, defend, love, cherish and"—he spreads his palms over my stomach—"be timeless with. I will love you both *unconditionally*. Lie to me, don't lie to me, I don't care. Just don't ever fucking leave me again."

I shake my head. "I won't. I'm yours. Timelessly yours."

EPILOGUE

(6 months later)

"WHERE ARE YOU TAKING me?" my wife asks with a groan.

I married her on New Year's Eve, mere days after we claimed our eternal love and commitment to each other. We gathered the people closest to us; my daughters, her brother, Cora, Jace, and Bruce. And checked into a luxury bed and breakfast for the long weekend, where we rang in the new year just after saying our vows.

"It's a surprise."

"Royce. It's a thousand degrees out. My ankles are swollen, I'm enormous. And we passed the ice cream shop three blocks ago."

"Yeah. I had a feeling you thought we were going there when you paused in front of it."

She pauses again. This time dropping my hand. "Are you making fun of me?"

"No. Last time I did that, I almost lost a finger." I check the time and sigh. Wishing I could text Angel that we're running late. But Nicky is already suspicious. Trying to get one over on her has proven to be quite the impossible undertaking. "Look, I promise we'll get ice cream today."

"Two scoops," she grumbles, walking ahead of me.

I huff out a breath and catch up. Relieved that we're almost there.

Nicole stops, scrunching her face as she looks up at the corner storefront. The *newly renovated* storefront. "Didn't this used to be a sandwich shop? I wonder what's here now."

I step up behind her and pull on one of the glass doors. "Why don't we find out?"

Stepping in, she scans the small, brightly lit lobby. The floors are glossy white tile with a narrow red carpet that leads to a dark hall. There's a welcome desk with no one behind it at the moment. But the stock photo images, flyers, and even some shadow-boxed souvenirs are already on display across the shelves and walls.

She gasps. "No way. They opened up a new dojo in town, honey."

"Hmm."

"You think anyone is here? It looks pretty closed."

I peek down the hallway. "Let's go find out." I lead her along the carpet.

"It's so dark, I don't think we should be going in there," she whispers.

"Who's stopping us?"

"I didn't dodge six arrests in my adult life just to be brought up on trespassing charges *now*. And eight months pregnant, no less."

I grunt just to keep myself from laughing. "Pipe down. Let me see if I can find a light."

I flick the lights on exposing the full expanse of the floor. It's padded in two tones. The back wall is fully mirrored and it's nearly twice as big as the one downtown.

"This place is amazing. Why isn't anyone here?"

"It's not open yet," I say, letting her pass me so I can watch her take it all in.

"Who owns it?"

I catch her hand and twist her to the wall along the hallway we entered. I point up to a framed photograph of her and Rory in uniform. One I snapped of them when Nicole was teaching my little girl the basics of self-defense.

I bend to her ear. "*You* are now the proud owner of *Rise Above Martial Arts*."

Her lips part before she turns to meet my eyes. "What?"

I take her hands. "I knew this is what you were meant for the moment you told me that every young woman deserves the knowledge of basic self-defense. When I noticed that you didn't keep going back to your karate classes just to brush up your skills. But to help others master it just in case...they were there for similar reasons you were."

"This place...is *ours*?"

I exhale a laugh. "Mostly yours but yes, it's ours."

She steps onto the mat and takes in the space. Her voice cracking when she speaks. "I don't know what to say."

I follow, sliding my hands in my pockets. "Say you love it."

Her face lights but she shakes her head, eyes wandering just to take it all in again. "You get me."

I nod. "I get you. And I love everything that makes you who you are."

She breathes in the space, then her eyes focus on something resting on one of the benches. "What's that?"

I follow her gaze and curse to myself. Looks like the girls forgot to grab it when they were setting up. Either that or Angel left it here on purpose because she knows her best friend.

"That...is a gift from Rory. She's supposed to give you that. I'm not sure why it's here."

"Oh." she pouts. She's been doing that a lot lately because she knows what it does to me.

"Buuut... I suppose if you could pretend to be surprised when she gives it to you..."

"Totally. I'll be the picture of pure shock."

I chuckle and take her to it, sitting with her as she places the red box on her lap and opens it.

There's a gentle frown at first and then a small smile. "Beaded bracelets?" She snakes her fingers through a bunch of pastel-colored bracelets. "There must be a hundred in here...what are they—" Bright, misty green eyes turn up at me.

"Fearless bracelets," I say, quoting my six-year-old daughter. "For everyone who joins on their first day."

She shuts the box, sets it aside, and whispers, "I love that girl." The she swipes at a few loose tears and stands, barely.

I help her up the rest of the way and take her hands. "This isn't all of it. There's a party room too. You know, for birthdays and sponsorship events."

"Sponsorship?"

I swipe my thumb along her jaw, knowing how important this is to her considering where she came from. "Sponsorships that will go toward children in the neighborhood who can't afford it."

She blinks as tears stream down her cheeks and reaches for me. "Are you trying to make me go into early labor?"

I hold her, rethinking taking her into the party room next. Where several of our friends, family, team members, and neighborhood store owners are waiting to yell surprise.

She gasps and pulls away.

"Yeah, I felt that." I chuckle, putting a hand on her round belly.

"He's hungry for ice cream."

I raise a brow. "Is he now?"

She looks up at me. "As much as I want it to be a boy, I'm going to enjoy laughing in your face if this is another girl."

For the fun of it, Nicky and I decided to not find out the baby's sex. And I've been regretting the decision ever since.

"Are you kidding? The amount of testosterone between you and me—it's definitely a boy."

The End.

Thank You

I hope you enjoyed Coach and Nicole's story
as much as I enjoyed writing them.
Please consider leaving a review. I read each and every one!

**Sign up for my newsletter to be notified about upcoming releases
and bonus epilogues**

Blades of Heart is a series of three forbidden love stories and can be read
in any order. If you're starting with this one, flip to the end for an excerpt
from Becoming Mine (Nick and Cora's story)

Books By

ROXANNE Tully

ROMANCE AUTHOR

The Roommate Deal
A fake relationship hockey romance
The Better Bully
An enemies to lovers college football romance
Sporting Goods
A single-parent hockey romance
Wrong Twin
A mistaken identity hockey romance
Mistaken
A mistaken identity billionaire romance

Connect With ROXANNE Tully
ROMANCE AUTHOR

ROXANNE GREW UP IN New York City, where she studied play and screen writing. From an early age, she loved storytelling and knew she wanted to be a writer. While her genre was never limited, she now enjoys writing billionaire and sports romance, creating strong realistic heroines and swoony alpha heroes.

Website: https://www.roxannetully.com
Newsletter: https://geni.us/rtnewsletter

Excerpt

Chapter 1
Nicolas

"What's with the pink hair, Cor? You got an audition for Jem and the Holograms or somethin'?" My best friend and teammate, Jace asks his kid sister Cora, when she breezes into the kitchen.

There's no other way to describe the way she flies in here when the two of us are working.

Okay, maybe working is the wrong word for athletes. More like planning, plotting, eating, and drinking enough Gatorade for the entire league.

Jace is my alternate Captain for the Buffalo Blades and one of the very few people in this world I trust. He's been my best friend since we met in junior hockey league when we were sixteen. And now, he's our most valuable player in the national league. I'm here quite often...and not just for the fridge he's always got well stocked, but because it's easier for me to drive the five minutes over than for him to leave his kid sister and meet me at the rink.

Before we each got our own place, Jace and I lived together—and when Cora turned eighteen and wanted to live on campus, Jace overruled that idea as soon as it presented itself. Laying out all the dangers of living on campus for a girl as "fragile" as Cora.

He'd never say that to her face, because if there's one thing in the world that scares Jace Knight, it's upsetting the five-foot brunette he'd been helping his father raise since their mother passed away.

But he had no problem pacing around our old living room telling me there was no way she was living alone. Or with a roommate that would potentially be toxic to her health, both physical and mental.

The sneaky result? We ended up agreeing it was time to be grownups and each bought our own house in a new gated community development. So Cora can "leave home" and live independently...in her big brother's new house...under his ever-so-subtle watch.

The convertible he got her might have sweetened the deal and Cora moved in the summer before her freshman year.

My place is merely a five-minute drive further down the road. I sprung for the lake house, while Jace—who's secretly afraid of reptiles—chose the street view.

But it's always easy to stop in—especially in the early mornings—to run through strategies and drills for the team before practice or a game.

We work best as a duo—it's why I recommended him as my alternate.

"It's a streak. Don't get your panties in a bunch over it," the now *almost* twenty-year-old in the room bites out.

I don't know why I remind myself of her age every time I see her or think about how long I've known her or become creepily lost in her presence.

"Is it the end of the month already?" he says with genuine curiosity.

I press my lips together but a part of me is instantly offended on her behalf. I expect her to turn pink as she would, but she deadpans him instead.

"And this is your only warning for the next three days." She grabs a bagel and heads for the back door.

"I can handle you any day of the month," he calls after her.

With astonishingly good aim, Cora turns and tosses the bagel at him. And the six-foot-four pro hockey player with bulging biceps winces as he rubs his shoulder.

I shoot him a look and he shrugs defensively. "Bagels are stale."

"Maybe you do have your panties in a bunch. Lay off the girl," I say casually, in what's become my continuous effort to get him off her back.

"Dude, I can't with her lately. She's testing me."

"She's also past the age of being your responsibility."

Jace runs a frustrated hand through his hair, and I know exactly what he's feeling. His next words confirm it. "She'll always be my responsibility."

I want to explain the logistics of how wrong he is. But when my twin sister Nicole comes to mind, my twenty-seven-year-old adult sister, who I will never stop looking out for, I bite my tongue.

But not for reasons that we both are protective over Cora—who lost a mother at a young age and needed to be looked after like no one else given her traumatic loss. Nicole's situation was different. Nicole unfortunately, inherited our mother's addiction gene. So there's no way I'd ever tell another brother that he's being too protective of his sister.

I'd give my life for mine. Heck, probably for both of them.

"Ready to head for practice?" he asks, eager to get his gear on and hit the ice.

"Yep."

Chapter 2

Cora

Jace: *Be home by sundown.*
Cora: *Why? Are we suddenly holding sabbath?*
Jace: *No reason to be out later.*
Cora: *I'll find one.*

"Where's your school spirit?" my friend Ava asks when she finds me stretching in the aerobics room in the Fitzgerald Gymnasium on campus. I'm not in uniform but I'm wearing leggings and a tank top and it will have to do.

I hate all sporting activities—unlike my brother, who's built for sports, waking up at the crack of dawn every morning and running. Why would anyone ever willingly run?

"I was too busy studying for my real classes," I say but it's not true. I left my gym bag by the door when I raced out this morning, feeling like a fool for trying something different. I push the artificial color strands behind my ear, self-consciously.

"It'd be a shame to lose that straight A average because you were too prissy to wear your uniform today," she points out.

"I left it at home with my reason for caring."

She leans in. "Is it the end of the month again?"

"The fuck is up with people?" I mutter as I stretch.

"Seriously you're usually the first in uniform, ten minutes early to class. What's going on?"

"Jace pissed me off today."

Ava tosses her duffle bag down and sits beside me. She pulls her bleach-blonde hair up in a ponytail and stretches her freakishly long legs out in front of her. "What else is new?"

"I hate how he treats me like a child. Especially when—"

"When what?"

I sigh, knowing there's no sense in hiding this little fact from the few friends I have. "When Nicholas is around."

"Ugh, you know you're the only girl I know who hangs around hot hockey players all day and is constantly miserable."

"One of them is my brother and the other...might as well be." I try not to sound melancholic when I admit this.

"Well, you're in your last year of school, you've got an awesome ride, and you're killing it at your internship at Tales for Tots, which is basically your dream job."

She's right. I've been interning since the summer at Tales for Tots which is a mental health center where children in foster homes come for counseling where needed. Not your everyday dream job, I know, but my major is adolescent therapy, and talking to these children every day and feeling like I'm a part of what's healing them and making them feel normal has been good for me. As an intern, I don't do much. I talk casually to kids in between their therapy sessions, play with little kids as they wait to be picked up, and occasionally do some light paperwork. It's not paid, of course, but it's a big step in my long-term career goals.

My mentor, Julia, has mentioned my sitting in on some sessions in the coming weeks, but just for observation, but there's a lot that goes into something like that apparently, including confidentiality, so I'm not holding my breath.

"So, what's with the streak, anyway?"

I shrug. "Trying something new. Maybe I wanted to piss off Jace."

"Just ignore him. I bet once you turn the big two-o, he'll back off. Then you can take that ridiculous color off your hair to prove a point."

"Don't count on it. If he treats me like an eight-year-old now, he won't suddenly realize I'm old enough to drink and have babies."

"Hope you don't plan on that in one night." Ava winces.

"Who's having babies?" Angel asks, jogging up to us in her perfect, toned, gorgeous body. Her dark blonde hair in a tight ponytail and her smile as bright as ever.

"No one," I answer promptly. I generally avoid talking about my brother with Angel since the two of them have been having a war for years and it's inexplicable. My luck, she'll use whatever I say against him on their next brawl. She's clever and sassy like that.

The two should just fuck and get it over with.

I smirk to myself as I picture Jace and Nicholas hearing my foul mouth. Then shiver at the thought. Angel could do way better.

"Yeah," Ava chimes in, ever in tune with my abruptness. "Cause Cora couldn't get a guy past Jace or his other half if her life depended on it."

It is gut-twistingly true. If Jace is distracted or otherwise unavailable, Nick is there to pick up the slack. It never fails when it comes to the subject of keeping me in a bubble—out of trouble, home by curfew, and as far away from anything with a penis as possible.

My existence isn't embarrassing enough that my crush of almost ten years is my part-time babysitter.

Angel nods with an understanding smirk. She scans me head to toe and I remember why she's here. She's the new gymnastics and yoga teacher at North Buffalo State.

And I'm unprepared for her class.

I look up at her. She's the first person all day I give a smile to. It's a sheepish smile, but it works. She smirks back at me and holds out a hand for me to stand.

I feel bad for Angel. Last year, at only twenty-four, she had an accident on the ice and hasn't gone back on since. She was an amazing figure skater with a part-time job as an ice girl cheerleader for the Buffalo Blades. Until she had a bad fall during a figure skating competition that ended it all for her.

No one knows if the ice burns on her calves healed, since she wears leg warmers all year round now.

With her 'never look back' attitude in full gear, she's here in the gym with a permanent smile on her face, working toward what she calls her 'new dream'.

"Where's the uniform, Cora?" she asks in spite of our little exchange.

"It needs to be washed." My response is dry and unconvincing. I wouldn't believe me.

She nods then leans in. "Do you need a medical excuse today?"

I grunt. "I don't have my period. Okay?"

She jerks. "You do now. Sit on the bench." She lowers her voice. "You can't work out in that, and I don't want you getting an incomplete for today's class."

No uniform is an automatic incomplete for class so I know she's helping me out with the 'medical excuse'.

"Sorry, Angel."

"All good. Hey, I'm not a stickler like my dad. The grump would use any excuse to bark at his team."

Did I mention Angel's dad, who's hot as hell for an older man, is head coach for the Buffalo Blades? Single too. Angel's mother is still around; sweet as honey, but according to Jace and Nick; Coach Collins and his ex-wife clashed like wild wolves when they were together.

She's had a rough year, but I've somewhat envied Angel for having two amazing parents—and no interfering older brother.

"Thanks. I'll have it for next class."

She winks. "Thanks, kid. Don't make me look bad around here, alright."

Kid? I frown and shake my head as I take a seat on the bench.

Do I have it written on my face?

Chapter 3
Nicolas

I put the car in park and take a deep breath, calming myself down before I blow a fucking fuse.

My sister Nicole has seen my temper lost more than either of us can count and is likely expecting one today.

But I'm different now. I have to be. For her.

Don't want to set a bad example, do we Nick?

Nicole is being released from rehab today. A place I was forced to send her months ago when she finally hit rock bottom in her addiction and my interventions and trying to care for her myself weren't enough. I knew it was time—and probably overdue—when she willingly agreed while crying in my arms that night I found her on the floor in her apartment.

In my opinion, ninety days wasn't enough. Or maybe, for her, it was too long.

Hell if I know what to expect from my twin these days. She could be a whole new person or she could be as big a cynic as me that this shit even works for people.

My chest aches. God, I hope she's alright.

I hope she doesn't hate me.

I watch the revolving doors from the inside of my car. I would have parked and gone inside if I thought I had a shot in hell of not being recognized. But neither Nicky nor I need that kind of spotlight right now. I can see the headline now;

NHL Buffalo Blades Center Picks Up Twin from Rehab.

It's her long dark hair I notice first when she emerges from the side door. Then her long legs that were a dead giveaway that I am looking at my twin. She's not as tall as me but noticeably taller than most of her friends.

I zero in on her eyes.

Is she okay?

She spots the big black jeep in the circular driveway.

Like me, she takes a deep breath before taking long strides toward the passenger side with her duffle bag.

That's all you need at this place. An average size duffle bag. No overstuffed suitcases with various outfits and shoes. No accessories. In fact, I remember being sent home with half the stuff I dropped her off with.

She flips her hair behind her shoulder and tosses her bag in the back seat before jumping in. "Thanks for the help, douche."

"You got this, Nicky."

"Yeah, I don't go by that anymore." She buckles her seatbelt.

"Oh sorry, *Nicole*," I stretch out.

"No. It's BadassBabe83."

I crack a laugh. "Can I call you BB-8 for short?" I joke, since Nicole's the only other Star Wars junkie I know.

Perhaps that's the wrong word to use right now.

"No. That's taken." She moves her seat all the way back and settles in comfortably. Once we leave the hospital grounds and get on the highway, she lowers her window and closes her eyes, breathing in the fall air.

I turn back to the road with a grin.

She's going to be fine.

"Have you thought about what you want to do?"

"Not now, Nick. I literally just got in the car."

"You knew you were leaving for two weeks now, you haven't thought about what you're going to do?"

"Not all of us have an athletic talent people pay a lot of money for," she says bitterly. But my sister has always been the only one cheering me on our whole life. Through injuries, through despair. We take turns being the "older" sibling for each other.

I don't mention her bartending as an option. That's not exactly a skill I want her going back to right now. I wrack my brain thinking of anything else Nicole might be good at. In college, she studied photography but it isn't the kind of thing that I could throw her back into.

"We'll figure something out, Nicky." My tone is casual, the way it has to be with her. But I hope she hears the promise.

On the drive home, I sneak glances at her every chance I get and hope she doesn't notice. There's no denying she seems calmer, more at peace, and ready for help.

My sister is a phenomenal liar. But she's also a fighter and I see that commitment brewing in her.

I convince myself I'm not imagining it. That I do in fact see that she's ready for this. That she'll make the right decisions if opportunities present themselves. That she'll stay away from toxic friends. And if not for herself, that she'll realize she's all I have in this world and will do it for me.

I just hope I'm enough.

We pull up to my driveway twenty minutes later. I jump out of the car and come around to open her door, but she's already stepped out and lunging herself at me. I catch her without missing a beat.

"Nicky," I whisper into her hair.

She tries to hold back but I feel the slight tremble and sob she releases, and I pull her tighter. "I'm so happy to see you."

The physical affection she's showing is new for her, but not surprising. I was told by her therapist to expect mixed emotions for a few days, maybe weeks.

"I'm good. I'm good." She pulls back and wipes her eyes, avoiding mine and eyeing the perimeters of my house instead. "Jeez, a three-car garage? What on earth for? You'll never drive anything but this stupid old Jeep."

"Let's go inside." I bought this house three years ago. Nicky's only been away for a few months. I don't bother telling her she's been here but was likely too high or wasted to notice anything.

I lead her through the double door entrance. My dog Max jumps at her immediately and she laughs, bending to scratch him in all his favorite places.

"Can I make you something to eat?" I offer, heading toward the fridge.

"No, I'm not hungry. I need to call my friends."

I turn and glare at her.

"Not *those* friends. My old friends. The ones...I guess the ones I've let down, who think I've dropped off the face of the earth."

"I have your room all ready upstairs. You're staying with me for a while."

I wait for her to argue. To tell me she can take care of herself and that I need to stop treating her like a child.

I'm mentally prepared for a fight.

To my surprise, she doesn't argue. She shrugs and settles into my couch like it's home. "It's just as well. I'm pretty sure my landlord changed the locks and donated all my stuff to Goodwill."

I cross my arms in front of me and lean against the wall, debating on telling her this. But I can't have her thinking she's lost everything. "Nicole, I've been paying your rent and utility bills. All your stuff is intact. I promise."

"My plants?"

"Dead."

"My cat?"

"You don't have a cat."

"Bubbles is gone too?" She feigns a sob and I can't help but chuckle, moving to sit next to her. Max jumps between us and rests his head on my lap.

"Glad you still have your sense of humor."

There is a glimmer in her eyes, and I can't tell if it's gratefulness...or just exhaustion.

But it's gone before I can figure it out. "Thanks Nick. Forgot you're loaded. You didn't have to do that."

"I'm not mom. Not trying to teach you a lesson on life the hard way by letting you lose the little you have left."

She shudders and her eyes turn dark. "You hear from her?"

"No. And we're not going to." I go to the kitchen counter and pull the drawer, retrieving Nicky's cell phone. "I'm monitoring this." I hold it up for her, keeping my tone sharp. "Don't think of it as an invasion of privacy, think of it as someone looking out for you." I take in a breath, ready for this to get difficult.

Her eyes go wide. "I get my phone back? Yeah—I'm good with whatever, dude."

"It's a new number...one that *she* doesn't have." I say, referring to our mother.

She nods. "Okay."

"You have my number in here. Coach Collins, in case you can't reach me, and a few other people I trust."

I see her skimming through the contacts.

"I deleted anyone I didn't know Nic."

She nods again. I see her taking it all in. Like I've just given her a new identity and she needs to get used to it.

I change the subject. "I'm heading to Jace's to drive him to practice. His car is in the shop."

She scoffs. "Like he can't just use his spare Maserati?"

I roll my eyes. "We're not cliche like that. Besides they don't make too many of the model he's got. I'm surprised he's let it out of sight."

"Hmm..." She eyes me. "He's the one with the kid sister who's got a crush on you, right?"

"Cora? That was like seven years ago and she's grown up."

A lot.

I clear my throat.

"Maybe I can hang out with her? She seems like the type who wouldn't judge."

She's right about that. Cora would never judge Nicole. She'd likely find every which way to keep Nicole distracted and then sit and plot ways of pissing the two of us off.

It seems innocent enough, but for some reason, I don't agree to it. The idea of Nicole with Cora is unsettling. Not that my sister would ever poison the young and innocent mind of someone who is like my kid sister, but for some reason, Nicole's like the bad influence friend I didn't want around my kid.

I don't deny that it's an odd thought to have and feel a little guilty over it. "Maybe lay low from Jace's kid sister." I avoid calling her by name. It's the little reminder I find quite helpful lately.

She frowns and I can tell I've offended her.

"For now."

It occurs to me on the drive over that I wonder if Cora's pink streak is still intact or if Jace had made her get rid of it.

Oddly, I realize that I hope not.

End Excerpt

Read the rest of Nick and Cora's story here
https://geni.us/blades_bm